STRIKE THREE

He couldn't tell how many times he was clubbed before hitting the floor, or even where the blows had landed. All he knew was that his entire body was screaming with pain.

"Stop, please stop!" He begged the boy to have mercy. But there was none, only the anguish of his battered body. He crumpled to the floor in a heap, his entire body soaked in sweat—or was it blood? And the bat coming down *again and again and again*....

The next explosion in his head told him that his nose was broken, and his few remaining teeth slithered down his chin, mixing with blood and spittle, while a gusher spurted from the hole that used to be his nose.

Silently watching the bat descending upon him, he was barely able to read the words "Louisville Slugger" burned into the white ash.

again and again and again....

SAL CONTE

Child's Play

LEISURE BOOKS   NEW YORK CITY

**For Mom.
Thanks for everything.**

A LEISURE BOOK

Published by

Dorchester Publishing Co., Inc.
6 East 39th Street
New York, NY 10016

Printed in the United States of America

Child's Play

BOOK ONE

Chapter 1

The old Mercedes moved cautiously along a deserted stretch of the Bronx River Parkway. The soft hum of its engine along with the hiss of tires massaging damp pavement were the only exterior sounds. Inside there was silence.

A soft drizzle had been sifting slowly from a nearly blackened sky, appearing like smoke, melting quietly into the pavement. Even the rain was silent.

Visibility was difficult, and the man switched on the headlights. The beam, rather than knifing through the mist, seemed to bounce off an impenetrable wall.

"It's pretty thick," he said, the first words he had uttered during the entire trip. The woman seated beside him stared straight ahead, her gaze falling on nothing in particular, her mind a tangle of thought.

"We'll be home soon," the man said, as if he

had to say something to keep the conversation alive.

The woman didn't answer. Her mind was on the boy. *Her* boy.

Stiffly the car took the curve that separates the Bronx River from the Sprain Brook Parkway. Then slowly it ambled past exit signs for Bronxville and Eastchester. They were nearly there.

"It's slippery as hell," the man said.

Silence.

The drizzle lightened somewhat, and as the car crawled up the exit ramp the woman could make out the sign pointing to Crandall. Turning off, the car headed towards town. Soon another sign came into view:

YOU ARE NOW ENTERING CRANDALL
HOME OF THE
LITTLE LEAGUE CHAMPIONSHIP
GIANTS
PLEASE DRIVE CAREFULLY

The woman's fists clenched involuntarily as she read the sign. A lump formed in her throat.

"I once had a boy," she whispered.

"Don't torture yourself like this," the man said. It was the first conversation between the couple in hours, one of the few they'd had in days.

"I once had a boy," she repeated louder. Anger gripped her voice.

"As far as everyone's concerned, we still have a boy," the man said. "You understand?"

Silence.

The drizzle was now a light, eerie mist, silhouetting the trees like an enigmatic aura. The end of a spring rain.

Visibility improved. The car increased to normal speed, gliding down Main Street, through the center of town. They drove past the tiny shopping center that housed the Walgreen's and the Shopwell. Flickering lights loomed in many of the windows. Evening life in Crandall.

The center of town had been designed to look like a tiny New England fishing village. The effect was brilliant, giving the impression that one was hundreds of miles from New York City, rather than in the city's own backyard.

The lights from the center were soon behind them. The car turned onto Evergreen Avenue, finally rolling to rest in a narrow driveway.

"I'm not too old, you know," said the woman, her gaze fixed on the windshield.

"What do you mean?"

"Children. I'm not too old for children."

"You've got to be kidding!"

She faced him. "We made a mistake."

"Don't you have any feelings at all?"

"Don't talk to me about feelings!" The anger flashed back, then softened. "We've seen what it's like. It could be perfect this time. No mistakes, right from birth. There are even ways of checking for birth defects, such as Down's syndrome, during the pregnancy. There needn't be any mistakes."

11

"You are unbelievable! Our son is . . . *gone* not two days, and you're talking of having another baby. You don't have a heart!" It was a cruel thing to say, and he regretted it the moment the words passed his lips. "This whole thing has me on edge. I'm sorry."

"It was a mistake," she said again. "But this time we can do it right."

"No!" the man blurted.

When the woman spoke again, her voice was a cracked whisper. "I miss him."

"Do you?" her husband asked, not believing.

"I miss him terribly. That's why I want to start over. You have your work to keep you busy, to fill your day, your life. All I had was him. Eleven years of my life. I need to know it wasn't wasted. I'm just thirty-five, this can't be the end." Silent tears washed down her cheeks.

"No," he said again. "No more children."

He turned off the ignition. Reaching across the seat, he squeezed her hand. It lay limp, like some small dead thing.

"Let's go inside," he said. Not waiting for her reply, he clambered out of the car, slam-locking the door behind himself.

For a moment she was alone, but never totally—a prisoner of her own thoughts. Memories.

"Our son is gone, damnit!" she whispered. It was still hard to believe. "I once had a boy, and now he's gone."

Pushing open the car door, she too climbed

out. The rain had stopped, and the sweet odor of damp earth filled the air.

A baby is a wonderful idea, she thought, following her husband into the house. This can be a beginning for us. It isn't over. It isn't. . . .

Chapter 2

"No one's ever been killed here."

"What?"

"In the hundred or so years that Crandall has been on the map, no one's ever been killed here. It's as safe a town as you can find anywhere," said Ruth Roberts, a thirtyish woman, with a bold streak of premature grey slicing through her jet black hair. She sipped at her coffee.

"It's quite comforting to know that. Really!" Dana said, trying to sound convinced.

"It's true. With New York so nearby there's always the threat of violence. I hate to say that but you know it's true. Here in Crandall, though, I feel totally and completely safe."

"Good," Dana replied, hoping to put an end to the subject. "More coffee?" she asked, rising. Ruth, seated comfortably at the new chrome and glass dining room table, offered her cup. "I think I'll like it here," Dana added, walking to the stove where she poured two fresh cups.

"Oh, you will. You already do, right?" There was no sense in answering.

Ruth Roberts was a highly opinionated, talkative woman, who in the single week that Dana had lived in Crandall stopped by every day—every single day!—foisting her opinions of the town, its people, and God knows what else on Dana. There wasn't much of a dialogue between them, and Ruth seemed to prefer it that way. She was a one-woman Tower of Babel, rambling on and endlessly on.

Ruth and Tom Roberts were the Evans' neighbors to their immediate left. A week earlier, when the Evans family first arrived in Crandall, Dana thought that she and Ruth might become friends. They were around the same age, had husbands who worked in the city, and each had one child—a boy. Ruth's son Ronnie was twelve and Todd eleven. The boys made friends immediately, but their mothers, Dana discovered that first afternoon, had nothing in common.

Ruth had appeared at her door that first afternoon wearing a smile, and carrying a bucket of Kentucky fried chicken:

Hi. Welcome to Crandall. I'm Ruth Roberts, your neighbor to the left. I know you're not going to feel like cooking tonight, so I brought some chicken. It'll keep the men-folk out of your hair, and give you some time to get settled.

16

*You're really going to like it here in Cran-
dall. It's a good town with good people!
Speaking of people, did you know . . .* And on
and on.

Dana had expected Ruth to be filled with
questions about her family and her own life,
but Ruth jabbered the afternoon away, nib-
bling at the chicken. By the time she had
finished, the bucket was half empty.

Dana tried waiting for an opening, but Ruth
didn't leave many. At one point she started to
blurt out all the things she'd been dying to
say: *My name is Dana Evans and I'm thirty-
one. And my husband's name is Rick. He's
slightly older than I. Our son is Todd. We
moved here from New York because we didn't
want to raise our children in a crime-ridden
city. And my husband is a business
consultant, and I'm a freelance journalist
when I can find a paper to write for.*

That would have floored Ruth! Of course
she didn't. She waited for Ruth to supply an
opening that never came, so Ruth knew absolutely nothing about her.

Maybe it's better that way.

I'll be civil, Dana decided returning with the
coffee. After all, she's my neighbor. *Thank
heavens for the good neighbor policy!* But we
could never be friends. Never!

"The town has so much pride," Ruth continued, without missing a beat. "Our Little
League team is the first from the United
States to win the crown since 1975, and the
only reason an American team won that year

was because foreign teams were banned.''

Dana's interest was suddenly piqued. *Maybe there's a story here!* "You mean the Little League World Series is actually a *world* series?"

"Yes. Teams from all over the world compete. But you'll find out all you could ever hope to know about Little League living in this town. It's what everyone talks about."

"That's nice," Dana said, her interest falling off as quickly as it had risen. A story about foreign teams being banned from Little League sounded interesting. She'd look into it. But she wasn't about to become a hard core Little League devotee. *No way!* Baseball was men's business. They invented the silly game—let them enjoy it. If Todd was interested in joining the Little League, Rick would take him. He had to spend some time with the boy. He promised. But their marriage was a string of broken promises, missed engagements.

Why should this time be any different? Because when we moved to Crandall Rick promised to spend more time with Todd and me. And this time he means it! Dana was optimistic.

Her mind suddenly shifted to something Ruth said. *It's what everyone talks about. Little League!* She hoped not. Crandall was to be an exciting adventure, filled with interesting new people and good times for all of them. Dana had looked towards moving to

18

Crandall with childlike anticipation. Even Rick seemed different—more caring. But she didn't want to live in a town filled with baseball nuts.

"Ronnie's so excited, and to tell the truth, so am I. Spring camp starts Saturday."

"That's nice."

When you can't think of anything to say, just turn up the corners of the old lips and say: "That's nice." It has an abject air of ambiguity about it. Dana smiled.

Ruth caught the smile. "You'll change soon enough," she added knowingly. "Last year I was just like you. I couldn't tell a fielder's choice from a fungo."

A fungo? Fat chance!

"It's really an honor for a boy to be a part of the team. They're quite selective," Ruth said. "Ronnie's on pins and needles over the whole thing. He's taking his physical tomorrow."

"Physical?"

"Oh, yes. All the boys are checked out thoroughly. Coach Dreiser is a stickler for things like that. He's a little eccentric, I know, but he's given us two straight championship teams. He really knows how to get the best out of the boys." She turned suddenly. "What's that . . . scratching?" Ruth's brow twisted oddly, as she glanced around the room.

Somewhere to their right the faint sound of scratching could be heard.

"SCRUFFY!" Dana had let the dog out in

the yard over an hour ago. Now she could hear his soft, high-pitched whine as he begged for entry.

She ran to the door that led from the kitchen to the back porch, throwing it open. "I'm sorry puddin'."

The small, shaggy mutt danced in, his paws skating across the freshly waxed floor.

"Dogs should stay outside," Ruth said.

Afraid of the competition, huh?

"He's an apartment dog. He doesn't understand his new life yet. He thinks the outdoors are for just one thing . . . or should I say two things?" Dana chuckled at her own humor. *Hey! We're almost holding a conversation. You're slipping, Ruth.*

"Well," Ruth said, draining her cup, "I really have to go. Tuesday is laundry day for me."

"Ugh! Laundry. Don't remind me. I've got a lot to do myself. Sorry you have to go," Dana lied.

"If I finish early I'll stop around later and give you a hand."

Me and my big mouth!

"All right."

Ruth left by the front door, Dana standing in the doorway, smiling politely and waving. She hoped she was rid of Ruth for the day.

Turning to reenter the house she noticed someone standing in the yard of the white stucco across the street. A boy, standing by the gate, with dark eyes and curly blonde hair, stared at her intently. She smiled, waving at him, but he made no attempt to wave back. Dark eyes, mysterious, stared on.

A sudden chill came over her, blanketing her like a soft winter's snow covers the earth. The eyes were cold, unfeeling.

Strange kid! Why isn't he in school?

Just then came the sound of Scruffy rustling newspaper.

"What are you getting into, dog?" Dana called. Turning, she disappeared back inside the house. The cold stare never wavered.

Chapter 3

In the evenings she often came to his room. It wasn't good for her. She knew it, but she couldn't resist. Like a magnet pulling in tiny grains of metal, she was drawn to his room daily.

On the edge of his bed she sat, gazing at the contents of the room. Things. His things—the poster of Reggie Jackson on the wall, a model Darth Vader, his baseball glove. His picture, taken at the Little League World Series last summer, seemed to reach out to her. The impish grin bathed her in memories, but she wouldn't cry. Not today.

She sat, silently waiting, as if any moment he would come running in and once again fill the room with his life and vitality.

She suspected that she should get rid of most of his things—make it a sewing room (or a nursery). But they had to keep up the hoax, although they both knew he would never return.

The shuffling sound downstairs startled her.

David! He shouldn't find me here.

Rising, she crossed to the door. Lately, everything had become more difficult. She had hoped that somehow the pain would subside, but instead it grew, and now the thundering within threatened to rip her heart to pieces.

She had decided to speak to him again. He had to realize that it needn't be over for them, that they could bring new life into the world. And this time everything would turn out all right. This time they'd be prepared.

Slowly she opened the door. "David," she called, starting from the room. She had to make him understand—soon. Before the loneliness destroyed her.

"Pick up the Cheerios!"

Todd had just dripped several milk-soaked Cheerios onto the new dining room table, fingering the milky designs onto the glass top.

"Clean up that mess, Todd. Please!" Dana implored.

"Okay," the boy answered. Then, reluctantly he dragged himself into the kitchen for a paper towel.

Rick, head buried in the business section of the morning paper, didn't look up.

"More coffee?" Dana asked in an attempt to snare his attention.

"Ummmmm," he nodded.

So this is our new life. Seems pretty much like the old!

Todd returned to the table, several towels bunched in his fist. He began smearing the mess into the glass.

"Let Mommy do that, hon."

"I got it. Look!" he said smiling proudly.

"Very good." The smoked plexiglass was now a mass of smudges. *Not bad, kid!* Dana would clean it later, after Rick and Todd had gone. "All right, now come back and finish. I don't want you to be late for school."

"Okay," said Todd, shuffling back to the table, a perfect imitation of a seventy-five year old man.

Old folks and kids. Maybe there is something to second childhood!

"Rick, hon," Dana tried again, "Ruth Roberts was here again yesterday. What a character!"

Silence.

"Rick?"

"Ummmmm."

"President Reagan called yesterday and was wondering if I'd be able to come in and help out around the White House—just for a few weeks, mind you. I told him it was okay. I mean there's no one to talk to around here. It might be stimulating."

"Really, Mom? What about me?"

"I was just kidding, Todd." He smiled. Rick hadn't heard a word.

"Ronnie's gonna teach me to throw a curve ball, Mom."

"That's wonderful, son." Mild indignation burned behind Dana's eyes. She wanted to snatch the paper away from her husband, force him to look at her.

He'd promised more involvement. Of course she knew it wouldn't be easy. He was so wrapped up in the business. She realized he was doing it all for them, but Todd needed a father, and she needed a husband—an active husband. She was sure he was trying and didn't want to press.

She consoled herself: *We just moved here. He'll come around.*

The local newspaper, a weekly, was delivered that morning, a complimentary copy for the new family. Dana picked it up, now glancing at the headlines, hoping to relieve some of the tension she felt between her husband and herself.

THE CRANDALL GUARDIAN

COACH DREISER PREDICTS
UNPRECEDENTED THIRD STRAIGHT TITLE

Ugh! Dana thought. *Little League. Little League. Little League!*

All the articles seemed baseball related. There was even one on the old man who kept the field.

Finally, on page three:

RUNAWAY STILL NOT FOUND

The tragedy of Mr. and Mrs. David Grote continues. After two weeks of searching, the Grotes have no clues as to the whereabouts of their son, Thomas.

Thomas Grote, age twelve, left his home on March twenty-third, leaving his parents only a brief note. Today marks the fourteenth day since young Thomas' disappearance.

The county sheriff's office and the New York City police department have been working on the case since the beginning, but both admit that the problem of runaways is a most difficult one.

"The poor woman," Dana mumbled.

What would she do if Todd ran away? Of course she knew he wouldn't. He was too happy. Still, the thought of losing him nagged at her.

She regarded her child as he fiddled with his breakfast. The dark hair and ice-blue eyes were his father's, but he had her lean, angular body. He would be tall, unlike Rick who was squat—although still quite masculine and sexy. Todd also would be quite handsome. This she knew.

But is he happy?

Looks ran in her family. Dana had always been considered pretty, with her long brown hair and flawless complexion. I was quite popular in school, she mused. Todd will be also.

The boy smiled at his mother, holding up the empty bowl. He had a beautiful smile.

Yes! He's happy.

"I better get started," Rick said.

Well, hello there; welcome back to the real world!

"Don't forget dinner, tonight. The three of us."

"I won't." Rising, he leaned across the table, pecking her cheek gently. The pleasant odor of 4711 tickled her senses.

"Promise?" she added cautiously. "On time?"

He smiled. "On time. And I'll bring a bottle of Asti Spumanti for the celebration."

"Great!" Jumping up, she reached over and hugged him. Things would work out just fine.

"See you later, tiger," Rick called to his son as he headed for the door. Todd waved. Dana followed him out.

Suddenly she felt exhilarated. Reaching the door, she wrapped her arms around his neck and kissed him.

"Hey! What's that for?"

"I love you," she said smiling into his eyes. *They really are ice-blue!*

"Love you, too," he said, and was gone.

Dana stood in the doorway watching her husband walk down to the corner, where he would meet his ride to the train.

Dinner will be wonderful, she thought.

Across the street, in the yard of the white

stucco, an elderly man played catch with the dark-eyed boy.

Strange! thought Dana. *Shouldn't he be getting ready for school?* But she was too happy to let the thought linger. Her mind danced to other things.

She dashed back into the house to get Todd off to school, then plan a menu for dinner. *Maybe a turkey! No, not a turkey. Well, whatever!*

Nothing would spoil this evening.

Chapter 4

The man was at the liquor cabinet when the woman got downstairs.

"Fix you one?" he asked.

"Yes. Scotch and soda."

"What were you doing?"

"Lying down."

"You all right?"

"Yes. I just had a busy day, that's all. I drove into the city to do some shopping. Macy's, Ohrbach's, Lord and Taylor. It was really quite a day. I picked up the most precious earrings."

"You went alone?"

"Yes. Then, when I got home, I fixed a surprise for dinner. Pot roast." She smiled.

Finished at the cabinet, he came over to her. Handing her the drink, he leaned closer, kissing her cheek lightly, antiseptically.

"Pot roast. With your special gravy?"

"Yes."

"You did have a busy day."

His fingers made a brief run through her hair, then he moved to sofa. She was coming along fine. She'd be all right. He was sure of it.

The woman went into the kitchen.

Sipping his drink slowly, he felt the warmth ooze into his belly. He was glad to see his wife getting out. Before, all she did was mope around the house. He'd even caught her, a few days earlier, in the boy's room, sitting on the edge of his bed, trancelike. She'd been crying, her eyes red and bleary. She wouldn't admit it, but he could tell she was still grieving.

He wanted to comfort her, but he had his own grief to deal with. The boy was his son, too. He wished there was some way to bring the boy back, but of course there wasn't. He was lost to them forever.

"Come and get it," the woman's voice chimed from the dining room. It was the way she used to call them to dinner. She was becoming more of her old self every day. . .

He wondered how much she thought of the boy. It was hard not to think of him, since his things were everywhere.

It was all a horrible mistake, he thought. A horrible mistake.

"David! Come on, now."

"On my way."

Rising, he moved towards the dining room. He was really glad to see her finally coming out of it. They were still young, with plenty of good living ahead of them.

Walking into the dining room, he seated himself behind a plate heaped with Yankee pot roast and mashed potatoes. His wife's special gravy had been poured liberally over the meat and potatoes.

"Mmmmm." He smiled, nodding his approval.

Helen Grote joined her husband at the table. They each ate in silence, David looking up occasionally and smiling his approval of the meal.

Finally Helen spoke. "David, let's bring some happiness into this house again."

"What do you mean?"

"There used to be talk at this table. Happy talk."

"Please, Helen, not that again." He put his head down and continued shoveling forkfuls of mashed potatoes into his mouth.

"And why not?" Helen slammed her fist onto the table. "What are you so afraid of? We've seen the worst. This time we can groom the child from birth."

"Helen, it's a dead issue."

"Why? Because you're afraid to try again? Afraid we might succeed this time? Is success what frightens you, David Grote? IS IT?" she screamed.

Abruptly David stood. "The food's good, but I'm not hungry." He started from the room.

"You're not going anywhere!" He was out of the room now. "Come back here, you coward." She picked up her plate and flung it across the room.

"Coward!" she screamed, her eyes filling with tears. "Coward!"

Scruffy had already eaten—twice—and was once again seated in front of Dana, tongue hanging out, his patented *I'm starving, feed me!* look scrawled across his shaggy face.

Dinner was ruined.

Dana couldn't wait any longer. She had to feed Todd.

Rick had promised. Promised! *Where is he?*

Dana gazed, through teary eyes, at the large starburst clock on the dining room wall. The clock had been a gift from her brother, Ted. 8:10. He was over two hours late.

"Mommy, I'm hungry."

"All right, hon."

And Todd looked so cute. She had goaded him out of his daily uniform of jeans and sneakers. He now wore a sport shirt—one she had given him for Christmas because it made him look so much like Daddy—gray slacks, and *shoes*, for heavens sake. *That took some doing!*

She'd worked all day, planning her menu and cooking right through Ruth's incessant jabbering. Not really minding Ruth today. Her mind was occupied with creating the perfect meal.

At five, she showered, singing. She slipped into her sexiest lounge dress, and daubed Tigress around her ears and throat.

At 5:40, she set the dinner out. On a large

platter, ginger beef surrounded a huge bed of rice garnished with sliced green peppers. Snow peas with pearl onions and a tossed salad rounded out the meal. She had borrowed the silver platter from Ruth.

Now, Rick would never see the beauty of the meal set out on the new chrome and glass dining room table. It was getting late, and Todd had to eat.

"Go away, Scruffy. You ate already," Dana said. She began piling food on a single plate.

The dog, cocking his head to one side, jumped up, wagging his tail.

"This isn't for you," she told him.

"Aren't you eating, Mommy?" Todd asked.

"I'll wait for Daddy."

"I wanna wait, too."

"You said you were hungry."

"I wanna wait," he said again.

"No. Eat now."

"I wanna eat with you and Daddy," the boy chided.

"Daddy has to work late. Eat now!" An ocean of tears gathered behind her eyes, and she fought to contain them.

"But we're all supposed to eat together tonight. I wanna wait!"

She slammed the plate down in front of him. "EAT!" she screamed.

Kicking the small dog out of her way, she raced upstairs for the bathroom. Already waves of hot tears were rolling down her cheeks. The dog's high pitched whine followed her up and into the bathroom.

It was to be a special celebration—a new home, a new life, no more ignoring his family. Rick had promised! He was going to start coming home for dinner. Keep regular hours. And he was going to start spending some time with Todd.

Not once had he spent a weekend with his son. Not once in eleven years. Dana had been both mother and father to Todd, but no more. And she also needed his time. Her own husband was a stranger to her.

All day she wanted to call him at the office, just to remind him. But no, she wasn't going to be insecure. It was up to him to remember. He didn't. If something had happened to him someone would have called. There was nothing the matter. He had forgotten.

And he promised!

Eight months ago she had given him an ultimatum: "Either you be around for Todd and me or we're leaving!" But nothing had changed—not really.

He was always thinking of the business—weekends with clients, evenings going over books and records. The evenings that he did come home he'd lock himself in the bedroom for hours, falling asleep holding onto some customer's report instead of his wife.

After he missed a circus date—leaving them waiting in front of Madison Square Garden for two hours, she knew she had to do something.

"I'm leaving!" she told him. She couldn't go home, not to Allentown. Her folks never approved of Rick anyway. It would have been too demeaning. So she and Todd stayed with Carly, a friend from college.

Then one day Rick came to her, telling her of his plan to buy a home in Westchester, to start a new life for the three of them.

"Take me back. I love you," he said on bended knee. It was a corny act, but it was just the type of thing he knew she'd like. He was a schoolboy again, proposing to her. And it took all of her will power to keep her smile from breaking through.

"I don't believe you," she told him. But she went for the drives in a rented car every weekend, all over Westchester county. *He's really trying.* Finally, he called one day from the office and said he'd found the perfect house. "The price is right, the town's good, and the people are wonderful, honey." He babbled the entire drive up, like a child with a new toy, and when Dana saw the house, she had to agree.

Staring up at her make-up stained face in the bathroom mirror, she now wondered if she'd made the right decision. She wasn't going to let it all happen again. *A new house to appease me?* But what good was a house without a husband?

No. Rick was either going to spend more time with his family, or he would have his new house all to himself.

Dana lay awake, staring into darkness. The silence that surrounded her was unnerving.

Crandall was so very unlike New York. It was just past eleven, yet it seemed the town had closed up shop for the night. Eighty-sixth street was practically a street festival at this hour.

There was always noise in New York—teen-agers with oversized radios blasting music all the way up to the twenty-third floor; a multitude of traffic sounds, with tires screaming against the pavement, shrill horns piercing the night, and garbage trucks munching their way up Second Avenue. There was also shouting, singing, laughing and heated arguments, all spilling together to form the cacophony that was New York.

Dana missed this hodgepodge of street sound. It was music to her, proof of the exuberance and vitality of life in the city. Crandall was quiet, too quiet. Secretive. It wasn't a place for a woman alone with a child. *Is New York?* If Rick didn't come around soon, she'd return to the city she loved.

She hadn't meant to fly off the handle with Todd. She apologized, both their eyes filled with tears. "I'm sorry. And yes, Mommy does love you. No! I'm not crying!"

Now, as she lay staring at the ceiling, the last of her tears dripping onto her pillow, she thought about the runaway she'd read of in the paper that morning.

Todd is happy! I know it. . . ? But it came out a question.

She had always been close to her son, closer than close. He was a good boy, and she rarely had to chastise him. She wasn't going to let Rick ruin their relationship. She came to a decision, arriving at it suddenly, like a flash summer storm abruptly coming to an end. She wouldn't sleep until they had had it out. Once and for all! One way or the other!

She wasn't going to be over-emotional or unreasonable. She was just going to explain to her husband the way she saw things. And when he saw that she meant business, that she was firm and wasn't giving in, he would straighten out. She was sure.

The yellow cab deposited Rick Evans in the driveway of his two-story brick home on Oakwood Avenue. After paying the fare, Rick left the driver a generous tip. Rick enjoyed being a generous tipper. He especially liked the look he received after tipping.

Awe? Gratitude? No. He couldn't describe it. Whatever it was, though, it always sent a glorious feeling washing over him, like a fresh morning shower or a cooling summer rain.

Once, after a small, hurried dinner at Victor's, he left the waiter twenty dollars. "Sir, this is a twenty," the waiter had said. "I know." And then the look, the waiter trying to act casual. "Thank you, sir." But he couldn't hide it. *That look!* It left Rick rejuvenated for the entire evening.

"Thank you," the driver said stuffing the money into his jacket pocket. Rick could see the look, the street lights illuminating the man's face. *The look!*

Rick smiled, as the cab backed slowly out of his driveway, then peered up at his bedroom window. Darkness. That was a good sign. He'd enter quietly, undress downstairs, not turning on any lights. Then he'd slip upstairs and gently slide into bed next to his wife. He'd be extra careful not to awaken her. Tomorrow's another day, he thought. In the morning things will be hectic, too hectic to really discuss anything, and by evening—after he'd had time to send her a dozen roses—the whole thing will have blown over.

He slipped his key slowly into the lock. It turned easily, silently. He was in, quiet as a church mouse. Quickly he was out of his things and noiselessly mounting the stairs. So far so good. Maybe he'd send her two dozen roses; he was in a very good mood.

The bedroom door crept open. It was Rick. Dana had heard the cab pull into the driveway and lay stiffly waiting to confront him.

The closing of the door was a whisper, and Rick came slowly towards the bed, moving like a dream figure in slow motion.

Dana flicked on the lamp, the light exploding into the room. Surprise streaked Rick's face, but he quickly gathered his wits and looked over at her, eyes soulful, an apologetic smile creasing his lips.

"I didn't mean to wake you," he said. He sat on the edge of the bed. "Sorry."

"If you didn't want to wake me, you should have come home earlier!" There was a sternness in Dana's voice that surprised even her.

Rick sat silently staring into his hands.

"I don't know what to say. I'm really sorry." His voice was a whisper.

"Why?" she asked, her tone softening.

Be firm, Dana.

He looked up. "A new client. I got involved. I forgot."

"Why?" she asked again. "Why did you bring us here? Why didn't you just leave us where we were?" The sternness was back. *That-a-girl!*

"Dana, you're my wife, Todd's my son. My family. I love you."

"Love?" she said incredulously. "If you love us, why do you want to hurt us?"

"Honey. . ."

"This type of love we don't need." The tears were coming. *I'm not going to cry!* Dana composed herself. "Do you want us here? I mean *really* want us?"

"Yes. I need you."

She sensed a wound opening somewhere inside of him. There was pain in his eyes. Dana didn't want to hurt him, but she had to be tough. It was her marriage she was fighting for.

"It can't be like this again," she told him.

"I know."

"We won't stand for it, Rick. Not again."

"I know." The ice-blue eyes seemed to be moistening. "I'm really sorry."

Dana looked deeply into the eyes of her husband. Windows to his innermost self, she hoped they would convey something to her, answer her questions. She wanted to believe him, needed to believe. She had believed him in the past and trusted him. But a trust betrayed is a difficult trust to regain. She reflected on the basis of that trust—eleven years of marriage. Over the years, though, the foundation had become shaky, and the marriage began to crumble, like so many sand castles washed away by the sea. Still, she wanted, needed, to believe him—and did.

"Don't let this happen again," she said trying to be tough, but the fight had gone out of her.

"I won't."

"Promise?" She suddenly remembered something her father once said. A proverb. Rousseau, she thought:

He who is most slow in making a promise is most faithful in the performance of it.

It was odd that she would think of it now. Her father wasn't an educated man, just a mill worker in a mining town, yet somehow Rousseau, Shakespeare and others had found their way into her father's life. And now one of the proverbs her father had eagerly spouted sneaked into her thoughts.

"Promise," Rick said, bringing her back. And then the warm, disarming smile. "What did you cook?"

"It's not important." She remembered the ruined dinner.

"I'd like to say that I'll make it up to you tomorrow, but..."

Here it comes.

"...I have to take Todd to Little League tryouts."

"What?" *Is he joking?* The look on her face was one of sheer surprise, and Rick laughed out loud.

"Little League! You know...baseball. This town is crazy over it. I was talking to Tom Roberts the other day, and he suggested I bring the little fella out. I was watching him throw with Ronnie. The kid's got a rifle for an arm."

Dana was staring wide-eyed at her husband. This time she couldn't help it; she was going to cry. *He really means it!* It was true. A new life for all of them.

She scrambled to the edge of the bed as the tears spilled down her cheeks. Throwing her arms around him, she delivered a long, wet kiss.

"What's happening?" he asked pulling back.

"Love!" she answered smiling. "Now, come to bed." She pulled him back to her, needing to feel his warmth.

His fingers began to dance over her skin, and tiny waves of ecstasy flooded her. Once again the room was dark. And they were naked.

He made love to her, wringing orgasm after glorious orgasm from her body. Afterwards, he lay in her arms until he fell asleep, the steady rise andf all of his chest feeling so good.

The night was still. They were engulfed in silence, and Dana had the feeling that at that moment the whole world was at peace. She smiled to herself, and her last thought before sleeping was that tonight had been the best in eleven years.

Chapter 5

PHOOP——PHOOP——PHOOP—
Dana was dragged up from the depths of a fitful sleep. She'd been dreaming of her mother, an overbearing woman who tried desperately to dominate the lives of her four children. Todd was also in the dream. He was going to live with her parents in Allentown. It was his own decision. Dana begged him to stay, but her mother kept saying, "He'll be happy here." Dana pleaded with her son to stay with his family in Crandall. "I'll be happy there," the boy told her.

PHOOP——
That noise, Dana thought. That's what woke me. What time is it? She glanced at the clock on the nightstand. 5:30. Rick had rolled over sometime during the night and now lay, his bare back exposed to her, in deep slumber.

PHOOP——
What is that? Dana gently stroked Rick's

back, her thoughts flitting back to the night before.

PHOOP——

It was coming from outside. Dana slipped from the bed and padded to the window.

PHOOP——

The graying man and the boy! The boy stood at one end of the driveway, dark eyes set and reflecting the streetlamps, pitching the ball to the man who crouched on the sidewalk about thirty feet away.

The boy held the baseball tightly in his tiny grip. He stared hard at the man who relayed a signal. *The windup... And the pitch.* The ball, a miniature missile slicing through the air, exploded into the glove of the man. PHOOP.

Dana again glanced at the clock. 5:37. Crossing the room, she slid back into bed, next to her husband. They were a strange sight, the boy and the man. The boy's intent stare sent a sudden chill spiraling down Dana's back. *Crandall really is crazy for baseball.*

PHOOP!

Chapter 6

Breakfast was the greatest. Rick and Todd talking baseball. *He's really trying!* Then the mad dash so no one would be late. And now that everyone was gone, and the breakfast dishes were done, and Ruth wasn't coming over until later, it looked like Dana was finally going to have a chance to do some serious work around the house, but—wouldn't you know it—the phone rang.

"Hello!" Dana said, a little too harshly.

"Hey, what did I do? That's what I get for calling my little sister all the way from Atlanta?"

"Ted? Is that you?"

"How many big brothers do you have?"

"Oh, Ted," Dana bubbled. "It's wonderful, really wonderful hearing from you."

"You didn't sound that happy a minute ago," he teased. His voice, Dana noticed, had picked up a slight drawl, the effect of three

47

years living in the south.

"I thought you were my neighbor, Ruth. She's latched onto me like fleas to a dog. I think I'm her only friend in town. But you don't want to hear about that. How have you been, Doctor Stephens?"

"I'm just fine, now that I know my little sister's doing all right. And you know how I just love it when my favorite sister calls me doctor, instead of Ted. How endearing."

"It sure beats some of the things I called you when we were kids," Dana said, laughing.

Ted was always teasing her about being his favorite, and she always called him doctor. It was a game they'd played since he'd entered med school. They were still close, even with so many miles between them. And they came from a close knit family, but now Ted was Dana's only link to that family.

They all had been so very close when Dana was a child, not only going to church together every Sunday but in so many other ways. But Dana's insistence on leaving Allentown to attend Colombia University in New York started her alienation. After she became pregnant with Rick's child, breaking the family's religious tradition (no premarital sex), Dana's mother forbade any member of the family to correspond with her. Only Ted, the oldest, dared defy his mother's decree.

Dana missed the family closeness. *At least I have Ted*, she thought. Still she missed Mom and Dad, and of course Liz and Ronald, her younger brother and sister. Ronald was just entering high school when she had left for New York, with Liz a year behind. She missed not being there to watch them grow.

"How are the kids?" she asked.

"Liz is expecting again. Everyone's banking on a boy, after the two girls. And the last I heard of Ronald, the calling had taken him to Africa."

"Africa?" she said, truly excited. "Don't tell me they still have missionaries bringing Christianity to the so-called savages?"

"Not exactly. It's a mission of peace for God, visiting thirteen different countries."

Liz and Ronald were adults now. *Is it really eleven years already?* When Dana left Allentown, they were kids. Ronald was just four years younger than herself, but to her he was still a kid, and probably always would be.

"How's mother?" Dana asked, stonily.

"Just as cantankerous as ever." They both laughed, brightening Dana's spirits all over again. Suddenly she was a geyser of information, telling Ted of her new found happiness with Rick and the town. She talked of Todd, Ruth and Little League, spilling forth like she hadn't in weeks. When she was finished, she felt even better and realized how she missed having someone to talk to. She promised herself to call Carly in New York more often.

"What's that coach's name again?" Ted asked after she'd told him about the championship team.

"Dreiser. Philip, I think."

"Philip Dreiser. I believe I've heard that name somewhere before."

"I'm sure you have. He's probably very famous, coaching Crandall to two straight championships. It's really quite a feat." She was surprised at her own sudden town pride. *Watch it, Dana. Pretty soon you'll be selling peanuts at the games!*

"No, I've heard it somewhere else. Philip Dreiser. I can't place it now. It'll come to me. Things like that always do when I least expect them. Like when I'm on the toilet or something." They laughed. Then he got serious. "Sis, I'm worried about you. Are things really working out?"

"If you'd asked me that question last night I would have said no. But I really wasn't giving Rick a chance. I was looking at it all wrong. He's really trying."

"Are you happy?"

"Yes."

"Todd?"

"If only you could have seen his face this morning—talking with his father about baseball. It was wonderful. Things are just fine," she said, smiling as much on the inside as on the outside.

"When I get back from the conference in Europe I'll be stopping in New York. I'll come by and give the new house my seal of approval."

"We'd all like that."

"I miss you."

"I miss you, too," she said. "And I love

you," she added, realizing how much she really did love her brother.

After she hung up, her fingers lingered on the receiver, trying to maintain the connection with Ted for a little while longer. I'm sure lucky, she thought. I have a loving brother, a loving husband who's really trying, and a son who's about to become a baseball player.

Doc Teasdale opened the Crandall Guardian and, for the third time today, read the article Max Richter had written about him. It was a good article. Honest. Fair. Good. He knew that, even though he didn't understand all the words.

He hadn't really asked Max to write the article—not really. Oh, he had told Max that some of the parents hadn't been fair about this mud thing. But all he had said was that the Guardian should print the truth about him. "A loyal public servant"—that's what he was, and that's how he wanted the community to view him. But he never asked for the article. Max printed it because he wanted to print the truth, not that pack of lies some of the parents had been telling.

Reading the article made Doc Teasdale feel good. He wasn't really a doctor. He hadn't even finished junior high, dropping out in the seventh grade. He'd always had trouble speaking, even as a kid, rolling his R's into W's, sort of like Elmer Fudd.

The seventh grade was the worst year of Ed

Teasdale's life. The kids would tease him so much that before you knew it he was in still another fight. So he left the seventh grade, but the fighting continued.

In the fifties someone started calling him Doc.

What's up, Doc?

And the "Doc" had stuck, following him throughout his life. Now, at age sixty-six, he had forgotten how he earned the distinction and thought the appellation truly an honor.

Doc Teasdale was all the grounds crew the Crandall baseball field had had for the past eleven years. He was actually the grounds-keeper for the whole park, but the upkeep of the baseball field had been his primary function for the past five years, since Dreiser took over as coach. He was proud of his job, and the mud thing really hurt him.

It wasn't his fault the field was muddy for the playoff game against Throgs Neck. The night before the big game a torrential rain hit Crandall, the huge drops falling in droves. Despite decent drainage on the field, the steady, saturating rain took its toll. Several times during the night he'd gone out with blankets, sopping up the water, to try and save at least the infield.

"I'm not a magician," he thought out loud. "What did they expect?" He'd done everything he could to save the field. Still, some of the parents blamed him, saying he was too old or incompetent for his job. It wasn't true.

"And what do I have to show for eleven

years of service?" he asked of no one. "Just this lousy house, and it doesn't even belong to me."

Teasdale lived in the ramshackle Peter Crandall house. It was large and drafty, a house that time had forgotten. But it was rent free, so Teasdale stayed on, using his small paychecks for necessities like food, which he bought too little of, and liquor, which he bought all too often.

Doc Teasdale hoisted the bottle of Irish Whiskey to his lips, swallowing the liquor in huge gulps. The burning sensation he'd once had from alcohol splashing into his empty stomach was now a kind of numbness, proof that the human body, wonder that it was, could get used to anything—even torture.

He chuckled to himself over the article. *It's really good!*

He was having a sort of celebration. Now the parents would know what a dedicated public servant he was. They'd speak of Doc Teasdale with respect, and once again justice would prevail. That's when he heard the knock.

It was a light rapping. "Who?" he said, staring up at the blur that was his door. The room started to spin, and Teasdale realized how drunk he was. "Who's out there?"

No answer. Then the rapping again, like tiny knuckles hammering against the mottled wood.

"Is somebody out there?" he called, rising and trying to steady himself.

"No."

"What?" he said, totally surprised.

"Just a waskily, wittle gway wabbit!"

And then it all came back. The seventh grade, the fights, and that being called Doc Teasdale wasn't really an honor at all.

Ehh... What's up Doc?

Anger raced through his body like the Irish whiskey that now coursed through his brain. He steadied himself, then shuffled over to the door. Yanking it open, he stared out into the night. *There's no one here!* Then slowly his eyes focused on the youth. *I know this boy.*

"What do you want?" he asked.

Smiling, the boy stepped silently into the room. He wore a Little League uniform with the word "Giants" emblazoned across the front in bright orange letters.

Seeing the uniform Doc Teasdale smiled, closing the door behind the boy. "Coach send you here for something?"

"What's up, Doc?" the boy said, munching an imaginary carrot.

And the anger returned. "You little kweep! What do you want?"

The boy chuckled. "Did you say *kweep*?"

"Shut up!" Teasdale demanded.

What does he want? It really didn't matter. Whatever it was, he was in trouble. Teasdale would make sure the boy's parents found out about this. *And they better punish him, too!*

"You better leave now," Teasdale warned. He moved to open the door, but the smiling boy stood blocking it. No, not smiling. There was a grin stretched across the boy's face, but he wasn't smiling.

Is he in trouble now! "Move!" Teasdale demanded.

He thought the boy was smiling, but now he could see the eyes, like stones, peering out at him from under the peak-bill cap. There was a dark stillness in those eyes, like a graveyard at midnight. They were cold, unfeeling.

Doc Teasdale was beginning to get nervous. There was something about this boy that wasn't right.

He's still in big trouble!

"Move!" Teasdale said again almost half-heartedly. The boy remained stark still.

Big, big trouble!

Something was wrong. The eyes, that was it! They weren't human. But there was something else wrong, different. Something in the boy's hand, in both hands. . . .

Oh, yes—a baseball bat.

Teasdale was about to say, "You'd better leave before you get in any worse trouble," but his eyes were glued to the bat slicing silently through the air, and the words got lost in his mind.

The bat caught him flush in the midsection. The pain wrenched his stomach, and his mouth dropped open, but he didn't scream. He was too surprised. Then he heard the loud crack, as the pain shot through his leg, climbing all the way up into his head before exploding—POW!

Ring the bell, win your lady a kewpie doll!

And he let out a loud, ear piercing scream.

His leg was broken; he could see the bone, a jagged stick, poking against his pants leg.

He couldn't tell how many times he was clubbed before hitting the floor, or even where the blows had landed. All he knew was that his entire body was screaming with pain.

"Stop, please stop!" He begged the boy to have mercy. But there was none, only the anguish of his battered body.

He crumpled to the floor in a heap, his body soaked in sweat—or was it blood? And the bat coming down *again and again and again....*

The next explosion in his head told him that his nose was broken, and his few remaining teeth slithered down his chin, mixing with blood and spittle, while a gusher spurted from the hole that used to be his nose.

Silently watching the bat descending upon him, he was barely able to read the words "Louisville Slugger" burned into the white ash.

again and again and again....

He didn't feel the blow that fractured his skull or the one that crushed his head like an eggshell. He was already unconscious by then, his last thoughts having come to him quite clearly, like bright sunlight peeking through the clouds after a summer storm.

They were:

1. The parents of Crandall will remember Doc Teasdale as a loyal public servant; and,

2. Maybe the boy isn't in trouble after all.

Chapter 7

Something's wrong! Rick and Todd were silent all through breakfast. Rick's head was buried in the newspaper, *of course*, but Todd—bubbly, fidgety Todd—sat machine-like, mechanically shoveling Cheerios into his mouth. Dana tried to get him to talk, to laugh—anything!

"How was Little League yesterday?"

"Fine."

"Excited about being part of a championship team?"

"Yes, Mother."

Mother!

She hadn't noticed it at dinner, but now it was apparent. Something had happened between Todd and Rick, something neither of them was ready to talk about.

I'll give them some time, she thought. I won't press or butt in. It was new, this father-son relationship; it would take some getting used to—for both of them.

After they had gone Dana cleared away the dishes, puzzling over the coolness between her husband and son. "It's nothing," she told herself. But something nestled in the back of her mind edged its way forward. Then Ruth came, with a whirlwind of chatter, driving the thought away.

"Isn't it horrible about that child running away? His parents must be heartbroken. I'll have to give them a call."

Dana remembered the article in the Guardian. She wanted to ask Ruth if she knew the people, but already Ruth had launched into another diatribe.

"I'm really so lucky. Crandall has been such a blessing for us. Tom was so different before we moved here. A compulsive gambler. He once lost our home. Imagine that!"

It was impossible for Dana to think of Tom as being that irresponsible.

"My mother warned me against him. But after she passed on, I just forgot her warning and married him. It was hell, those first eight years. Then struggling with Gamblers' Anonymous. But when we moved to Crandall he changed overnight. Now, he doesn't even think about gambling."

"Coffee?" Dana asked, managing to squeeze in a word.

"Thank you." And Ruth was off again, reliving the first eight years of her marriage. "These are secrets, mind you. But I know you're not one to gossip, right?"

Secrets! I didn't know you had any!

Before Dana could utter a sound, Ruth was into her tale.

Five minutes into Ruth's autobiography Dana's mind began to wander. Crandall had been so very good for Ruth. She'd gone through so much, but in the end she was happy. Dana hoped Crandall would have the same results for her. Rick would change as Tom had. He was changing already. Didn't he take Todd to Little League? And then a further torrent of questions flooded her conciousness. *But, what happened yesterday? And will they spend time together again?* The hidden thought in the back of Dana's mind inched closer to the surface. Something about love.

"Ronnie and Tom were all I had," Ruth went on. "I don't have any family, no brothers or sisters, just an aunt that lives in El Paso. I hung in there through all the hell, and now I'm glad I did." Her story was coming to an end.

"I don't have any family either," Dana said suddenly, caught up in the emotion of her thoughts.

"You don't?"

"Not really." The two women sat staring at one another. The silence that hung over them surprised Dana.

Don't tell me she's swallowed her tongue!

"Go on, tell me!" But Dana couldn't. She was sorry she'd spoken in the first place. "A secret for a secret," Ruth implored.

Not on your life, sister. "Descretion is the better part of valor," Daddy used to say. In other words, "Keep your big mouth shut!"

"Has all of your family passed away?" There was sympathy in Ruth's eyes.

"No."

"Your parents?"

"No!" Memories of her family slowly filtered in. Talks with Dad, Sunday dinners, picnics on the Fourth of July. She loved her family, really loved them, and now she'd never see them again.

For heaven's sake, Ruth, say something!

Ruth stared on silently, and Dana could feel tears bubbling to the surface, along with the bottled-up pain of being separated from her family for so long.

Here she is, ladies and gentlemen, the town crybaby!

"I have a family," Dana blurted. "A wonderful family in Allentown, Pennsylvania, but I'm the family outcast. I haven't seen them in years." The tears rolled down her cheeks. "There's no one that I can turn to—just a brother in Atlanta. So far away. But I have a close friend in New York . . . I think."

"And you have me." Ruth smiled. "We have each other." And before Dana could say anymore, Ruth was off on the merits of friendship.

A smile creased Dana's lips, ending the emotional storm. Her problems with Rick and her family were quite small compared to what Ruth had gone through. She was sure Crandall could have the same wonderful effect on her marriage that it was having on Ruth's. Then the alienation from her family in Allentown wouldn't matter. They just needed a little more time to get things together here, and they had all the time in the world.

"I don't wanna play Little League!" Todd was seated at the dining room table, stuffing Oreos into his mouth and scowling.

"Why not?" asked Dana. He'd come in from school as solemn as when he'd left. Dana was determined to find out why. After she'd plied him with milk and cookies, he began to talk.

" 'Cause I don't like baseball."

"You play baseball all the time."

"But I don't like it anymore."

"Don't you want to be part of the famous team and get a nice uniform?"

"No!"

Was it Rick?

"Are you angry with Daddy?"

"No."

"Sure."

"Yes."

"Then why?" she blurted.

" 'Cause I don't like baseball! Leave me alone!" He was up and running from the room, Scruffy barking behind him.

She had badgered him. She knew it, but she couldn't help herself. Little League was an opportunity for Rick and Todd to get acquainted, to become friends. If this failed Rick might never spend time with him.

Has Rick alienated Todd purposely? Suddenly she laughed out loud. The thought was ludicrous. "Dana, you're becoming a paranoid old hen," she said, still laughing. It's because I'm not working, of course. I have nothing to do but worry. She thought back to all the tears she'd shed recently, her constant doubt, and her sudden feeling of loneliness. She needed something to occupy her time, something more than the house. She needed to work again.

The Guardian came to mind. Max Richter was its editor, but Ruth had told her he was a cantankerous old man who didn't like anybody. Still, it was worth a shot. She'd stop by the office and chat with him tomorrow.

The Guardian could use a little sprucing up. The people around here must be interested in something other than—ugh, Little League. A follow-up story on the runaway boy and an interview with the boy's parents was a good idea. She hoped Max hadn't thought of it already. It was the kind of human interest story that readers loved. Or how about uncovering a Little League conspiracy. *Crandallgate?*

Dana smiled as she walked from the kitchen. The idea of working again excited her. The interview would be a perfect assignment. Her smile broadened. She was feeling good, and all of the little things that had been nagging at her all day now seemed unimportant. Even Todd's not wanting to play Little League. Baseball was a stupid game anyway. Hitting a ball and running in circles—ridiculous! Rick would just have to find another way to get close to Todd.

But that was unimportant now. Dana's thoughts were on tomorrow. She was looking forward to meeting Max Richter, presenting her idea, and most important of all, getting back to work.

Rick called and asked Dana not to fix dinner for him tonight. "I'll be eating in the city, hon. Sorry. It can't be helped." It was enough to start the doubts all over again, but not tonight.

Dinner with some gorgeous ledger, I'm sure.

"All right." Then she remembered Todd. "Todd says he's not playing Little League anymore."

"What? Why?"

"He doesn't like baseball anymore."

Silence.

"Rick?"

"Yeah?"

"Did anything happen out there yesterday?"

"No. He loved it. We had a great time. I don't understand what brought this on." His concern surprised Dana. "Let me speak to the little fella."

A first! Dana thought as she called Todd to the phone. "You can take it in our bedroom."

"Okay."

She was tempted to listen in, but thought better of it. *It's between them. I won't listen.* She waited until Todd picked up, then recradled the phone. A few minutes later Todd called down to her.

"Daddy wants to talk to you, Mommy."

"All right." She picked up. "Rick?"

"Change of plans, hon. I'll be coming home after all."

"You will?" She couldn't hide the surprise in her voice.

"Something's eating at him. I don't know what it is, but I think it's worth losing the Digby account to keep my son happy. Of course this means no villa in Rome."

She chuckled. "With the interest payments on this house, who can think about a villa in Rome?"

"I can." He laughed. "Expect me in a little over an hour. And Dana. . ."

"Yes?"

"I love you."

"I love you, too."

A miracle! And a welcome one. Worrying never solved anything. The moment Dana stopped worrying, all of her problems seemed to come to an end. And the thought that had inched its way to the surface earlier now retreated to a safety zone somewhere deep in the recesses of her mind.

It was wonderful watching Rick handle Todd. He had a way with people. She knew that from experience, but the way he handled Todd was different. She'd never seen him so caring, so loving.

Rick teased his son throughout dinner, and

afterwards they all went into the livingroom to watch TV. Then Rick picked away at the problem like an expert sculptor, seeking out and finding a bust of Homer buried in a slab of hardened clay.

"Mommy tells me you don't want to play baseball anymore. Is that right?"

Todd stared at Dana accusingly, and she felt as if she'd betrayed him. "Yeah."

"Why?" Rick's voice was soft yet firm.

" 'Cause."

"Now, ' 'cause' isn't a reason for anything. Is it?"

Silence.

"Well, is it?"

"No."

"Let me see." Rick cupped his right hand to his chin, resting the elbow on his thigh—his thinking position. "Is it because you don't like being with Daddy?"

"No! I *do* like being with you, Daddy." Dana was glad to hear that.

"Is it because you don't like baseball?"

"No."

"Could it be that you want to start your own team? Todd's Tigers. And challenge the Giants all by yourself. . ."

Todd smiled.

". . . And go on to win the Little League championship of the world single-handed. Maybe even play against the Yankees?"

Todd giggled, then broke into a laugh. "Aw, Daddy."

"Come on, son, tell me what it is. I won't

make you go if you don't want to."

And to Dana's surprise Todd told him everything. He didn't even need milk and cookies!

"They're so good," the boy said. "They're better than any of the kids I've played with. They never drop the ball."

"That's because they practice, son."

"And Adonis. He throws so hard. Daddy, he even throws harder than you!"

An obvious exaggeration.

"Practice harder, son. Tell you what, I'm going to come straight home from work every day for the next few weeks and we'll go out and practice, just you and me. And I promise you, if you keep practicing you'll be as good—better than any of them."

"Really?"

"Promise."

Then it was over. Rick turned on the TV and they never mentioned it again. He switched on the video game, threw in the Pac-Man cartridge, and he and Todd became immediately absorbed in the little yellow figure gobbling up energy dots.

Dana was dumbfounded. She couldn't get over the change in her husband. She knew the team couldn't be as good as Todd had said. She'd watched him throw with Ronnie, and at best that boy was average. She knew that if Rick kept his part of the bargain, Todd could be as good as any of them, and hopefully the family would grow much closer.

Then she thought of the mysterious boy

across the street. He was *very* good. She didn't know much about baseball, but she could tell. He had to be the exception. Most of the boys were probably average, just like Ronnie, and with a few weeks of practice Todd could be as good as any of them.

Chapter 8

Ruth simply had to go. Dana didn't want to be rude, but she could't sit and chat this morning (listen to Ruth chat was more like it). She'd planned on getting an early start. She was going to shower, don her gray tweed suit, and march off to the office of the Crandall Guardian to ask for a job.

She wasn't going to call before hand. She wanted to surprise Max Richter, to sail in and sweep him off his feet with her knowledge and enthusiasm. *And I'm not above begging!* She realized that he might not even be there, but this was the way she was going to do it, and it was worth the risk.

"I'm sorry, Ruth. But I have some errands to run."

"Oh, really? Well, maybe I'll just tag along."

"They're kind of personal."

"Are you pregnant?"

"No, nothing like that."

"Well, what could it be?"

"Personal!" Dana said, a hint of finality in her voice. "I'll call you when I get back."

"I have to take Ronnie for his physical this afternoon." She seemed dejected. "Maybe I'll see you tomorrow."

Is she pouting?

"Sure. Tomorrow. We'll spend the morning together chatting. All right?" And Ruth was gone.

For some reason Dana felt as if she'd just done something horribly wrong, especially since Ruth had reached out to her yesterday. Ruth really was her friend, her only friend in town, but she had to do what she had to do. *I can't sit and listen to her forever.*

Once showered and dressed Dana felt better. She grabbed her copy of the Guardian on the way out, hopped into the 1975 Ford Pinto wagon Rick had bought for her to get around town (he was going to buy himself a *real* car, maybe a Porsche, when he got the chance), and headed for the newspaper office on Eastchester Road.

It was a small brickfaced building on East-chester Road, with the window blinds drawn so you couldn't peek in. Wisps of light spilled through cracks in the blinds so Dana knew there was someone inside, even though her first knock had gone unanswered.

She knocked again, louder, and waited. Still, no answer. "I know he's in there, damn him," she mumbled. "MISTER RICHTER!" And then she pounded.

"Nobody home," said a gravelly voice from within.

"Mr. Richter, my name is Dana Evans and I'd like to talk to you."

"What the fuck about?"

Dana was startled, but only momentarily. She wasn't going to let him throw her. "I'd like to talk to you—face to face."

"Go the fuck away. Come back tomorrow. I'm busy."

"It's important."

"Then go the fuck ahead and talk!"

Dana was not going to let this cantankerous old coot spoil her day. She'd been up all night planning what to say.

"Face-to-fucking-face, Mr. Richter!"

Silence. And then slowly the door opened.

When Dana saw Max Richter for the first time, the word that popped into her head was gray. Max Richter was gray. He was about five-seven in height, between sixty-five and seventy, with tufts of gray hair scattered over his balding pate. He wore steel rimmed glasses, covering tiny gray eyes that regarded her with distaste. A bulky gray cardigan covered a white shirt, (she would discover that he always wore the sweater) and his baggy black pants and black shoes were covered with gray dust from the floor.

"Well?" he said.

Dana smiled. She knew she had a selling job

ahead. *Okay, buster!*

"I'm Dana Evans. I'm new in Crandall, from New York City. I'm a freelance journalist and I was. . ."

"Can it, girly." He started to close the door in her face, but she pushed her way in.

"Mr. Richter, you're being rude. I'm a newspaper person, just like yourself."

"Sure, sure. But I've had it with fucking newspaper people . . . just like myself! Where'd you ever work?" he barked.

"I've done some freelance work for the Chelsea, and The Smith, a literary journal. And last summer I had an article in the living section of the Sunday Daily News."

"Well, at least this one's had some fucking experience."

Dana looked around the office. It was small and seedy looking, with a large metal desk in one corner that was so cluttered the top was virtually hidden. The air in the room was stale, as if the windows hadn't been opened in years. Dana didn't like the place, and she didn't like the "gray" man in front of her. But she wanted a job, and this was the only game in town. She pressed on.

"Mr. Richter, I've brought samples of my work." She reached into her handbag.

"Save 'em, girly. I'm sure you're good, but to tell you the truth, there's no work around here for you." He moved to his desk and began poring over some papers. "Sorry," he said, in an attempt to dismiss her.

"But all you have in the paper are articles

on Little League. Surely the people around here are interested in more than that."

"They're not," he said without looking up.

"But, Mr. Richter, there must be something happening in this town." Then she launched into her presentation. "The Grote family, Mr. Richter. Their neighbors want to know more. . ." He interrupted.

"Another runaway kid. A few years ago I covered them in depth, but the last few I just ignored, and everyone was all the happier."

Dana hadn't taken into consideration that there had been other runaways recently. How could she have known? But she wasn't going to let even this ruin her sales pitch.

"But Mr. Richter, there's a wonderful tie-in here—the Atlanta murders, the kidnappings in Los Angeles. The story would have national appeal." Richter looked up, faintly interested, and Dana went on.

"Mr. Richter, an interview with the tragic family, a look at young Thomas' room—that's the kind of thing that sells newspapers. Stories with some emotion."

"You're right, girly. But in this town the only emotion folks expend is on baseball. For the past five years this town has been interested in nothing but Little League. If I didn't donate most of my copy to the team and the kids, I wouldn't have a fucking newspaper."

"You can't mean that!"

"It's true. I'll give you a break, though. If you want to work, cover the games."

"Games!" It wasn't exactly what Dana had in mind.

"That's it. Take it or leave it."

"I guess I have no choice."

"There's a schedule on the wall. All copy must be in by Friday at six P.M. If you can't be on time I don't need you. Understood?"

"Understood."

"I think you're going to turn out okay. At first I thought you were another bored housewife looking to fill time. But I can tell, call it instinct and it's been wrong, that you're a real professional."

"Thank you."

A quick smile crossed Max's lips but was gone in an instant. "Don't thank me. Prove it!" Then he thought of something. "Busy now? Want a quick assignment?"

"Sure." Even baseball beat not working.

"Doc Teasdale hasn't done the baseball field for a few days. Some of the parents have been bitching, saying I'm wrong about him. I went out on a limb for the old bastard, and now he disappoints me."

"A doctor?"

"Doc Teasdale, it's just a name. He got it because . . . Ah, shit, it's just a name. Go by his place right next to the field. He'll be there, probably drunk. Tell him if he doesn't do something to that field by this afternoon, I'll lead the charge to run him out of town."

Some assignment! "Sounds more like an errand than an assignment."

"A good newspaper woman can generate

her own story. Right, girly?"

Dana had to smile. He was a sharp old coot. "Right."

"Good. I'm sure you'll come up with something."

Max put his head back into his work, and Dana realized that she was dismissed. She started for the door. "Hey, girly. I want you to know I don't cuss as much as you think I do. I was just trying to scare you off." Just then the phone rang. "Who the fuck is that?"

Dana laughed out loud as Max picked up, then she went out the door.

Dana had plans. She was sure Max was overdoing it when he said the people of Crandall were only interested in Little League, and she was going to prove it to him. No, not right away. Max Richter was a stubborn old geezer, set in his ways. It would take some time, but little by little she would show him that the people of Crandall were like people in any other part of the country—interested in a variety of things.

Dana stepped out of the darkened little office and into the sun. It was early spring, a strange time of year, for it was no longer winter yet not quite summer. Mornings were frosty, and often when Dana arose there would be ice on the ground and tiny dew crystals on the windows. By afternoon the frost was gone, replaced by a steady warmth that seemed to increase daily.

By the time Dana had left the office of the

Guardian the temperature had already risen into the mid-sixties, a mild heat wave for late March. The trees had not yet begun to show their buds, but it was obvious that would be remedied in a few short weeks.

We'll be having an early summer, Dana noted as she climbed into the Pinto wagon. Probably a hot one, too.

It was too nice a day to go home. If she went home she'd spend the morning listening to Ruth, and she already had to look forward to that tomorrow. She'd also decided to visit Doc Teasdale later in the afternoon, after Todd came in from school. That left the rest of the morning for herself. She was going to spend the time exploring and enjoying the mild day.

She pointed the car in the direction of the Hutchinson River Parkway, one of the most beautiful stretches of road in the state. Absent-mindedly she headed for the city. *Why did I come this way? That city's like a magnet.* She automatically followed the road, letting her mind wander. Her thoughts touched on many subjects, but settled on nothing in particular. A feeling of triumph spiraled through her. She'd set out to wrestle a job from old Max Richter and had done it. She was entitled to celebrate her victory.

When she saw the sign, LAST EXIT IN WESTCHESTER COUNTY, she got off the parkway immediately, not wanting to go into the city at all. The city was the cause of all her problems, and a good dose of suburban life was the cure.

The exit ramp emptied onto Sanford Boulevard in Mount Vernon. She drove down the boulevard for about a quarter of a mile and stopped at the Colonial diner, where she treated herself to a leisurely lunch. It wasn't anything like lunching at Friday's or any of her favorite eastside restaurants, but it was good.

Afterwards she drove through Mount Vernon to the Bronx River Parkway and headed for home. She thought of Todd. *The bus usually drops him off at two-twenty*. She checked her watch—one-thirty. She had plenty of time, so she stopped off to browse at the tiny Crandall shopping center. It was a day of leisure, and surely not one to worry. Worrying was something Dana wasn't going to do any more. It never solved anything. Besides, it was obvious that all of Dana's problems were behind her.

Someone's in the kitchen! Dana had rushed in the front door and was about to drop her packages on the sofa (she'd purchased a bottle of Jergen's lotion, fake crystal salt and pepper shakers, and a "darling" set of placemats) when she heard the noise. It wasn't her imagination. *I'm not being paranoid! Someone's in the kitchen. A burglar!*

They had been burgled once before, just

after they had been married. They were living in an old five-story apartment building on Amsterdam Avenue, not far from Columbia University, but bordering Harlem.

Dana had come in early that day. She'd gone to class but was feeling queasy from her pregnancy, so she decided to take the rest of the day off. When she arrived home she found the door unlocked and open just a crack. Rick, she figured, and pushed in, all smiles for her new husband.

The apartment was in shambles, and it took her all of two minutes to realize they'd been robbed. The portable TV and a borrowed radio-cassette player were missing.

She ran from the apartment into the street screaming like a maniac.

"Hey, lady, what's wrong?" asked an aging black man, with bloodshot eyes and a gray stubble of whiskers.

"My apartment's been robbed!" she screamed.

"Hell, s'that all? Everyone lives round here gits robbed sometime, lady. It's the law of the land. This ain't Scarsdale, you know! The way you screamin', I thought you was raped or somethin'." Already a small group had gathered, and Dana could hear a chorus of chuckles springing up around her.

It had been a horrible and embarrassing experience, but at least she hadn't walked in on the burglar.

Now, a flurry of thoughts and fears flashed through her as she stood, petrified, by the sofa. *Should I run? Scream? Call the police? And where's Scruffy?* She heard the soft clunk of the refrigerator door closing. *Strange.* Then the sound of liquid sloshing into a glass. *Sounds like someone's pouring a glass of milk.* She checked her watch. 2:15. It was still too early for Todd, and he didn't have a key. *Who?*

She ran a list of possibles through her mind: Rick, Todd, Ruth? But it couldn't be any of them. No, their home was being robbed. *The city doesn't have a monopoly on burglaries.*

She was certain of the next sound she heard. Someone had taken down the cookie tin and was opening it. *Well, whoever's out there likes milk and cookies.* Her list of options turned over in her mind, and she came to a decision. She wasn't going to run, scream or call the police before she had a chance to see who was in the kitchen. Burglar or not, this was *her* home.

Gingerly, she placed her packages on the sofa—*God, those bags are noisy*—and began creeping towards the dining room door. The entire house was silent, save for the soft munching and slurping sounds coming from the other side of the door. *A child?*

By the time Dana reached the door her nerve had begun to falter, and she wondered just what the hell she thought she was doing. *The hero type, I'm not!*

Abruptly the eating sounds stopped, and the sudden quiet that shrouded the room slipped over Dana like a net. Her feet were frozen, as if she'd been standing in quick drying cement; they refused to move forward or backward. The only recognizable sound was her heartbeat, thundering through the silence like a booming bass drum.

What am I doing? she thought. There couldn't possibly have been a child out there. And if it was a cookie munching burglar, what could she do? That's when she told herself to run.

She turned and started a hasty yet silent retreat for the front door—and hopefully safety.

Then the dining room door burst open.

"HEY!"

"Ahhhhh!" She screamed as she stumbled on toward the front door.

"Dana!" She was almost out when she recognized the voice. *Rick?*

She turned, not knowing what to expect, and was ecstatic to see her husband's smiling face.

"You scared the hell out of me," he said. "Why didn't you tell me you were home?"

"*I* scared *you*! What are you doing home so early?" The fear began draining out of her.

"I took the afternoon off. Figured I'd get in early, so I could have a little extra time to work out with the tiger."

Scruffy's high pitched yelp could be heard coming down the stairs. He had been cuddled up in the master bedroom, taking an afternoon nap. "Some watchdog!" Dana said, throwing her hands up in mock despair.

And suddenly it was all so very funny. It was silly what Dana had thought. *A cookie munching burglar. Ridiculous!* She wouldn't even bother to tell Rick of her silly fear. The more she thought of it the more ridiculous it seemed. She broke into a slow, steady laugh, and Rick joined in. As their fears diminished, their laughter increased.

Crandall was "as safe a town as you can find anywhere." Hadn't Ruth told her that? And it was true. This was just another case of paranoia. *Watch it, girl, or you'll be a cardiac victim.* And even that was funny.

Then Todd came through the door and stared, puzzled, at his laughing parents.

"What's so funny?" But neither answered. They just couldn't stop laughing.

Todd wanted Ronnie to work out with him and his dad, but since Ronnie was going to have his physical today, Todd asked Jimmy Warren, the team's second baseman, if he could come over, and Jimmy said yes.

"He's a nice boy," Rick told Dana. "I met him at team practice the other evening, and he was a perfect gentleman."

Rick decided the boys should have a snack of milk and cookies before working out—"to boost their strength. "Ronnie came over for a few minutes, and Rick escorted all of the boys into the dining room, laughing and kidding along with them.

The happy sounds coming from the dining room added to Dana's already good mood.

These were the sounds of home, the first real home she'd had since she left for college over eleven years ago. At that moment Dana felt truly blessed. These were the happy family sounds she'd be hearing regularly from now on.

She stepped into the dining room to tell Rick that she was going out on an assignment. *Oh, my goodness!* Puddles of milk were scattered over the chrome and glass table. It reminded her of Broadway after a rainstorm.

Rick had joined the boys in their snack, and cookie crumbs lay everywhere, except in front of the new boy.

The place in front of Jimmy Warren was spotless. And while the other two boys were joking and making an utter mess, the Warren boy sat silently munching his cookies, as if he were trying to impress someone with his good table manners.

"This is Jimmy Warren, hon. He's our all-star second baseman. Right, Jimmy?" Rick smiled boyishly. Jimmy smiled and nodded.

He had piercing blue eyes that seemed to stare right through Dana—*I've seen those eyes before*—and a hideously close haircut.

"Pleased to meet you, Jimmy." *He reminds me of that strange boy across the street.* "Honey, I have some great news."

"Really? What?"

"Today I went over to the Guardian, the town newspaper, and the editor gave me a job. I'm leaving right now for my first assignment." Rick didn't seem impressed.

"You work for the Guardian, Mrs. Evans?"
Ronnie asked, all excited.

Well, at least someone appreciates it.
"Yes."

"You gonna cover the games?"

"Why, yes, I am."

"You must know baseball real good, huh?"

"I know it well enough."

Rick laughed. "Well, guys, don't be surprised if you're hitting touchdowns and running the bases for field goals this season." Everyone laughed except Jimmy, who sat munching his cookies, followed by short slurps of milk.

It was an old wood-frame house on the south side of Crandall Park, opposite the baseball field and just off of Edgemont hill. It had obviously seen better days. A gift from Edgemont Crandall to his son Peter on the boy's twenty-fifth birthday, the house then had been painted a sparkling pearl white, with gold trimmed shutters and a huge oak door. It was one of the loveliest homes in Westchester county, second in beauty only to the Crandall mansion. But that was ages ago, long before the town of Crandall itself had existed.

Today the house was an eyesore, a ghost of its former self.

As Dana walked across the winter-hardened earth that separated the house from the field, she thought of the old Harley house in Allentown. The Harley home had been abandoned for as long as Dana could remember. All the kids called it haunted, each generation telling their own tale of how the house got that way.

I'd never live in a place like this, Dana thought, wondering what kind of man Doc Teasdale was. She was hoping to find out, and she'd brought along pad and pen, just in case the inspiration for a story hit her.

She mounted the old wooden steps and stopped on the porch. The house was quiet, deathlike, and she remembered the foreboding stillness of the Harley house. Slowly she approached the door, not believing that anyone could live in such a place. *Doc Teasdale must be a spook.*

She pounded on the door. Nothing. The house seemed like a tomb, and she decided never to come out here alone again. She knocked a second time. *Max said he'd be home, "probably drunk."* She knocked again, louder. She wanted to leave but didn't want Max to think she was incompetent, uncapable of carrying out the simplest of tasks.

She decided to try the knob. If he were drunk, he may have fallen asleep. She turned the knob. The door clicked open, and gently she pushed forward. "Mr. Teasdale, don't be alarmed."

Suddenly the door was yanked open from within.

"What do you want here?"

"I'm here to see Doc Teasdale."

"Who are you?"

"Are you Doc Teasdale?"

"No. Who are you?" asked the elderly man

with distrusting eyes. He wore a gray sweat-suit, with the word "Giants" across the front in bright orange letters.

"I'm Dana Evans..."

"Evans?"

"I'm new in town. Max Richter sent me here to see Doc Teasdale. I represent the Guardian. Is he in?" She tried pressing on into the house, but he blocked her way. Then he stepped out onto the porch, swinging the door shut behind him.

"Yes, of course, Evans. I live across the street from you. The white stucco." She now recognized him as the man she'd seen playing catch with the strange boy. "I'm Philip Dreiser." He smiled, extending his hand, but the expression in his eyes never changed.

"Coach Dreiser?"

"Yes."

"I've heard so much about you." He didn't strike her as a baseball coach. He was tall, at least six feet, with a full head of salt and pepper hair, and he wasn't at all out of shape. But there was something non-athletic about him. The outfit he wore was right, but somehow it didn't fit the man. She tried telling herself it was his age (maybe sixty-five) that had prejudiced her, but she knew it was more than that.

He ignored her compliment. "Your son... Tommy... will be joining us, I hope?"

"Todd. And yes, he's looking forward to it."

"Good. He shows promise. Maybe not this year, but next year I'm certain he'll be on our tournament team.''

"He'll be glad to know that."

"Just watch his diet. No fatty foods, plenty of protein. It's the right foods that make successful athletes. Steak, lean, serve it twice a week, no more. Do you hear me?"

"Yes." *Pushy, isn't he?*

"I'll be giving him a special diet. See to it that he follows it."

"All right." *Todd will eat like the rest of us!* "Can I see Doc Teasdale now?"

"I'm sorry, but there's been a tragic accident." He took Dana's arm and escorted her from the porch, guiding her towards the car.

"What? Is he all right?"

"No, my dear, he isn't. He's dead."

"I'm sorry to hear that."

"To tell the truth, it isn't totally un-expected. A man of his age drinking the way he did. I found him this morning. The body's already been taken to the coroner's office." They reached her car. "Tell Max to say something nice about him in next week's paper. He will be truly missed." But his voice lacked sincerity.

He opened the car door for Dana. She hesitated, then climbed in. *I've heard of the "bum's rush" before, but this is ridiculous!* Dana excused his brevity with her. The two men probably had been very close. He needed to be alone.

There was something that momentarily touched her about Dreiser. Concern for his dead friend made her notice something fatherly about him. Although she tried to remain removed from the man, something slowly pulled her in.

"Well, I have to get back," he said. "There's still some tidying up to do. Give my regards to Max." He turned and started back for the house.

"Coach Dreiser, how did it happen?"

He spun around slowly, his eyes narrowing. "A massive stroke," he said sorrowfully. "What a horrible way to die."

Chapter 9

"Outside, dog!" Dana was putting Scruffy
out. She'd been trying to get him to walk himself since they'd moved to Crandall, but he
still was having trouble adjusting. "This is
not an apartment, and we are not living in the
city. Understand?" Scruffy stood playfully
wagging his tail. "Out!" She pushed the dog
out the back door and closed it behind him.
His high pitched whine rang out from the
other side. *Dumb dog!*

Dana's spirits were still quite high—a
family dinner two nights in a row. And although franks and beans had been tonight's
menu, Dana felt it was the best family dinner they'd ever had. Rick and Todd were
back on good terms, and Dana bubbled with
tales of cantankerous old Max Richter—"such
language!"—and the sad news about Doc
Teasdale.

She had just finished the dinner dishes and

was tidying up when Scruffy started begging to be taken out. "Go by yourself—in the yard. You're not afraid of the dark, are you?" She had let him out and was returning to her chores when she heard a knock. No one had ever knocked on the back door before. She pulled back the curtain and saw Ruth.

When she opened the door, Scruffy rushed in.

"I'm going to start keeping that dog tied in the yard."

There was something wrong. It was all over Ruth's face. "What's the matter?"

"I know I'm just being silly, but I have to take Ronnie to the hospital."

"What happened?"

"His physical. It seems he has a heart murmur. Doctor Warner called and said it's probably nothing serious, but they want to look at him right away. Tonight. They practically insisted."

"It can't be serious," Dana consoled. The boy had been with them that afternoon and seemed fine.

"That's what they say, but they seem so urgent about it."

"Ruth, they're just practicing preventive medicine."

"I suppose so. Coach Dreiser must have something to do with this. He's really concerned about the health of the boys, and when he says something, everyone around here jumps."

Not everyone! "Just be glad he has that type of influence."

Ruth smiled. "You're right. I should be glad that Coach Dreiser takes such interest in the boys." She broke into an embarrassed laugh. "I knew I was being silly, but thanks anyway. Like that man in the commercial, 'I needed that!' "

"My pleasure."

"I have to get him over to Community General tonight. I guess this means a day out of school."

They laughed together, and Dana realized just how much she cared for Ruth.

"We're still on for tomorrow?" Ruth asked. "Ronnie's big enough to be left alone for a few hours."

"I'm looking forward to it."

"Great. See you then, and thanks again for the reinforcement."

After Ruth had gone, Dana wondered about Coach Dreiser. He was probably a very good father, she thought, remembering her own father's lack of influence over the family.

Her father should have been more like Dreiser, she mused. Still, his interest in this heart murmur thing gave her a funny feeling. She couldn't put her finger on it, but one thing for sure was she didn't like the man.

Chapter 10

Philip Dreiser finished cleaning up the bloodstains from the old wood floor. It had been a hard job considering the mess he'd found that morning, taking practically all day. Then he had to dispose of the body.

They were lucky and he knew it. Teasdale had no family or friends, no one to claim his remains. But luck or not, Dreiser was worried, more worried than he'd been in five years. Things were going so well. A scandal could ruin it all.

"This couldn't have been done by one of my boys," he thought out loud. But there was an odd prickling at the base of his skull, a hunch that contradicted his words.

One of my boys has gone bad. The thought inflicted itself on his consciousness. And as much as he wanted to believe that Teasdale had been murdered by some wandering maniac, he knew it just wasn't true, knew it in his guts. This heinous thing had been done by one of his boys. And now, before it happened again, before everything was ruined, he had to find out who!

Chapter 11

Dana checked the big starburst clock on the dining room wall. It was almost 11:30. She was laboriously vacuuming, as news filtered from the radio of another tragic kidnapping in Los Angeles. Dana was sorry for the poor girl's parents but couldn't help be pleased by the comparative security she felt living in Crandall, where Todd was safe.

This morning Dana had a chance to get a jump on her work, a chance she hadn't had since they'd moved to Crandall. Ruth wasn't there to slow her progress.

After she'd finished downstairs, she decided to have a cup of coffee, and then tackle the upstairs bedrooms.

I hope there's nothing seriously wrong with Ronnie. If Ruth didn't come over by the time Todd got home from school, Dana was going to knock on her door, just to make sure everything was all right.

* * *

Todd was running away.

"I'm not happy here, Mother! I'll be happier in Allentown." He'd packed a bag and was heading for the door. The woman in black stood waiting for him.

"No, Todd, don't go!" He wasn't happy in Crandall. She thought he was happy, but he wasn't.

He reached the woman and turned back to his mother.

"I want to be with *her*," he said, pointing to the woman in black.

The woman spoke. "He'll be happy with us, and he won't run off against our wishes. We'll be a family again." Dana now recognized the woman. It was her mother.

"No, you can't have him!" she screamed. She tried to reach out to her son, but the woman's baleful eyes held her back.

"Todd will be happy in Allentown."

"I'll be happy in Allentown, Mother!"

"No, please. Take Scruffy instead." The dog's incessant barking irritated her.

"I'll be happy there," Todd said taking the woman's hand.

"NO!" And they were gone. "Take Scruffy!" His barking and whining bounced around inside her head.

She sat up with a start.

She was in her bedroom, lying across the bed. Perspiration washed over her body. Scruffy's yapping had awakened her.

Dana had cleaned all morning, and after

Todd had come home, she decided to take a nap. *And then I'll knock on Ruth's door.*

Scruffy was in the backyard. The dog simply had to learn that this wasn't an apartment and that it was fun to be out of doors.

She went to the window. Todd, Jimmy and a new boy, also with a hideous haircut, were throwing the ball around.

"Todd?" Dana called down. "Please bring Scruffy around the front with you. Can't you hear him whining? He wants to play."

"Aw, Mom, Scruffy can't play baseball. He'll just get in the way."

"Todd, get the dog!"

"All right," he groaned.

Dana went back to the bed.

What a horrible dream—Todd running away to Allentown with her mother! She hadn't seen her mother since Todd was a baby.

She'd gone back home once, when Todd was four months old. It was supposed to be a week long visit, hopefully to make amends, but her stay lasted just three days. Everyone was glad to see her except her mother. She was cold towards Dana, rarely speaking, and when she did speak, she scolded Dana for leaving home in the first place. She didn't even go near the baby; *that* hurt the most.

And now in Dana's dream her mother was taking Todd. *Fat chance!* But still the dream had unnerved her, had seemed so real.

"Mommy," Todd called from downstairs.

"Yes, what is it?"

"Can we have some milk and cookies?"

"Okay."

He *was* happy. This was his home, and he was happy. He would never run away from home.

Dana again wondered about the runaway boy. There had been others before him. *How many?* There was really no problem with Todd, though, especially now that his father was taking such an interest in him. Those other boys probably were neglected, and this certainly wasn't the case with Todd. He wouldn't run away, and he wasn't going to disappear mysteriously. Those kinds of things happened in cities like Atlanta, Los Angeles, or New York. But they were living in Crandall and were well protected from urban trauma.

Then Scruffy started to scream.

That dog! He was becoming more of a pain than he was worth. His high pitched whine punished her ears. *Stop it!* she thought. You'd think he was being murdered.

"Todd, get Scruffy!" No answer. *That boy!* I don't know what to do with either of them.

The dog was screaming louder, begging. *Something's wrong!* She raced to the window.

Downstairs, Jimmy Warren was kicking Scruffy like a football.

Whack! The little dog's fuzzy body lifted easily into the air and crashed to earth. There was already blood running from the dog's mouth.

"Stop it. You're killing him!" The boy

ignored her pleas as well as the dog's high pitched whine.

Playful Scruffy, slumping on the ground, wagged his tail. He tried to lick Jimmy's shoe, a sign of forgiveness.

Whump!

Dana ran downstairs to the dog's aid.

Whump! Jimmy Warren kicked the dog in the teeth. *Whack!* Then in the behind, and the dog flew almost three feet. *A third kick!* The dog's bladder let go, and a stream of urine trailed him, as Jimmy Warren again applied his foot.

When Dana reached the front of the house, the poor dog lay heaped on the ground. The boy's foot was on his head, and he was applying slow pressure.

A low involuntary groan escaped Dana's lips: *"Ohhhhh!"* She could see the dog's head steadily flattening, his eyes bulging from their sockets, as if any moment they would pop out.

A soft purring sound eminated from somewhere deep in the dog's throat. It was a plea for mercy.

"Stop it . . . *Please!*" Dana was practically on top of the boy when she heard the soft cracking sounds. It almost was like someone crinkling a piece of cellophane—but she knew better. By the time she'd wrestled the boy away, the dog was dead.

Dana was sick. She'd thrown up twice already, but there was still a violent churning in the pit of her stomach.

The day had turned into a nightmare.

Scruffy was dead. One of the neighbors had called the police, and soon after Dana had wrestled the boy to the ground (she had wanted to stomp his face), the police came and took him away. Then she called the A.S.P.C.A., and they sent out a truck to pick up poor Scruffy's remains. And Todd cried an ocean of tears and kept asking, "Why, why?"

"Mommy doesn't know why." *The boy just plain went crazy!*

She'd seen it in the boy's eyes the day before and now recognized that piercing stare as the look of a madman.

She had thought of phoning the boy's parents—whoever the Warrens may be—but was too disgusted for any confrontation and decided to leave it in the hands of the police.

Rick called around five and said there was just "no way possible" that he could make it home for dinner. She didn't mention the dog. *Why spoil his day, too.* When he came in there would be time enough to tell.

Dinner, of course, was trying, with neither she nor Todd speaking and Scruffy's absence billowing over them like a cloud of doom. Now that she was ready for bed she once again felt the hot bile bubble up into her throat. And she still hadn't been in touch with Ruth.

David Grote sat patiently in the Dreiser living room, waiting to speak to the coach.

Dreiser, who a few minutes earlier had

popped a cartridge into his VCR home video unit, was seated on the sofa, staring at the TV. His attention was riveted to the screen, and Grote didn't dare interrupt.

On the screen was a scene from the 1976 Montreal Olympics. Tiny, smiling, fourteen year old Nadia Comaneci, pony tail bouncing, trotted out confidently onto the main performance area. The crowd went wild.

All that week the fans had been awed by young Nadia's performances, and by now they had fallen totally in love with her. This was the finals of the balance beam competition, and they were ready for another miracle.

As Nadia mounted the balance beam, the crowd grew silent.

"Watch this," Dreiser said.

David Grote continued to watch, but of course, he'd seen it all before, back in '76, and he knew the outcome.

"Did you see that!" Dreiser said, after Nadia had performed a graceful, seemingly effortless routine. "The sons of bitches have it, David!"

David Grote had no idea what Dreiser was talking about, and he didn't really care. He wasn't there for a social call, but he knew better than to interrupt when Dreiser was preoccupied. So David Grote waited for the proper time to discuss his wife, Helen.

When the scores for the balance beam competition went up, young Nadia had tallied a perfect ten. The crowd was ecstatic.

The two men sat silently watching as Nadia Comaneci went through her floor exercise, the uneven bars, and the vault. Nadia was sparkling in each.

Everyone knows all this, Grote thought. He wondered why Dreiser suddenly had become enamored with the girl.

Finally the tape ended, and Dreiser clicked the TV screen to black. Yet still he sat staring, as if he were mesmerized by what he had just seen. Grote wanted to snap him out of it; he had to discuss Helen.

"Did you see that?" Dreiser said suddenly, his eyes still hazy.

"Yes. She was very good . . . Say, Coach, I'd like to discuss my wife."

"They have it, you know."

"Who? What?"

Dreiser looked up. "The Soviet bloc nations. They know my little secret. Didn't you see it in her eyes?"

"No."

"The eyes always give it away."

Suddenly what Dresier meant registered in Grote's mind. "You mean they. . ."

"Precisely," Dreiser said nodding. "You didn't think our secret was reserved only for little Crandall."

"I guess I never thought about it. But isn't that against Olympic rules?"

Dreiser regarded him with a tolerant smile. "I'm still ahead of them. They haven't gone public with it, and I doubt if they will before the end of the summer," he said, ignoring the question.

"You think they've had it since 1976, and they're holding back. Why?"

"I'm developing a theory, but it's only a theory, mind you. Suppose in 1972 the Russians tried it with Olga Korbut. It was a mild success. Then in 1976 the Rumanians have Nadia—a greater success. Now suppose in 1980 they had planned to launch a full scale program, and after Eastern Communist nations swept the Olympics, they would announce to the world what they had done."

Dreiser paused as the thing solidified in his mind.

"Are you following me?"

"Yes," said Grote.

"Now, what if the CIA found out about it—that wouldn't be hard—and they told someone in the state department. Something like this could reduce our country's influence from a world power to practically nothing overnight."

"Of course," David agreed. He'd finally latched onto Dreiser's train of thought.

"So if the U.S. couldn't counteract it, what would be our country's only defense?" Dreiser asked.

"To pull out of the 1980 Olympics."

"Precisely. To find a good saleable-to-the-rest-of-the-world reason, and then pull out."

The two men sat silently, as Grote digested what Dreiser had said.

"I'll tell you something, David. We're not just dealing with baseball. We're dealing with the leaders of tomorrow."

David Grote was well aware of the benefits of Dreiser's program. "I know."

Dreiser smiled. "But I'm going to get all the credit for it, ALL of the credit, and nothing is going to stand in my way!"

There was a quiet confidence in Dreiser that unsettled David. At that moment Dreiser seemed ruthless.

"Now, what can I do for you?" Dreiser suddenly had returned to the everyday world.

Finally! "My wife, she wants to have a baby."

"Really! What did you tell her?"

"That it was out of the question. But she desperately wants to try again."

"How is she holding up?"

"She's been a little withdrawn."

"Do you think she'll crack?"

"I don't know."

Dreiser's eyes pierced David. "David, I don't care if you and Helen have a million babies, but Helen mustn't crack. Have you ever thought of leaving Crandall?"

"No," David said. He loved Crandall and had no intention of leaving.

"Helen must not crack! Do you understand?" Dreiser's eyes sliced into him.

"Yes."

"Good." Dreiser relaxed. "Seven tens."

"What?"

"In the National Olympics, Nadia Comaneci was awarded seven perfect tens." Dreiser's eyes again had hazed over, but his mind was far from the Olympics.

Chapter 12

Dana couldn't sleep. She was lying there staring at the ceiling when she heard the cab pull up below. An hour earlier she had checked Todd, and he'd finally fallen into a fitful sleep. When she had put him to bed, he'd sworn he'd never again sleep without a light burning.

Then Rick was in the room, and suddenly it was time to tell him. She watched him walk over to the armchair by the window to set down his briefcase. It was practically a ritual with him since they'd lived in Crandall—crossing the room to that chair, where he would sit before undressing.

He's a handsome man, she thought, her mind temporarily avoiding the issue at hand. She thought back to when she'd dated Rick in college, she a lowly freshman and he a knowledgable junior. He was handsome, intelligent and a good dresser, and she was the small town girl on her first trip to the big city.

It was the type of cornball cliche you'd see in an old movie on the Late Late Show. She practically idolized him, and he ate it up. Her adoration was prime grist for his ego. That was eleven years ago. A lot had changed in eleven years, but she still found herself admiring him. He was determined to make it with his business, and she knew he would.

"Hi, hon. Nice of you to wait up. Nothing wrong, I hope." Rick's statement snatched Dana's mind from the past to the present. He was smiling and walking towards the bed. Then he stopped. "What's wrong?"

She stared at him silently for what felt like a lifetime. Several minutes passed before she spoke. "Scruffy's dead."

"What?" He rushed to the bed and instinctively threw his arms around her. "Hit by a car?"

"Hit by Jimmy Warren."

"Huh?"

"Or should I say kicked by Jimmy Warren? Yes, I will say it. Scruffy was kicked to death by Jimmy Warren." She said it slowly, shaping her words to give them added impact. But an icy numbness had crept over her, and what spilled from her lips were words, just unattached words without meaning.

"I don't believe it ... I mean, I believe it but ... When? Why?"

And suddenly it was all so very funny, too funny to discuss further. "No more Scruffy," she said lightly. "No more dumb dog—apartment dog. He was an apartment dog, did you know that?" A soft titter escaped her lips and slowly rose into full blown laughter.

"Dana," Rick called, but her mind had traveled to some other galaxy where things were all so very funny. "DANA!" he screamed. Laughter rolled around the room.

Grabbing her shoulders, he shook her violently, like an angry child shaking a rag doll. Slowly the laughter abated, turning into spastic gasps and sobs. She put her head on his shoulder and wept bitterly.

"It's all right, honey. How's Todd?"

"Holding up better than I am, I'm afraid."

"What happened?"

Slowly she told the tale, finishing by adding, "I noticed it yesterday, that look in his eyes. The boy's crazy, Rick.

"Maybe you're overreacting, just a little."

His statement angered her. "Overreacting! The boy kicked the shit out of Scruffy and then stood on the poor dog's head. What if that had been a person? It could have been one of his teammates. It could have been Todd!"

"Okay, okay, maybe you're right. I wasn't here. What did they do with him?"

"The police took him to the hospital for observation. The last I heard he was still there, and I hope he stays there forever."

"Dana, he's just a kid."

"Forever!"

Breakfast was strained, but Rick was really trying to bring both of them around. For once his head wasn't buried in the paper.

"Pancakes on Wednesday! How about that, tiger? Mom's really something, isn't she?"

"Yeah." Todd wasn't eating. Pancakes were his favorite, but this morning it was as if his plate were filled with brussel sprouts.

"With a breakfast like this, what could possibly be for dinner?"

Dana smiled silently at her husband. She didn't have an answer; she just didn't know.

"Practice today, Todd. They'll be choosing your position."

"Coach Dreiser says he thinks I'm a pitcher."

"Hey, I have another Fernando Valenzuela, rookie sensation."

"You think so?" Todd was smiling.

"Son, if we keep working out, they just *might* rename that team Todd's Tigers."

The boy laughed. At least he's coming round, Dana thought.

Breakfast picked up a little after that. Since kids had excellent recuperative powers, Dana was sure that Todd would be back to normal by evening. As for herself, she knew it would take a little longer. But it was consoling to know that there was always Ruth to keep her mind off this dreadful thing.

It was 10:30 and Ruth still hadn't come by. Now, Dana was beginning to worry. She'd finished her third cup of coffee, which only made her more jittery.

No more coffee today, she thought. When

Ruth came by she'd have tea.

At 10:45 she dialed Ruth's number, and let the phone ring sixteen times. Then, just to be certain there was nothing wrong with the phone, she went over and knocked on the door. No answer.

She hoped everything was okay and that Ruth had just gone shopping or something. She thought of doing her own weekly marketing but decided to wait until Saturday, when Rick was home and they could go to that new grocery warehouse in White Plains. She heard prices there were so reasonable it was really worth the trip.

Guess I'll drop by the newspaper office and see what Max is doing. Oh, brother! she thought. She hadn't told Max about Doc Teasdale. She had planned to tell him yesterday afternoon, but this horrible thing with Scruffy made her forget.

She hurried home to change. She had some explaining to do. *For a newspaper woman I'm sure getting started on the wrong foot.*

Stoop shouldered Max Richter sat behind the metal desk silently staring up at Dana. When she had arrived at the office a few minutes earlier, she immediately had launched into the events of the past two days, making sure she didn't give him a chance to get a word in edgewise. Now, she was nearing the end of her story.

"... It was a horrible day, and I'm not normally forgetful, and if you think that my not getting back to you about the death of Doc Teasdale is an inexcusable offense, then you're a cold-hearted bastard, and I wouldn't work for you if you paid me, which by the way, you're going to have to do if I stay." She stopped abruptly, staring down at him, expecting the worst.

"Damnit, girly, you sure talk in long sentences. I hope you don't write that way."

"I don't."

"Good. Then I guess you can stay around." A smile began to form on her lips. "To cover the games, of course."

"Of course."

"I heard about Doc Teasdale the night it happened. Dreiser called me. He wanted to make sure you were who you said you were. He said you didn't look like no fucking newspaper woman."

"What! Well, he sure doesn't look like a baseball coach either."

"That's the spirit, girly. That's what we need more of around here."

Dana smiled. "You instigating old bastard."

Max thought that was funny, and he cackled away. "He really did say that, girly. Said he thought I could make a better choice. What the fuck does he know about newspaper people?!"

"Right," Dana barked in agreement.

"You and me, girly. We're gonna get along just fine."

"I believe we are."

"Listen, I'd like you to get a fix on how we cover the games. Downstairs is what I call my archives. Down there is a copy of every edition of the Guardian since I took over. Why don't you browse around down there and get an idea of our format.

"Papers from the last two years are filed by issue number. They're all down there, though—twenty-two years worth, but not in any order. If you want anything earlier than two years ago you'll have to hunt for it." He looked at her hard, as if he had to justify his poor filing system. "I'm a newspaper man, not a fucking record keeper."

"How do I get downstairs?"

"The pressroom is through that door. I do all the printing here myself. I have a small electric press. I don't use any of that photo offset bullshit, although I would if I could afford it. Anyway, in the back of the pressroom there's a door that leads downstairs. Don't make a mess."

"I won't."

At the bottom of a flight of old rickety steps Dana found the light switch to illuminate the archive room.

"Don't make a mess!" she mumbled. The room looked as though a hurricane had recently passed through.

It was much larger than any of the rooms upstairs, running the entire length and width of the building. Down the middle of the ceiling ran a column of fluorescent lights that adequately illuminated the bare middle of the room but did little to brighten the corners and walls, where the papers were stored.

Around the entire room, except for the back wall, were old wooden, floor to ceiling, bookshelves, with four or five racks on each shelf. The shelves were crammed with newspapers. Against the back wall was a smaller, newer bookshelf. "The 1980s" was written on masking tape and stuck to the top of the shelf. A three tiered file cabinet sat next to the bookshelf, and alongside the cabinet was a card table and four chairs.

Scattered around the floor were newspapers, some in bundles, and some, old and yellowed, thrown helter-skelter.

Dana headed straight for the back wall. She decided to quickly scan a few issues, then get the hell out of there.

As she walked across the stone floor, the chill of the place enveloped her. The heat obviously didn't work well down there, and the room smelled of mildew. Her initial impression of the place was "dreary," and that was being generous.

Reaching the wall, she sorted through a random stack of papers. TOURNAMENT TEAM CRANDALL'S FINEST was the headline on the June 15th, 1981 edition. She quickly scanned the article, then aimlessly grabbed another paper which proclaimed DREISER PITCHES SHUTOUT. Dreiser? Carefully she perused the article:

* * *

'Adonis Dreiser, pitching with the fine form that led Crandall to winning the world's championship last year, today pitched his first near perfect game of the young season. Playing again for Harvey's Cleaners, Adonis struck out ten batters on the Walgreen's team, as Harvey's chalked up their third victory of the year.

Last season, young Dreiser pitched six shutouts, including two in the championship playoffs. . .'

Dana stopped reading. The format was basic, but she realized she had a lot to learn about Little League. The Giants was the name she associated with Crandall, but the boys seemed to play for other local teams. Obviously the best were chosen to play for the Giants, at least that was how she figured it. She had a lot of questions. She'd go to Ruth. Ruth would know. She smiled. Surprisingly, Little League *had* piqued her interest.

Her thoughts drifted to Ruth's absence, and she hoped everything was okay.

She again focused on the paper. The big surprise was the name Adonis Dreiser. She pictured the strange boy across the street and wondered how he was related to old Coach Dreiser. Suddenly she was very curious about Crandall and Little League baseball.

Well, I've seen enough. Turning to leave, her gaze fell on the metal file cabinet, and she wondered what it held. Some type of records, no doubt.

She went to the cabinet and pulled open the upper drawer, which slid along its bearings with a soft "woosh." Surprisingly, the files in the drawer were extremely neat. There weren't many—maybe ten or twelve yellow folders with names neatly typed on each of the tabs. She recognized the name on the first folder in front—Thomas Grote. She'd seen the name before. *Where?* She reached for the file, hoping a glimpse at it would refresh her memory. As her fingers locked onto the yellow folder she heard the soft creaking of the stairs. Max was coming down. Instinctively she returned the file and was about to slide the drawer shut when Max entered.

"Uh-oh, just as I thought. You're a newspaper woman all right." Slowly he shuffled towards the rear. "Thought I'd look in on you, and it's a good thing I did. The one thing that's off limits, and you find it." Reaching her, he smiled. "Those files are private, girly. But feel free to look at anything else down here your little heart desires."

"I'm sorry. I . . ."

"My fault, girly. I didn't tell you." He stepped in front of her and pushed in the gray button at the top of the cabinet that locked the three drawers. "Like I said, feel free to look at anything else." He looked in her eyes. "Any luck with the papers?"

"Yes. I found a few articles. I'm sure I can handle the style. It's pretty basic."

He turned and headed back. "Gotta get

back, girly. I've got to fill this week's paper with some bullshit. I'll sure be glad when the season starts."

Moments later Dana was standing alone, wondering about the file and wishing she'd glanced at it. *Thomas Grote*. The name was very familiar. Maybe Ruth had mentioned it. She couldn't remember.

Chapter 13

There was an awesome stillness in the house. The house had been quiet before, but today it was different. It weighed on Dana, and she dragged it around from room to room. Often Dana had hoped, prayed, that she would get some quiet time for herself. But this quiet wasn't welcome.

It was a screaming silence, that wailed like a banshee in her ears. It was the lack of Scruffy. This time he wasn't upstairs napping, ready to fling himself into her arms when she stepped into the bedroom. This time he was gone for good.

Ruth still wasn't home, and sitting in the house alone was suddenly a chore. She needed companionship—now! Ruth's words flashed through her mind: "We have each other." But she needed Ruth now. *Where is she?*

A little while later Todd came in, making things somewhat easier, but when he asked for milk and cookies she again thought of Scruffy. She wondered what would have happened if she had said "no" to the boy yesterday. She chastised herself for ever forcing Scruffy to stay in the yard.

"I miss Scruffy, Mommy."

"I miss him, too."

"You think he's in heaven?"

"I don't know."

"Do dogs go to heaven?"

"I guess so."

"I don't think so. I think there's a special place where animals go. Sort of like animal heaven. Maybe he's in animal heaven, huh?"

"I guess so."

"But I'm not really sure there is a place like that. . ."

"Todd, please! Wherever he is, he is not here!" Todd looked hurt, and she was immediately sorry for her outburst. "I'm sorry, hon. Maybe there is an animal heaven." She tried to smile, but Todd sat silently eating a cookie.

She excused herself and went upstairs to lie down. I'll be glad when the baseball season starts, she thought. She needed to work. Now, more than ever, she needed not to be in the house alone.

Rick was home by 3:30.

"Surprise!" Dana was on the bed, lying silently. "You okay?"

"Yes." She smiled. "What brings you in so early?"

"Big day for Todd. Today they choose his position. I think he's got the right stuff to be a pitcher. Anyway, I want to be with him when he tries out. For moral support." He came to the bed and kissed her.

"Hold me," she said suddenly.

"What's wrong?" he asked throwing his arms around her. "Scruffy?"

"No," she lied. "I just want to be held, that's all." His arms felt good around her. "I'll be glad when the baseball season starts. Then I can cover the games for the Guardian."

"That's good," he said, but his arms stiffened. "Well, it's almost time to get down to the field." He got up and started to change his clothes.

"You don't want me to work, do you?"

He stopped and looked at her. "Dana, we've been through this before."

"But I thought we'd come to an understanding."

"You came to an understanding!" he said suddenly, then ducked into the closet to find his sneakers.

"What? You agreed! Rick, I can't sit home all the time. I tried that, remember? It was no good. We were all miserable."

"We don't need the money."

"Even if we did, you'd say we didn't."

"What's that supposed to mean?"

"You want to do it all by yourself. No help. You want to show the world that Rick Evans can do it alone!"

119

"That's ridiculous." Finding his sneakers, he put them on, then rummaged in the closet for his baseball glove. He took the glove and his jacket and headed for the door. "Dana, Todd and I need you here. If you *must* work . . . fine . . . but don't expect me to get all excited about it."

"Let's go, Dad," Todd called from downstairs.

"Be right down." He went back to the bed and kissed Dana on the cheek. "Let's not make a big deal over this thing. Work, honey. We'll love you even if you can't make it home for dinner." She smiled, and he kissed her, lingering. "The master calls," he said after the kiss was broken. Minutes later he was gone.

Rick had never wanted her to work. She knew that. There was a strange quirk in his personality. He constantly had to prove himself. When she'd met him at college she thought it was just a tough determination, but it was more—as if he feared people would think him less of a man if he didn't constantly prove himself.

He hated Dana to even mention working. Even when Todd was a baby, and they both had to drop out of Columbia, he did all but forbid her to work.

He worked days, while getting his degree at City College during the evenings. It was a tough three years, and Dana offered to help. She found a job at D'agostino's, working part time at the cash register eight hours a week.

When she broached the subject to Rick, he flew into a rage.

"Todd needs you at home."

"It's just eight hours a week, hon."

"He misses you. I don't like him being left with strangers."

"I wouldn't exactly call Carly a stranger. She's my best friend and practically lives here. Besides we can use the money."

"I can manage!" he insisted.

She didn't want to argue. She decided to wait for Todd to get bigger, more independent. But it wasn't Todd, it was Rick.

Even when they looked for the house, Rick insisted on proving his worth. They could have found cheaper homes in Mount Vernon or White Plains. But Rick insisted on looking in exclusive Scarsdale, Purchase and Katonah, finally settling on near-exclusive Crandall.

"A home is an unreasonable investment, today," one of their friends had told them. "With interest rates so high, why not wait a year for the edge to be taken off of inflation?" Of course he was right, but Rick needed to prove he could afford it.

Dana had few complaints about Rick. He was a good man. He worked hard (maybe too hard), didn't drink or play around, and his new found interest in his family pleased her. If only she could correct that one little quirk.

Dana left the bed and headed downstairs to prepare dinner. Part of the problem is me, she thought. She knew there were lots of women who would love not having to work. Her own mother never worked a day in her life. Her job was the family. But this wasn't Allentown, and Dana was different.

"I'm no women's libber, but I'm not a *hausfrau* either. I don't want to upstage my husband. I just want to work. I enjoy reporting—snooping." She giggled.

She pulled a shrink-packed frying chicken from the refrigerator and opened it. She didn't want to fight with Rick, but this time she was going to work, and she wasn't going to back down.

He's spending more time with Todd, now. I might as well go for it all, she thought. And then she laughed.

Dana sat, sipping coffee and trying to get her husband to take his head out of the newspaper. Rick, poring over the paper, occasionally raised his head to take a bite of toast before diving back into the print. And Todd splattered huge globules of milk onto the once clean dining room table. Business as usual.

"Rick, you're going to have to come shopping with me on Saturday. I hear we can get some real bargains at the new food warehouse in White Plains."

No answer.

"Rick, sometimes I wonder if you're among the living?"

"Mommy," Todd blurted, "Coach Dreiser gave me a special diet. He says I have to be real careful about what I eat from now on."

"Really? Are milk and cookies on that diet?"

"I don't think so."

She smiled. "Have you decided never to eat milk and cookies again?"

"Milk's on the diet. So I guess it's okay to have milk and cookies sometimes. There's milk in cookies, right?"

Suddenly Rick's head was out of the paper. "Hey, tiger, I'm coming home early today. Maybe three o'clock. We've got to get that pitching arm in shape for the season." Todd grinned.

"It seems baseball is the only thing that can get your mind off business," Dana said.

"Not the *only* thing," he said, smiling slyly. "You did pretty well last night."

Dana thought back to the night before, cradled in Rick's arms, making gentle love. She smiled.

"Mom, I'm gonna be a star pitcher. Right, Dad?"

"Right, tiger." The father and son grinned at one another, like two boys about to embark on some wild adventure.

"Shopping Saturday, Rick. How about it?"

"We'll have that arm in tiptop shape by the start of the season, tiger."

"Daddy, Ronnie is so much better than before. He's almost as good as Adonis."

"That's practice, son."

"I practice all the time. Am I better?"

"You sure are."

"RICK!" She'd had it with being ignored.

"Yeah, hon?"

"Shopping Saturday, at the new grocery warehouse in White Plains—all right?"

"Saturday morning I'm coaching the boys."

"Coaching?"

"Yeah. They need extra hands and I volunteered."

"Dad'll be one of my coaches, Mom."

"As a matter of fact, hon, there's a coaches meeting tonight. So when I bring Todd in from practice, I'll head right back out, over to Dreiser's."

"What about dinner?"

"Dreiser says his wife makes sandwiches for the guys. That'll be fine."

Lately Rick was full of surprises. Coaching a boys baseball team was more than Dana expected of him. It was a pleasant surprise, and she decided that she could make it to the food warehouse alone.

"Rick, that's really wonderful. I'm proud of you—of both of you." She smiled at her two men. "Maybe Ruth will come with me. You two saw Ronnie yesterday, so I guess he's all right."

"He looks fine to me," Rick said. Dana felt relieved, knowing that Ruth's initial panic had been a false alarm.

"I haven't seen Ruth for a few days. I guess I'll pop in on her later."

"I saw Tom Roberts yesterday, and he said that Ruth had to leave town for some family emergency."

"Family emergency?"

"Yeah. Her mother's taken ill. Just a bug, nothing major. But she's an old lady, living by herself, and Ruth wanted to make sure everything ran smoothly. I guess you'll get a welcome break from all her chatter." He laughed lightly. Dana smiled.

Why would Tom Roberts tell Rick such a story? She remembered the morning Ruth confided in her, telling of Tom's gambling and her mother's death. Whatever the reason, she decided not to mention it to Rick. What Ruth had told her was in confidence. She was sure when Ruth returned she'd find out the truth—with blow-by-blow details.

"Well, time to shove off." Rick was heading for the door, and Dana trailed after him. They shared a wet kiss at the threshold, and Rick dashed off to meet his ride.

Dana glanced at the yard of the white stucco across the street, hoping to get a glimpse of Adonis and Coach Dreiser. The yard was empty. As she was about to back into her house, her eye caught movement in the second floor window of the stucco. She stopped and looked up. The window was empty. But briefly, she was sure, she'd seen an elderly woman staring down at her. Probably Mrs. Dreiser, she thought. Again she wondered what Dreiser's relationship was to young Adonis. *Grandfather?*

She returned indoors to get Todd off to

school. Afterwards she hoped to begin her plan of generating her own story for the newspaper.

Chapter 14

After sifting through the recent Guardian,
Dana found the article on the runaway boy.
Quickly scanning the story, the name Thomas
Grote leaped from the page—and then connected. It was the name she'd recognized in
Max's file cabinet. *Why does Max have his
name on file?* The question bothered her, but
not for long. Her thoughts were on pursuing a
story on young Thomas Grote and then
selling the idea to Max.

She picked up the phone directory, searching for the name: Grote, David C., 41 Evergreen Ave.

She wasn't going to call and give them a
chance to say no. If there was a story, she was
going to get it.

She moved quickly, now, heading for the
bathroom. After a piping hot shower, she
would dress and go out on her first *real*
assignment.

* * *

She was in the room again.

Last night, David had spoken to her about moving, leaving Crandall.

"A fresh start, dear. This place has too many bad memories."

She'd only nodded then, but now she laughed. "Bad memories! I have no bad memories. He's the one with the bad memories!"

Lately, she'd been seeing a doctor, and he too suggested that a move would be beneficial. But these were all *David's* ideas, and she'd had it up to here with David and his ideas. Now, all she wanted was to be left alone.

Tommy had been the center of her life. She was lost without him.

She'd always wanted more children, but they'd never gotten around to it. They never agreed that there would be only one, but by the time Tommy was nine, there seemed to be an unspoken agreement that Tommy was enough.

Helen Grote sat on the edge of the boy's bed, thinking about her son. David refused to even discuss a baby, and without the prospect of bringing a baby into the world, Tommy once again became the center of her life. She could almost feel his presence. Just last night she thought she'd heard him walking around.

"Don't you hear him?" She'd awaken her husband several times during the night.

"I don't hear anything."

"Well, he's there!"

"Helen, get some sleep, dear."

"Of course you can't hear him! You never were a good father. You wanted to get rid of him all along!" she said, accusingly.

Actually, David wasn't a bad father. He tried, but he had to work so hard. Times were bad, and money was tight.

They both worked throughout Tommy's early years, but since David wanted her home with Tommy, he took a night job in a service station. She began staying home with Tommy, and the two of them developed a closeness, more than a mother-son relationship. They were friends—good friends.

"Mommy, who's your best friend?" Tommy would ask, smiling.

"It ain't the man-in-the-moon," she'd say, tickling up waves of laughter. Then, their home was filled with laughter.

Two years ago when they moved to Crandall, she knew things would be even better. David was taking an interest in Tommy, and the house and town were lovely.

Then she thought of the day she lost her son. *If Tommy were alive, imagine the riches we all could have shared!*

The chiming of the doorbell dragged her mind grudgingly back to the present.

David wouldn't ring! She'd had very few visitors since Tommy was gone. She hoped it was a friend. She didn't have many friends, but today she needed one. She had to talk to someone—anyone.

* * *

"Hi. Mrs. Grote?"

"Yes."

"I'm Dana Evans. I'm with the Crandall Guardian." Dana smiled, hoping her introduction was enough to grant her entry.

"Yes?" the woman said again. She stood by the door like a sentry, protecting the fort from interlopers.

"I've come about your tragedy, Mrs. Grote. The parents of Crandall all grieve your son's disappearance. We'd like you to share your feelings on this tragic ordeal with us. Maybe we can even do something to help bring Tommy back."

"Back?"

"Yes." Dana noted the surprise on her face.

"Did Max Richter send you?"

"Yes," she lied.

"He should know better."

"Why?"

"You want to talk about Tommy?" she blurted out.

"If that would be all right. The hearts of the parents of Crandall reach out to you, Mrs. Grote. They want to share your ordeal." A strange, unbelieving smile crossed Helen's lips.

"Come back later, when my husband is home." She started to close the door.

"Wait! What time?"

"After six."

"All right. I'll look forward to speaking with both of you. Say, around 6:30."

"Good." Again the door was swinging shut, but stopped. "Are you new in Crandall?"

"Yes, I'm. . ."

"Do you have a child, a boy?"

"Why, yes."

Quickly the door shut.

Dana wondered about the woman. *Is she frightened?* She was obviously still very upset, and justifiably so. But when she'd asked Dana about having a child, there was something in her eyes that didn't reflect grief, something, that to Dana, looked very much like anger.

Helen Grote sagged against the door. *She had a son, too!* "Everyone has a son!" Her voice was tinged with bitterness.

She wanted to tell the woman her own story, what it could have been like with Tommy. But, no—she was sworn to silence.

Anger pervaded her, as she thought of the woman with a son. She didn't like her. "They'll get her son, too," she mumbled. "They'll get hers, like they got mine." An evil, yet satisfied smile crossed Helen's lips, as she turned and headed back upstairs.

Rick was home early.

"Rick, it's just one o'clock!"

"I know, but I wanted to be here when Todd got home, and the next train would put me in Crandall about 2:30. So I'm early instead of late."

She was glad he was home. She didn't want

to be in the house alone.

"Rick, don't you think Coach Dreiser is kind of strange?"

"How?"

"Oh, I don't know. Eccentric."

Rick laughed. "Yeah, the old guy's a little wacko, but he's a genius."

"Genius may be pushing it."

"The guy has this thing down to a science, honey. Training, diet, mental preparation. He doesn't leave one stone unturned. You have to see him at practice, the way he stresses discipline to the kids. I sure wish I'd had someone like him when I was a kid."

"Do you?" Dana was surprised.

"Maybe I could have been the big league baseball star I'd always wanted to be."

"You played baseball?" Dana laughed; she just couldn't picture her husband running the bases. The more she tried picturing him in a baseball uniform the funnier it seemed.

"I was pretty good!" Rick said with a smile, but Dana continued to laugh. "Hey, we were talking about Dreiser. He's really great. This year, when Crandall's the Little League champion for the third consecutive time, the world will take notice of him. We may even lose him to the pros."

"I've never known you to be such a baseball fanatic."

"It's for the tiger, hon. Hell, it's for both of us. I admit I was a baseball nut when I was a kid, and I guess I'm just reliving my childhood through Todd. There's nothing wrong with that, is there?"

"I think it's wonderful."

"I'm a Dana fanatic, too," he said. Taking his wife into his arms he kissed her passionately. "Everything's going to work out just fine," he whispered.

"I know."

"I forgot to tell you, there's a meeting tonight," Rick said, as he began to change into his baseball outfit.

"Another one?"

" 'The better prepared the coach—the better prepared the team.' Guess who said that, hon?"

"Don't tell me—Dreiser?"

"The man's a genius."

After Rick and Todd had left for practice, Dana thought about her brief talk with Mrs. Grote. She seems very wary, Dana thought. But I guess if Todd had run away I would want to protect my privacy, too. *Of course, Todd wouldn't run away!*

Dana remembered the anger in the woman's eyes, and wondered what she meant about Max Richter knowing better. *Is there a secret about these runaways that Max shares? Is Max's file a runaway file?* "Slow down, Dana," she mumbled. "You've had your share of paranoia for the year."

She decided not to even think about the Grotes until later. Now, she was going to write her brother, Ted, a nice long letter. She'd received one from him that morning. He was in London, headed for Switzerland, but his mail would be forwarded. He was quite far away now, much further than Atlanta. She missed him, but the loneliness she'd felt last week was gone. She was in the bosom of her family, felt very happy, and wanted to share that happiness with her brother. "Dear Ted. . ."

At 6:25 sharp, Dana was standing at the front door of the Grote residence, looking professionally solemn. She rang the bell. A minute or so later, the door swung open, and a brown-eyed, medium built man in his late thirties stared out at her.

"Mrs. Evans?" he asked.

"Yes. Mr. Grote?" She extended her hand, but he ignored it.

"Mrs. Evans, I'm sorry you had to come all this way for nothing. You didn't leave your number with Helen, and. . ."

"Nothing!"

"Yes. I'm afraid Helen and I really have nothing to say. The loss of our son is a very personal thing. I. . ."

"I realize that, Mr. Grote. And the parents of Crandall realize it too," Dana added quickly, in an attempt to stave off the rejection. "We don't want to impose on your grief; we want to share it. Maybe we can help in getting Thomas back."

"I don't think so."

"By working together there might be things we can do, Mr. Grote."

"Mrs. Evans, my wife and I appreciate your concern . . . really! But we'd prefer not to talk. Does Max Richter know you're here?"

"Yes." She lied again. He seemed surprised.

"Well, tell Mr. Richter that we just aren't ready to talk."

He stepped out and swung the door shut behind himself.

"Mrs. Evans, this whole thing has been very hard on my wife. Your presence here this afternoon upset her. We're planning to move away from Crandall before she has a total breakdown. I hope you understand."

"Yes. I'm sorry." She extended her hand, and this time he grasped it firmly.

Dana turned and headed back to her car. There was something oddly secretive about the Grote family, especially Mr. Grote. She realized the tremendous pressure they were under, but in Mr. Grote it wasn't visible. In him she saw something guarded. It seemed to her that he wanted to keep her from talking with his wife.

She got in the car and drove off. There was something else nagging at her. She felt that neither parent believed that Thomas would ever be back. The boy simply ran away from home and could return tomorrow. But they were acting as if he had died.

She turned the car off Evergreen Avenue, down Peter Street, enroute to Oakwood. For some reason she felt that there was something very secretive about most of the people of Crandall. Dana dismissed the thought as easily as it had come to her, because, of course, it was nonsense.

The man came back into the living room. His wife, seated on the sofa, looked up. "She's gone," he said.

No answer.

"What did you tell her?"

"Nothing. I told her absolutely nothing."

"Still, I should let them know that she was here." Moving to the table, he picked up the phone, and dialed.

At 7:17, Philip and Adonis Dreiser came in from practice.

"David Grote called," the old woman said. "It's important."

Philip Dreiser went to his study, closed the door, and finding the Grote number on his note pad, dialed it.

"David Grote? This is Dreiser."

He listened intently.

"Evans. I know her."

He paused.

"All right. No problem. I'll take care of it. You did the right thing. Thanks again, David. And don't worry about it." He hung up and felt the veins in his neck slowly begin to tighten.

"So close," he said softly. He was so near the goal that the least little thing made him nervous and jumpy. Dana Evans was no threat. Still, he had to take precautionary measures. The season would open in three weeks. Everything was running so smoothly; they couldn't let anything spoil it now. They'd found out about Jimmy Warren in time. The worst was behind them. He smiled.

"So close." He started from the room, then came back to his desk, picked up the phone, and dialed.

Chapter 15

"What the fuck did you get yourself into, girly?" Max Richter, clad in his faithful gray cardigan, was seated behind the cluttered desk, staring up at Dana over the rim of his glasses.

"I was just trying to create my own story, trying to get this paper to take an interest in something other than baseball."

It was Friday afternoon, and Dana had had it with being in the house. The day was gorgeous. By noon the temperature was in the mid-seventies, and signs of spring were everywhere—birds chirping, trees slowly beginning to show their spring colors. From her window, Dana had seen a young mother pushing her newborn in a stroller. Budding signs of life were all around.

It was too nice a day to be indoors, so Dana took a drive. When she wound up at the paper, she decided to look in on Max—but she wasn't expecting this.

"Damnit, girly, I told you this town wasn't interested in anything but baseball." He had a nasal way of talking that Dana hadn't noticed before. When he was excited, which seemed to be all the time, the twang in his voice rose an octave.

"You talk as if I broke the law or something. All I did was go after a human interest story."

He smiled. "Girly, I like you. You got *chutzpah*. But I got three calls that said I should fire you. Now, *I* want you around, but this paper keeps me going. Social Security don't go too far these days, you know. And the town supports the paper, so I need the town. But you keep this up and I'll have to let you go. Why not generate a story that's baseball related?"

"Three calls!" Dana said suddenly. "From whom?"

"I'm not at liberty to say, although I'll tell you, in confidence, mind you, that one of them came from Dreiser."

"Dreiser!"

"He's got a lot of influence in this town, girly."

"Not with me! What business is this of his, anyway?"

"A friend of the family, I guess. Now, girly, you got to promise me that you won't pursue a fucking story without clearing it through me first!"

"I have to clear everything?"

"Well . . . anything that isn't baseball related. Why don't you go down to the archives and dig up a story on last year's team? We're a little short of copy this week. I sure will be glad when the fucking season starts."

Dana was more suspicious than ever of a conspiracy of sorts. *But why?* She decided against mentioning it. *He'll probably just give me the run-around.* "Max, just what is Dreiser's relationship to Adonis?"

"Father."

"Father! The man must be close to seventy."

"Hey, you think us old timers can't get it up or something?" She laughed. "Actually, the boy's adopted."

"Oh." She remembered thinking that Dreiser once had made someone a good father.

"Now, what say you go down and find me a story?"

"Sorry, Max, I can't. I have to be home when my son gets in from school, which is. . ." She checked her watch. ". . . in about half an hour."

"Damnit, girly, I need some copy. How about covering practice in the morning? Interview some parents, get their predictions on the season, some stuff on the kids."

"Sounds exciting."

Max cocked his head and stared. "Sometimes I can't tell if you're being serious or sarcastic."

"Good, that'll keep you on your toes."

"You'll cover the practice?"

"I might as well. This town isn't interested in anything but baseball—right?"

"Don't let it get you, girly."

"Don't worry, I won't." She started for the door. "Gotta run, Max. Don't want to keep Todd waiting."

"Say, I'll need that fucking copy tomorrow. Hustle it over here as soon as possible."

"Yes, your highness." She dashed out of the tiny office, banging the door shut behind herself.

"She's a tough one, all right," Max said after she had gone. "Maybe too tough."

Of course, the house was quiet. It just wasn't the same without Scruffy—or Ruth either, for that matter. Dana was adjusting to spending the time alone, but it was a slow adjustment. It was gratifying to know that Ruth would be back soon. She'd spoken to Tom Roberts on the phone last night. He told her that Ruth would be home in about a week.

"Says she nursed the old lady back to good health. Now, she just wants to make sure there isn't a relapse."

"Where does her mother live?"

"Oh . . . uhh, Philadelphia." Tom's stammering was obvious, even over the phone. "She moved there a few years ago."

"Can I have her number?"

"Why?"

"I miss Ruth. I thought we might be able to

chat over the phone. You know, 'The next best thing to being there.'"

"Dana, the old lady's kind of senile. Doesn't believe in too many modern conveniences. Ruth has to call me from a booth every-night—collect. I can imagine what my bill's going to look like." Dana pictured him rolling his eyes.

"Tell Ruth I asked about her. I know you'll be glad when she gets back."

"I sure will."

"And tell her I'm glad her mother's feeling better."

It was obvious Tom was lying. Maybe they'd had a fight. *Oh, well, I'll find out soon enough.*

Dana went into the kitchen and turned on the coffee pot. Seeing Scruffy's water dish still in its spot by the door brought back memories.

Carly had given Scruffy to them five Christmases ago. He had been given to Carly by another friend, but the building she lived in didn't allow pets. At first Rick didn't like the idea of having a dog around.

"You don't have to walk him," Dana argued. "Todd and I will feed him, walk him, everything."

He was a cute little fuzz ball of a puppy, not quite two months old, and he whined nearly every night for a week.

"Dana, this dog just isn't working out."

But after ten days Todd and Scruffy had become attached, an inseparable pair. Rick knew that his argument was futile and eventually gave up.

We've been through a lot together, Dana thought. A chill went through her as she pictured Scruffy lying dead in a puddle of blood and urine, his still open eyes reaching out to her.

A knock jolted Dana's consciousness.

It was already 2:35. *Todd's late!* She rushed to the door. Throwing it open, she stepped back and stared into the distrusting eyes of Philip Dreiser.

"Mrs. Evans, how are you?" Coach Dreiser asked, a phony smile stretched across his face. He was wearing a blue peak-billed cap and a green windbreaker. The smile on his face reminded Dana of a child who'd been caught with his hand in the cookie jar.

"Fine," Dana said. She was still a little stunned, and stood silently, while Dreiser waited for her to invite him in. "I thought you were my son," she said finally.

His smile widened. "Todd. A fine boy. He has the makings of a really fine pitcher."

The silence again. Dana felt awkward. There was an air of confidence, of power, about him that seemed to throw her off balance. She immediately thought of the power her mother wielded over the family and wondered what it would have been like to grow up with a dominant father.

"What can I do for you, Coach Dreiser," she asked. It was obvious he wanted to enter, but this was *her* home, and she didn't want him here.

"I thought we might talk for a moment," he said and stepped forward. It was an old salesman's tactic.

Dana stepped back, and he walked in.

"A lovely place you have here."

"I'm kind of busy, Coach Dreiser. What can I do for you?" She could have kicked herself for letting him in, but that didn't mean she had to be polite.

He walked to the sofa and seated himself. He gazed up at her from under the bill of his cap, his dark eyes laughing. *I'm in control here!*

"Is it about Todd? Little League?" She was becoming annoyed with him.

"No, Mrs. Evans, it's about Thomas Grote."

Her eyelids danced up in surprise. "Thomas Grote?"

"Yes, Mrs. Evans. You're new in town, I realize that. Maybe they do things different in New York, but around here we respect one another's privacy." He crossed his legs.

"What!" Anger flushed her cheeks.

"A child running away from home is a tragic occurrence, Mrs. Evans. There's no need for anyone from the Guardian to come around and open old wounds. At least Max Richter should know better."

"So I've been told. Just why are you here, Coach Dreiser?"

"Mrs. Evans, it just seems in the best

interest of Crandall, and the Guardian, for you to leave the paper." The dark eyes stared up, challenging.

"I appreciate your interest, but what I was doing could have benefited the family, as well as Crandall. I was only trying to help." *My God! I sound like a child begging her father for forgiveness.* "With more exposure we just might solicit help from other newspapers. Someone, somewhere may have seen young Thomas."

"We don't need that kind of help, Mrs. Evans."

"If his family wants him back, they'll take any kind of help they can get!"

Dreiser rose. "Your kind of *yellow* journalism isn't wanted here."

"If you're asking me to stop working for the paper, the answer is no. And if that's the only reason you're here—good afternoon, sir!"

"Mrs. Evans, I hope you'll reconsider, at least until you've lived in Crandall a while longer and can see how we do things here."

The soft rapping at the door ended the conversation.

"That's Todd." Dana went to the door and let him in.

"Coach Dreiser?" Todd said as he stepped into the living room. "Did I do something wrong?"

"No, no," Dreiser chuckled. "I was just having a friendly chat with your mother. Excited about the season?"

"You bet. I can't wait. Mom's gonna report

the games for the newspaper, and Dad's gonna be one of my coaches."

"I know." At that moment Dreiser's eyes locked onto Dana's. They were distrusting, but there was also an awesome power in them, a power that resented defiance. "I have to go. See you tomorrow, Todd."

"Right, coach."

"Mrs. Evans, it's been a pleasure."

"Just lovely." She escorted him to the door.

He started to leave, then turned back and remarked, "Maybe I'm being a little hasty. You probably have the boy's family at heart, just as I do. After all, we both know what it is to have a child. Please forgive my impassioned plea. I only had the safety and well being of the parents of Crandall at heart, but I'm sure you'll work out." He tried on a smile, but it didn't fit.

"You're forgiven." Her voice was flat.

"Thank you," he said. Then nodding, he headed down the walk.

Who died and made him king? As Dana watched him leave, she involuntarily began squeezing the doorknob, and she could feel her dislike for the man slowly intensify.

That night Dana dreamt.

In the dream she was a child, younger than Todd, although at times also a woman. Todd was there, too. Her mother was taking both of them to church.

"God punishes little boys and girls who don't listen to their mothers." She was holding their hands. They were walking down a street, past a row of ramshackle old buildings. Dana recognized the buildings from her childhood. They were along the route she'd traveled to church hundreds of Sundays ago.

"Where are we going?" Todd asked.

"To church," his grandmother replied. "It's Sunday, and we're going to church, of course."

"Mommy doesn't take me to church."

"She doesn't?"

Dana felt her mother's grip tighten around her tiny hand. "We worship privately," Dana said, but the woman's eyes tore into her.

"God wants to be worshipped in his *own* house."

"We feel differently about it, Mother. Church doesn't make a person religious, or even good. We believe in God. . ."

"Todd will stay with us."

"No," Dana said.

"Yes. It already has been decided."

"By who?"

"By a higher authority." Suddenly they were in the house in Crandall. Dana stared beseechingly into the face of her mother. "There are rules that must be obeyed. It's like baseball."

The voice Dana heard was her mother's, but the face suddenly belonged to Philip Dreiser.

"You can't have him," Dana said.

"I'm sorry," her mother-Dreiser said. "It's already been decided. He's coming with me.

He'll make a fine pitcher."

"I wanna play baseball," Todd said.

Dreiser took Todd's hand, and they walked to the door. Dana wanted to move, to get her son, but she was frozen, as if she'd been dipped in quick drying cement.

"He's coming to Allentown with me." And then he-she began to laugh. The laughter was intermittently her mother's and Dreiser's. It rose in a steady, raucous wave, bouncing around the room and off the walls.

"Todd!" Dana called, but he looked back and smiled.

"I'll be happy in Allentown."

"No!"

She awoke, jerking upright with a start. Her heart raced, perspiration waxed over her body, and her head whirled as she took in the familiarity of the room. It was a dream, of course. Rick lay next to her, his hair askew on the pillow. She marked the silent, reassuring rise and fall of his chest.

The dream slowly receded from her consciousness. She barely remembered it, but she knew it was bad.

Her heart rate was slowing down, and rising, she padded over to the window. She threw up the shade, and moonlight from a nearly full moon splashed into the room.

It was something about Todd, she thought. About Todd, mother and Dreiser. Her eyes fell on the white stucco across the street. The house was dark.

Leaving the shade up, she came back to bed,

where she lay on her back staring at the ceiling. She lay like this for nearly an hour, until finally she again fell asleep, drifting into a world of black dreams.

"The nerve of the man," Dana said, staring across the table at Rick, who for once wasn't at all interested in the newspaper. "He doesn't run this town."

"But he's pretty popular. Maybe some of what he says is right."

"You're not siding with him, Rick?"

"I'm not siding with anyone. But maybe you should get a feel for the town before you go writing stories about the people who live here." Rick picked up a slice of toast, buttered it, then slopped on a glob of marmalade. "Honey, the old guy knows what he's doing. You should see the discipline he imposes on the boys."

"I see the way the boy across the street moves like a robot."

"Dana, please! Not in front of you know who." They looked at Todd and he smiled.

"You're right."

"Besides there's a lot to be said for discipline."

"Why! Because it makes the boys better ball players?"

"Not just that. Most kids on the team are also excellent students. Adonis is a prodigy with the violin. Jim Spencer has almost total recall. . ."

"And Dreiser gets the credit?"

"You're darned right!"

"All right, maybe there is a lot to be said for his methods, but Rick, it was as if the man were saying the Grotes didn't want the boy back! Somehow I feel there's some kind of conspiracy."

"What do you mean?"

"Everyone wants to drop the issue of Tommy's running away."

"Honey, the parents have seen enough grief."

"What I was doing could help."

"I guess they just don't see it that way."

Todd, who had been silently gobbling his bacon and eggs, said, "I like Coach Dreiser."

"Me too, tiger."

Dana stared at her two men. "It seems to be unanimous."

"Honey, I'm sure you've misjudged him. Give him a chance."

She laughed, tossing her head back and shaking out her hair. "Father always said I had a suspicious nature. Maybe it's just the snoop in me that's upset because I didn't get a story."

"You'll get a story today, Mom. Watch me practice." Todd jumped up and mimed throwing his fastball.

"Save it for later, tiger," Rick said. He reached over and tussled his son's dark hair. "Steak for dinner tonight, hon?"

"Steak?"

"Yeah, today's Saturday, and we've only had steak once this week."

"Rick, are you aware of meat prices these days? And steak! We might as well eat gold!" Dana stopped sipping her coffee and buttered a piece of toast.

"It's for the tiger, hon."

"Are we supposed to follow that silly diet?"

"Yeah, Mom!" Todd bawled.

"It can't hurt," Rick said. "All those things are good for him. And maybe Todd does have the stuff to be a big league pitcher—right, son?"

"Yeah, Mom, like Guidry, 'Louisiana lightning.' " He mimed throwing his fastball again.

"All right, but if we wind up in the poor house, Todd's fastball is going to have to bail us out!"

Breakfast was light and breezy. The conversation was up, and it was obvious to Dana that the family was really pulling together.

Although covering a Little League practice wasn't exactly Dana's idea of how to spend a Saturday morning, she actually was looking forward to it. She'd not only get a chance to see Todd play but also see Rick interacting with children. And the three of them would be there—not together, but the closest thing they'd had to a family outing since Todd was a baby.

A few minutes later Ronnie Roberts knocked on the door. When Dana answered, at first she didn't recognize him. He stood at the threshold with his cap in his hand, a perfect gentleman.

"Hi, Mrs. Evans, are Todd and Mr. Evans ready to go yet?"

"Oh, Ronnie! When did you get that haircut?" She now recognized him as the boy she'd seen the day Scruffy was killed.

"I got it the other day, ma'am," he answered softly.

"Oh." It was a hideous haircut, like Jimmy Warren's, and for some reason, today Ronnie reminded her of Jimmy Warren.

She led him to the kitchen where he sat silently, waiting for the others to finish breakfast. Dana offered him a glass of milk, but he refused.

"No, thank you, Mrs. Evans." He was being so polite.

Immediately after breakfast—Todd didn't even brush his teeth—the three of them left for the field. Dana stood in the doorway, staring after them as they walked towards Crandall Park and wondering what made Ronnie seem so different.

I'm sure it's the haircut, she thought. But still there seemed to be something else.

The ringing of the phone intruded on her thoughts. She turned and headed back into the house to answer it.

"Hello?" At first there was silence, and then a muffled voice. She recognized it almost immediately.

"Hello, Mrs. Evans?"

"Yes."

"This is Helen Grote."

* * *

By the time Dana had arrived at the field the morning chill had begun to lift, and it was already too warm for the jacket she was wearing.

The field was like a miniature version of a professional baseball field. It even had an electronic scoreboard. It was obvious to Dana that after the spring thaw, when the earth had softened and the outfield was covered with lush green grass, the ballpark truly would be a vision of beauty.

She decided to walk around and get a feel for things. The boys were so cute in their baseball caps and jeans, all trying so hard to look like adults. Todd and several other boys were with Rick, and he was going through different throwing motions with them.

Dana was glad that Todd wasn't with Dreiser. She didn't like him being so close to the man. Of course Dreiser was harmless; she realized that. It was obvious, even to her, that he took a great interest in the boys, but still she preferred that Todd stay away from him. *Todd doesn't need all that discipline rigamarole.*

Walking across the newly sprouting grass of the outfield, Dana made her way towards a group of parents.

"Hi," Dana said to a youngish woman who was gazing off to the right of the field, staring intently at a small cluster of boys. "I'm Dana Evans." The woman smiled.

"Eunice Graham. You're new here in Crandall."

"Yes."

"That's my son over there. Petie. This is his year. He's going to play second base on the tournament team." Her face was a picture of intensity.

"That's my son over there. Todd. And I don't even know what a tournament team is." Dana laughed lightly.

"It's the best. Coach Dreiser calls it the best of the best. Sometime in June they will pick the best boys from the local teams. Those boys will represent Crandall, and Petie will be one of them."

"I hope he makes it."

"He will! You'll see," she said defiantly. Dana knew how some parents were about their children when it came to competing, and she quickly decided to change the subject.

"Eunice, I'm with the Crandall Guardian, and we wanted to get some parents' feelings on the season."

"What do you mean?"

"How do you think Crandall will do this year?"

She fixed Dana with an incredulous stare. "We'll win, of course!"

"Of course." And Dana moved on.

The parents were all adamant in their feelings about the outcome of the season. *It sounds like manifest destiny!* This was not going to do. She had to get more of a story.

Then she saw the boy. Adonis. He was on the little hill—I think they call it a pitcher's mound—his dark eyes, set deep in their sockets, staring intently at the catcher's glove. Dana stood mesmerized, watching the boy pitch. The ball gunned through the air and exploded into the glove. He threw several pitches, all hard and straight—like a machine.

As Dana looked around the field, she saw several boys with eyes that were set hard. She also noted that laughing or fooling around was not tolerated. The boys were drilled repeatedly in the fundamentals of baseball. *Don't they have any fun?* The boys who made mistakes were scolded and seemed flustered, but even those who were complimented showed no signs of pleasure. To them the game of baseball had become a deadly serious business.

A creepiness invaded Dana's spirits. It was sad that these boys somehow had lost the true spirit of the game. But this wasn't what was causing her uncomfortable feeling. Dana's wandering glance had connected with Dreiser's and he stared back defiantly. In him she saw the same controlled behavior she'd seen in the boys, and she realized that it was this man who had perpetuated their robotlike demeanor.

Suddenly she didn't know if she wanted Todd to be a part of this team—or if she wanted to be a part of this town. The lunatic ravings of Helen Grote over the phone that morning could not have been true. Still, something Helen had said stuck in her mind, clinging obstinately. Maybe Helen was right.

Maybe through her cloud of lunacy an ounce of truth had come shining through.

Helen had told Dana to flee for her life. Dana had laughed, but now she wondered about what Helen had said. Standing there, staring at Dreiser, Helen Grote's words reverberated in her mind. Maybe the lady wasn't crazy after all. Maybe the town was evil.

BOOK TWO

Chapter 16

Baseball was the game, and the town knew games.

Crandall knew many games, like the games of men and boys acted out on a playing field, where you could come and root for your favorite team; or the games of physical strength and sweat, with clearly defined rules and obvious winners and losers. The town knew these games well. These were the surface games, and they had their place.

But the town knew other games, games where the playing field was the mind and rules were thrown out the window. And the winners were all the folks still around in the morning, when the sun came over the horizon, signifying the start of a new day and a new game.

These were the games concocted in the minds of men. And everyone played—had to play—for playing was the only way to survive.

Bill Hutchinson played down at Hutchinson's market, when he bought a truck load of milk—back in '78—that was infested with rat urine. The FDA was looking for that milk, three thousand gallons of it, inspected in a plant in southern New Jersey and ruled unfit for human consumption. But the milk disappeared before it could be seized, and wouldn't you know that five hundred gallons wound up in Hutchinson's market.

The stranger gave Bill a real good deal on the milk—thirty-five cents a gallon—and Bill didn't ask no questions, but of course Bill didn't drink the milk either. Purchasing that milk was survival. What with Shopwell moving in a few years back and underselling him all the time, Bill had to survive anyway he could.

Tom Roberts played, squirreling away a portion of his paycheck each week, so he could sneak off to Atlantic City one weekend a month and fritter it away on the gaming tables. Tom had credit at every casino, and eventually the control he so carefully exercised over his gambling would slip away, as easily as his savings.

Of course, Doc Teasdale played. For him the game was to forget, which he did. Teasdale forgot his childhood—the beatings he received from his old man, the jokes about him in school. All he remembered from his past was that to be called "Doc" was a distinction. Still, Teasdale was a loser, but for every loser hustled into the ground, there were several new players being ushered into the game. *There's a sucker born every day!*

The games started long ago, long before Abner Doubleday took a hunk of wood and a hardball and invented what would become the national pastime. For Crandall the games started with a young entrepreneur named Edgemont Crandall, who wore prissy white suits and dabbled in the genteel life by day. By night Edgemont practiced white slavery, taking his wagonload of young girls up to the state capitol, then down to Washington on weekends. Crandall supplied girls for the combined administrations of Jefferson and Madison. He catered to a high-class clientele and was known for being discreet, but he gave up the business in 1813, when the war with Canada made travel too risky. By then Crandall had amassed a fortune, and the Crandall Estate stretched for miles, lying somewhere between White Plains and what is now Mount Vernon.

He lived out his life playing the role of a respectable farmer. Folks said that Edgemont Crandall was an honest man, who'd earned his fortune from the soil. Of course they knew otherwise, but it was just a game.

So, on that day when Carl Stotz got three teams of boys together to play something he called Little League, people rejoiced—rejoiced because it was a game, and man is a gaming animal. And on that muggy day in mid-

August, 1980, when the town of Crandall won its first Little League championship, America rejoiced. There were fears that maybe, just maybe, countries from the Far East were taking over what was rightfully ours, taking away our technology and our profits and yes, even our national pastime. But for one day in mid-August that fear was put to rest. Our American boys had showed 'em, all right. We were still tops. When the boys did it again in 1981 it was apparent that America was regaining her position of dominance. Now, if we could only do it again.

Somewhere in his guts, where survival is more genetic than cerebral, man knows that all this life is just a game. And no matter in what arena the game is being played tonight, no matter what the size or shape of the ball, no matter if you hit it, throw it, kick it or knock it into other balls, there's still only one game.

In the town of Crandall *that* game is baseball, and the town knows games.

The pressure was getting to her.

Helen Grote had tried to be a good mother and a good wife. When Tommy had been snatched away from them she tried not to miss him. And when David refused to have another baby, she tried to shed all of her mothering instincts, like a butterfly shedding its caterpillar cocoon. But she couldn't.

On the Saturday morning that Helen Grote called Dana, she had given up trying. She had always tried to do what was right for the family. When she discovered that someone in Crandall could help Tommy, she goaded David into moving there. When she was told of all the riches the family could reap, she had tried to make the best decision for all of them. But they filled her head with lies, the evil people of Crandall, and for all her trying, Helen Grote lost her only son.

She had tried, struggled, to hold onto her sanity, but no more. She had been fooled by the people of Crandall. There was nothing good in this town. The town was evil.

Crandall was evil, and she didn't care who knew nor what she destroyed. Helen Grote had cast her fate into the wind. She would act on whims now, allowing destiny to blow her in any direction.

When Helen Grote woke up Saturday morning she wanted to talk to someone, and she remembered the woman from the Guardian. She got the number from directory assistance and dialed.

Saturday was a turning point in the life of Helen Grote. Her sanity was beginning to recede, and Helen didn't try to stop the downward spiral. It was bad enough knowing that the town was evil, but it was even worse that she'd made a costly mistake. Helen Grote did not want to remember.

Chapter 17

"Steinbrenner's an asshole!"

"Rick!"

They were sitting at breakfast, when Rick's head bobbed up from the newspaper and he bellowed out.

"Sorry. I just got carried away." He smiled sheepishly, and they both looked at Todd who was grinning like it was Christmas.

"Who's Steinbrenner, Dad?"

"The owner of the Yankees." He turned his smile towards his son.

"Oh?" Dana said.

"First he lets Jackson go." He looked at Dana. "The guy wasn't the greatest, but, *Christ*, Reggie Jackson! The kids loved him. He was worth keeping around for the gate alone."

"Re-gie, Re-gie," Todd droned.

Rick went on. "Then he makes some great off-season deals. He gets us Griffey, and our outfield looks so solid you couldn't drive a tank through it. And I say to myself, 'Maybe this guy isn't so dumb after all.' But now he pulls this!" Rick slammed the paper down.

"Re-gie."

Dana couldn't believe it. Rick was reading the sports page.

"I didn't know you were so interested in baseball."

"Yeah. 'Baseball fever—catch it!' That's the major leagues' slogan. I guess I did."

"Re-gie, Re-gie."

Dana shook her head and told Todd it was perfectly all right with her if he stopped the chanting. Her eyes were threatening. He stopped.

She looked at Rick again and still couldn't believe it. How long had he been reading the sports page? Baseball fever was catching, all right. In the short time they'd lived in Crandall, Rick had gone from hard core workaholic to Little League devotee. The transformation was amazing. She didn't know how long he'd been reading the sports page, but this sudden change in him was unsettling. He was like a different person. He not only came home from work on time, but some days he didn't bother to go.

I hope there's nothing wrong with the business. She didn't believe there was. Rick had just gotten caught up in Crandall's Little League mania.

"Opening day tomorrow, tiger. You ready?"

Todd mimed his fastball. "Louisiana Lightning, Dad."

"Hey, look at the time. I've got to run."

Rick was up, tussling Todd's hair and planting a wet smooch on Dana's lips. He even seemed lightfooted this morning as he raced for the door.

Dana stood in the doorway watching him run for his ride. He was halfway down the walk when she noticed it.

"Isn't that something," she mumbled, looking at her husband who was clad in a three piece Glen plaid business suit. No wonder he seemed so light on his feet. He was wearing sneakers.

Opening day! And Todd looked so cute in his baseball uniform. "Not cute, Mom. Macho." And Dana looked at Rick. "Macho?" And shaking his head, Rick said, "Not from me!" And they all laughed.

The morning was overcast, but the forecast was for mild, breezy weather, the temperature supposedly reaching near seventy. A perfect day for baseball.

The electricity of the whole thing had swept through Crandall like a lightning storm. Banners and pennants were hung in many of the shop windows, and a local stationery store ordered two hundred bumper stickers proclaiming, "I'm from Crandall. Home of the World Champion Giants." Citi-Bank had a sign in their window that wished the team good luck in their quest for an unprecedented third straight title. And word was going around that this year's team would be the best ever.

Dana felt herself getting caught up in the furor, as she made sure Todd was eating all the right foods. And yes, they even were having steak twice a week!

When Todd's uniform came Friday night and Dana saw that the pants were much too big for his little waist and seat, she sat up until two in the morning tapering them. They were still quite baggy, but at least they wouldn't come rolling down when Todd rounded the bases after he'd hit his first home run.

"Nervous, tiger?" Rick asked, as he slipped into his yellow coach's sweat shirt, that said "Hutchinson's" on the front and "coach" on the back.

Todd smiled.

"You get to start on opening day, son. That's an honor. Let's hope you make out better than Tommy John did for the Yanks."

The boy's smile widened.

Dana was busy stuffing herself into the new Gloria Vanderbilts she'd purchased just for the occasion. She was surprised at how excited even *she* was about the game. And it wasn't just that Todd was pitching, or that she was covering it for the Guardian. Little League actually seemed important. She even had a navy blue peak-billed cap, with a bright orange "G" plastered smack in the middle.

The importance of Little League was beginning to make sense.

She was watching the boys warming up when she noticed him—the boy on the opposing team, taking practice catches at second base. He looked familiar.

She moved along the sideline, stopping by the dugout, hoping to get a better view. Now she was moving again, stopping along the third baseline, her feet nearly touching the red clay on the infield.

She was sure. The youth standing at second base was Jimmy Warren, the boy who had killed Scruffy.

Anger bubbled up inside of her. She stormed into the dugout and called out to her husband, "Look who's out there!"

"Where?"

"There!" She pointed.

Rick's gaze followed her finger. "Jimmy Warren. He's the best second baseman in the league."

"He's the boy who killed Scruffy!"

"I know."

Did he hear me?

"Rick, there's something wrong with that boy. He belongs in a hospital!"

"Come on, Dana, you can't mean that."

"I do!"

Rick was alternately scribbling something on his clipboard and looking at Dana.

"Dana, he's a boy. What do you want?"

"He could hurt someone!" Rick's casual

attitude annoyed her. "Aren't you going to do something?"

"What the hell can I do?" He flung the clipboard to the ground.

"Tell someone!" she screamed.

"They know! The hospital released him weeks ago. He had to be ready for the season, hon. They say he's fine. He's not going to hurt anyone." He forced a smile.

"You knew he was out?"

"Dana, he's a boy." His smile widened. "Sometimes boys go apeshit, that's all."

She opened her mouth to speak, but the anger inside strangled her words and all that came out was empty sound.

She couldn't stay. She knew it as well as she knew her own name. *What kind of people are they?* What kind of people would allow a killer to be released just to play baseball?

She was running from the field just as Councilman Adler threw out the first ball. As she reached her car she heard the man's voice rise up above the noise of the crowd, calling the words that would start Crandall along its inevitable path of destiny.

"PLAY BALL!"

Rick solemnly watched as Todd walked his fifth batter of the inning. The boy had done poorly in the first inning. Not controlling his pitches, he gave up five runs on an assortment of hits and walks. Now it was the second inning, and with the bases loaded he walked still another batter.

Rick knew he was going to have to take him out. The boos were just starting, and he couldn't humiliate the boy any longer.

He took the long walk out to the mound.

"Sorry, son."

The boys eyes were filled with tears.

"I stink," he said softly, throwing the ball into the dugout. He ran to the end of the park, where he sat under an oak tree, crying.

When the game resumed, Dreiser came over and put a consoling arm around Rick's shoulder.

"His first time out. Don't worry."

"I knew he wasn't specially good, but I thought he was ready. I wanted to show you."

"You did."

Silence.

"Is he following the diet?"

"Yes. And we've been working out regularly. I'm sorry."

"Rick, I think he'll make it. He's got what it takes. I can see it in his eyes."

Rick looked at Dreiser, and a fatherly expression came over the old man's face.

"We'll work harder," Rick said. He smiled, and his team went on to lose 15-4.

"I don't wanna play baseball!"

Dana was in the living room, thumbing through a magazine when they came in. Todd was crying and throwing a horrible tantrum.

"You're going to play, and you're going to like it! Now quit acting like a baby!"

Todd raced into the living room and dove

into his mother's arms.

"That's it, Dana, mollycoddle him. That's why he's such a baby now."

"What's the matter?" she asked, wrapping her protective arms around her son.

"He just had a bad day, that's all. And now he's talking about quitting. Well, he's not going to!"

"I hate baseball!"

"You'll be letting all your friends down," Rick said.

"I don't have any friends. I hate baseball!"

"Isn't Ronnie your friend?" Rick asked.

"No. Ronnie's mean."

"Rick, I've been thinking about it. There's something wrong with the premium this town puts on Little League."

"What are you talking about?"

"Jimmy Warren is sick!"

"A boy kicks the hell out of a floppy old dog, and you're trying to pin a murder rap on him. The kid just went apeshit. THAT'S ALL!"

"Rick, watch your..."

"APESHIT!" He stared threateningly at Todd. "You're going to play baseball, and you're going to be good!"

Monday morning, after Rick had left for work and Todd for school, Dana drove over to the newspaper office.

The weekend had been a disaster. Rick and Dana had divided into warring factions, with Todd being wooed by both sides. Saturday night Rick reached for her in bed, and she stiffened to his touch. Rick was different. The last few times they'd made love it was totally lacking in warmth or sincerity. It was just a mechanical thing, done by a mechanical man.

When she got to the office she threw her story on Max's desk. She wasn't going to tell him she wasn't at the game. *Let him guess!*

"Harvey's won, 15-4," she snapped.

"What the fuck is bothering you? Husband been cutting you off?" He laughed, and she glared at him.

"I want to know more about Crandall and Little League, Max. When did this town fall in love with baseball?"

"Five years ago, I guess. Say, what's eating you?"

"And how long has Dreiser been here?"

"Six, maybe seven." Max started reading her story.

"Did Dreiser bring Little League to this town?"

"Of course not. What the hell's the matter with you, girly?"

"Little League!" she snapped. "I want to know what makes Little League so important around here. There's no money in it, is there?"

"No."

"It doesn't bring tourists to Crandall, that's for sure."

Max broke into rousing laughter. "Your son was the losing pitcher Saturday, and you're pissed. Girly, you can't get personally involved with this thing."

"Personal! I don't give a damn about Little League!"

"Sure."

"You have twenty years of newspapers downstairs, right?"

"That's right. Richter's chronicles. Not bad for the title of my life story."

"I'm going downstairs, and I'm going to find out what the hell makes this town so interested in baseball. You want a baseball related story? You're about to get one!"

Chapter 18

Dana had rummaged through several stacks of newspaper, looking for a clue as to what Crandall was like before the Little League craze. She had just pushed a large bale over to the table and was fraying at the cord with her nail file when she saw it:

ROGER DREISER BASEBALL SENSATION

'The town of Crandall was truly blessed when the Dreiser family moved here last year. Since that time our little town's name has constantly been in the headlines, as high school baseball sensation, Roger Dreiser, breaks and continues to break all the county pitching records. Young Dreiser, who has been named to the high school all-American team, is one of the most sought after athletes in the country.

Roger, who was sixteen on his last

birthday, is not only an excellent athlete. His grade point. . ."

Dana's eyes quickly found the date: June 1, 1976. *Dreiser has another son. He must be twenty-three now.*

Dana raced upstairs and found Max in the pressroom running off some circulars.

"Gotta do this side work just to pay the fucking rent."

"Is Roger Dreiser also coach Dreiser's son?" She pushed the paper under his nose.

"What's with you, girly?" He turned off the press.

"I feel there's a story here, Max."

"I hate to disappoint you, but Roger Dreiser died about five years ago."

This surprised her. "Was he the coach's son?"

"Yes. His pride and joy. I'll tell you something, the day the Dresiers moved to this town things around here started to change. The name Crandall suddenly seemed important, and everyone around here loved it, what with big league ball players and scouts passing through just to get a glimpse of the teenage sensation. It was really exciting. I even interviewed him myself a couple of times, with the old man sitting in monitoring every word. He was really protective of that boy. He sure loved him."

The sincerity in Max's tone touched her, and Dreiser suddenly acquired humanistic qualities. She'd never thought of the man as being capable of love.

"Did they adopt Adonis after he died?"

"Yes."

She felt sympathy for Dreiser. "How did he die?"

"Girly, there's no story in it, so why don't you just go back downstairs and find something else." He turned the press back on.

"I just want to know. I'm curious," she said over the hum of the press.

"It really ain't important, girly."

"Is it a secret?"

"I just don't want to talk about it!"

"Come on, Max."

"Damnit, girly. Any questions you want answered is in them papers downstairs. I got work to do!"

It was obvious Max had told her all he was going to. *So what's the secret about Roger Dreiser's death?* She didn't know. But she was going back downstairs to find out.

She stayed in the basement until it was time to go home and meet Todd. The papers were in such disarray that she couldn't track down anything further before she left.

Crandall is nothing like the city, she thought driving home. The city with all its filth and crime is still open. Everything in Crandall seems a secret. The warnings of Helen Grote played back in her mind.

"Mrs. Evans, you have to leave here, before

they take your son like they took my Tommy."

"Who?"

"Them."

"Your son ran away from home, Mrs. Grote."

Wild laughter spilled through the phone. "Run for your life, Mrs. Evans."

She sounded to Dana like a reject from some horror movie, and after the conversation was over, Dana couldn't help but laugh. *No story here.*

The more Dana saw of Crandall, the more Helen Grote's words seemed to ring true. As she slowly probed and uncovered the town's secrets, she intuitively felt herself embarking on a voyage that could change the course of her life. And now that her course had been set, she couldn't turn back.

"Listen to me, Rick. Coach Dreiser had another son, Roger, who was a great high school baseball player. Dreiser really loved him and he died. Now Dreiser is trying to make every kid in Crandall into his first son."

Rick had come in from work and raced upstairs to change, so he and Todd could work out while there was still some sunlight. Dana had followed him to the bedroom.

"What are you talking about?"

"Look at Adonis. He's not a normal, carefree little boy. And there are lots of others like him. Haven't you noticed?"

"He's good, I'll tell you that." Rick

removed his city clothes.

"Is that how you want Todd to be?"

"Yes." He slipped into a grey sweatsuit and donned his baseball cap.

"Well, I don't!"

"Dana, Todd is going to play, and that's all there is to it." He didn't raise his voice, and there was no threat in his words. This made them sound menacing. "Where did you get this crap anyway?"

"From back issues of the Guardian."

"What is this, research for some story?" He started for the door then stopped. "Since you've been working with that paper you've been thinking crazy." Again, he started for the door, then turned back. "Coaches meeting tonight; I'll be eating out." He left.

Normally she would have called after him to continue the argument, but there was a controlled peacefulness in his voice, a calmness in his demeanor that made her stop. For the first time in her life Dana was afraid of her husband.

She was going insane. Slowly but surely, like grains of sand, her sanity was slipping silently away.

So this is how it feels.

She'd often wondered if crazy people knew they were crazy, and if insanity was something only others could see. Or could you watch it creeping up on you like a midnight freight train? Now she saw it in herself, and knew the answers to her questions.

It started when she looked in the mirror and didn't recognize her own image. It wasn't Helen Grote. She didn't like this stranger in the mirror, so she stopped looking, stopped combing her hair, and just last week she stopped sleeping with David.

"I'm going to spend the night in Tommy's room," she told him. When he questioned her she hurled a barrage of accusations at him, and left.

Yesterday she didn't bathe, and this morning she didn't brush her teeth. *Why brush? I haven't eaten all week.* And when she asked herself why these things were happening, someone, not her, but someone inside of her had answered: *Because you're going crazy.*

When the knock came on the door, and she stood staring into the smiling face, she wasn't surprised that he had finally come for her.

I've been waiting for you.

It was finally over. She could feel it. That person inside could have her body. She didn't need it anymore. She was going to join her Tommy. The two of them would be together again.

So when she opened the door and saw the smiling face on the other side of the threshold, she knew instinctively what she must do. And without a word, she welcomed him in.

No one would listen to her. She tried talking to Max and to Rick, but both seemed to think that she was whistling in the dark. She wasn't sure, but she thought there was something terribly wrong with Crandall's obsession for baseball. Coach Dreiser was turning the boys into machines, and if it was okay with the parents of Crandall, fine, but it wasn't all right with her. They weren't going to turn Todd into an Adonis Dreiser.

First she had to prove it to Rick. She knew if she could just show him proof of how bad this thing was for Todd, he'd swallow his pride and take his son off the team. Then if she could prove it to Max, maybe he'd run a story, and she could show the whole town how Little League possibly could ruin their children.

It all came back to Dreiser. He wasn't a bad man—he seemed a decent father—but he was obsessed. He'd lost his beloved son, and now he was trying to turn every boy in Crandall into Roger Dreiser.

It began with crazy workouts, army-like regimentation, and strange diets. And just two weeks ago a supply of special multi-vitamins was delivered to every boy in the Little League. *At the parents expense!* What would he do next? How far would he carry his obsession? She didn't know, but she had to stop him. Already he had had a murderer released to play baseball.

He's not going to ruin Todd.

Her thoughts drifted to the dream she'd had, where Dreiser was taking her son. *He's coming with me. He'll make a fine pitcher.*

Dreiser was *not* going to get him! *No way!*

Then she remembered Helen Grote. Young Thomas had run away from home. He was part of the Little League, and Helen seemed to blame the town. Maybe. . . .

She found her phone book, looked up the number, and dialed. The phone rang eleven times before she hung up. She wouldn't call this evening. *I don't want to speak to Mr. Grote.* She decided to call again tomorrow, and while she was still at the phone, she'd try Ruth again.

She had to come home eventually!

Chapter 19

It was dark time. Mommy had snuggled Todd securely under the covers, crinkling his sides with fluttery fingers and then smooching him with a big old wet one. Laughing, he tried to wriggle free, but she'd gotten him again. She smiled, said, "Goodnight. I love you." And was gone.

Then came Daddy, talking baseball, and telling him how Dave Winfield had belted one out of Fenway Park. He reminded Todd of how proud of him he was, before tussling his hair and walking out. "Goodnight, tiger."

And now that the room was empty, and Todd was alone again, the fear came rolling in. It moved slowly at first, like the early stages of an incoming tide. But soon it swept in, covering Todd and leaving him thrashing about—like the time he accidentally fell into the roof-top swimming pool when they lived on Second Avenue, and Daddy had to jump in and save him. That day he was really scared. But this fear was far worse.

Todd lay silently gazing around the room, as shadows bloomed in the darkness.

The fear was coming more rapidly now, and Todd wanted to call out to his parents: *"Mommy, Daddy, save me!"* But he knew they'd only come in and muss up his hair, before tucking him away again and leaving.

He was afraid—really afraid! And he wanted to know how do you tell the grown-ups?

How do you tell them that you're lonely because there's no one left to play with? And that you don't want to play like men all the time, but sometimes, only sometimes, you'd like to play like a kid again, with toys—a racing car, Micronauts, or even a doll.

How do you tell them that your best friend is different? And no, it's not that he plays baseball better, or that he's more grownup, but that he's just plain mean.

Can you tell them that the monsters they say are all in your head seem so real? And that you're sure one night when you're not watching and have slipped off to sleep, that the bogeyman is going to finally come out of your closet and want to play?

Can you tell them about fear—real fear, the kind Todd was sure grownups could never imagine?

Todd rolled over and tried to sleep, but he remembered Mommy and Daddy, and how they used to talk to each other in loud voices.

Now that he was playing Little League they hardly talked that way anymore. He didn't want them to yell ever again. But how could he tell them?

He was going to keep playing baseball, and like it or not, he was going to be good, and Mommy and Daddy were going to smile a lot and be happy. Daddy would be so proud. He wanted Daddy to be proud, more than almost anything, but he didn't know how to tell him.

'Cause how do you tell grownups about the things that go on inside kids—about meanness and fear and being lonely, and that you want everybody in the whole wide world to smile a lot and be happy? How do you tell them that being a kid is harder than anything grownups could ever do?

Todd lay snuggled away under the covers, long shadows dancing around him, threatening to pounce on him any moment, and he kept wondering how to tell them. The answer, of course, was obvious, so he squinched shut his eyes and tried to push the scary things out of his head.

For you didn't tell them about all of the things that made being a little kid and growing up so darned hard. You went on laughing and playing—but telling? No. These were kid things, and you never ever told the grownups anything about them. You just plain didn't.

"Trow da bum out!"

Dana Evans stood watching Adonis Dreiser

hurl his fastball past still another batter. He'd been throwing hard all morning, like an adult, and was much too good for many of the boys.

Adonis had fired once again. This time, although the ball seemed to slice down the center of the plate, the umpire called it a ball instead of yelling "strike!" This prompted a chorus of jeers from several parents, like the remark from the beer-bellied father of Mike Perotti: "Da guy needs glasses!"

The day was hot, eighty-two degrees, and the elder Mr. Perotti came ready for the heat, wearing a Crazy Eddie T-shirt that looked about two sizes too small as it curled up over his gut. His Giants baseball cap shielded his dark hair from the sun. He slurped on a cool, frosty Rheingold.

Mike Perotti senior was a pipe-fitter, and from the talk Dana had heard around town, he'd been drinking more than beer lately—drinking because business was bad. What with the economy so sluggish, housing starts were fewer and fewer, and Mike Perotti was feeling the pressure.

When the umpire yelled ball a second time, the protests of the crowd became louder, as more parents joined in.

The score was 10-2, it was the fifth inning, and it was obvious that unless a miracle occured Harvey's was going to win. Still, the Harvey's parents protested vehemently, and Mike Perotti senior led the charge: "How much dey payin' you, umpire?"

He looks like such a nice man, Dana thought, staring sympathetically at the umpire. He was medium build and in his early thirties. He was someone from the town, a neighbor, probably someone they all passed on the street and called out to with cordial greetings. Today, however, he was the enemy, and several of the parents were not going to let him forget it.

Dana moved through the crowd, trying to get out of earshot of Mike Perotti senior.

"Hi. How are you?" The woman wearing the green jogging suit looked familiar. "Remember me? We met out here at practice once."

Now Dana remembered her—the woman who'd boasted that her son would be the second baseman for the tournament team.

"Hello," Dana said extending her hand. "Dana Evans. I'm afraid I forgot your. . ."

"Eunice Graham."

"Yes. Your son's name is Petie, right?"

The woman smiled proudly. "Yes. Have you seen him play this season?"

Dana had seen him play. He was good, but not nearly as good as Jimmy Warren.

"I think I have," she said.

"He's good, isn't he?"

How's that for a leading question? "I don't remember," she lied.

"He's going to be on the tournament team this year, at second base."

There was a momentary awkward silence between them, during which Dana vacantly smiled.

"Didn't you tell me you worked for the Guardian?"

Dana sensed what was coming and wished she'd stayed where she was, listening to Mike Perotti.

"Yes, that's right." She shuffled her feet nervously.

"Well, why don't you do a story on my Petie? He's the next great superstar of the Crandall Giants."

"Really!"

"Definitely."

The woman stared into Dana's eyes, challenging. *Answer the woman, Dana!*

"I don't think it's the kind of thing we're looking for."

"Why not? You've done stories on Adonis Dreiser. You wouldn't be playing favorites because he's the coach's son?"

"I can't speak for what happened before I came to Crandall."

"Well, you represent the paper today. I think you should do a story on my son. He's really good!"

Dana felt the stinging onset of a migraine.

"Mrs. Graham. . ."

"Eunice."

"Eunice, I just don't have the authority. Why don't you ask Max Richter?"

"Don't you think my son is good enough?" There was a flash of anger in her eyes.

"I don't know," Dana lied again. The headache was getting worse. "But Mr. Richter

gives me the assignments, and I cover them."
The pain pulsed into her neck. Eunice Graham
was grating on her nerves. She wanted to end
this conversation as quickly as possible.

"Why don't you tell Mr. Richter about my
Petie?"

Dana saw a way out. "All right, I will." She
looked over at second base. "Is that him?"
Little brat can't even throw.

"No. That's Arnie Cahn."

Dana glanced into the Walgreen's dugout.
"Which one is he?"

"Petie's not here today."

"What!" Dana felt her control slipping.
"Well, I'd like to see him play before I rave to
Mr. Richter about him." Her voice was tinged
with sarcasm. *Come on, girl, hold it down!*

"You will, soon. He's just in Community
General for a few days."

"Really! The hospital!"

"Nothing serious. Just a check-up. When
we went for his physical, Doctor Warner discovered he had a heart murmur, that's all. But
come to our game on Wednesday and see for
yourself. Pete's the best. At least he will be,
and. . ."

Eunice Graham was launching into another
harangue about her son, but Dana wasn't
listening. Her concentration had honed in on
the subject of heart murmurs. And somewhere in her mind a connection was being
made.

Dana had let the phone ring fourteen times,

and still there was no answer.

She replaced it on the receiver and checked the clock. 3:15. She'd been trying Helen Grote every fifteen minutes since she'd come in. Now, she wanted to talk to Helen more than ever.

It was a gorgeous Saturday afternoon, the kind you dreamt about all winter and waited to enjoy. Rick had left early with Todd. Since they had no game today, they took the station wagon and drove into the Bronx to catch the Yankees playing a double header at the stadium.

Rick had gotten two tickets from a client, and when he told Todd, the boy lit up like a Christmas tree.

Dana was feeling good and had walked over to the field to cover a game. But since she'd spoken with Eunice Graham, an eerie sensation had crept over her.

There really is something wrong with the boys of Crandall. The thought incessantly pushed its way into her mind. *Not all of them, just a selected dozen or so.* It was a silly thought, probably caused by some ridiculous paranoia. *I know they're not monsters!* But she couldn't shake the feeling.

There were secrets in the town of Crandall, secrets kept by David and Helen Grote, Philip Dreiser, and maybe even Max Richter. The secrets concerned the boys.

Dana didn't want to believe it. It sounded like the plot of some juvenile horror movie, but intuition told her there was definitely something wrong.

She didn't want Todd to be a member of the team, but she couldn't influence Rick or anyone with meaningless suppositions. She needed hard cold facts.

She picked up the phone again, and this time dialed Ruth's number. This heart murmur thing really had shaken her. Ronnie Roberts had a heart murmur, just like Petie Graham. And she remembered how different Ronnie had seemed the last morning she'd spoken with him.

Did Jimmy Warren and Tommy Grote have heart murmurs, too? She needed to know. *And where the hell is Ruth?* Ruth had been gone for nearly a month.

As the monotonous ringing of the phone droned in Dana's ear, a cold chill came over her. Ruth was definitely not at her mother's. And suddenly she felt—no, knew—that wherever Ruth was, she was in danger.

Dana was down in the archives, searching through stacks after stack of newspapers. She'd been there since early morning, leaving home soon after Rick and Todd. It was 12:15, and still she searched doggedly through the stacks.

Around eleven Max came down, trying to lure her upstairs with a cup of coffee.

"Come on, girly, you gotta take a break sometimes."

Why? Because you don't want me to find what I'm looking for?

Dana refused. When she found what she wanted, she was going to rub their noses in it.

Then she finally stumbled on something. A small column, in the April 17, 1980 edition, mentioned a runaway boy. The article was about the same length as the one on Thomas Grote, containing about as much information.

The boy was Jeff Mulligan, aged twelve. Little league age, Dana thought, as she ripped the column of print from the paper. She knew the article wasn't enough. It meant nothing, but in her mind another section of the puzzle had fallen into place. There was a connection between these runaway boys and Little League. The puzzle, of course, was still a jumble of errant pieces scattered throughout her mind, but slowly things were beginning to come together.

"Lunch time, girly," Max called down. "I got us a couple of tuna sandwiches and some apple juice. Come on up here, now. You're gonna need your nourishment if you plan to be down there all day."

Dana was a little hungry, but more than that, she wanted to talk to Max. Lunch was as good an excuse as any.

Upstairs, she pulled a rickety old folding chair up to the desk and bit into her sandwich.

"Thanks, Max."

"Don't mention it. You find anything?"

Is there a hint of wariness in his voice?

"No. Not really."

"You gonna keep trying?"

"Yes." She'd thrown him off guard, and they ate in silence for the next fifteen minutes. "Isn't it horrible about that thing in Atlanta?" she said finally. She stared into his gray eyes, searching, and saw there was still some fire left in them.

"What thing?" He peered at her over the rim of his glasses.

"The trial for the murderer of all those boys."

He was absentmindedly devouring the sandwich, but suddenly his head jerked up. She was on the subject of news. *I have him now.*

"Damnit, girly, it's a crying shame. This is supposed to be a democracy. I'd hate to see this guy convicted on circumstantial evidence."

"The murders have stopped!"

"Shit! Whoever did it, and I'm not saying they got the wrong man, but whoever did it ain't no idiot. If he was, he'd have been caught a long time ago. I wouldn't be surprised if this thing started up again somewhere down the road."

"Do you think something like that could happen here in Crandall?"

He paused in thought, and she searched his eyes hoping to spot a flicker of something—anything!

"No. I don't think so."

"Maybe the runaway boys were murdered," she said, and he nearly choked on his apple juice.

"So that's what you're leading up to. You're a newspaper woman, all right." He chuckled, and she knew she was losing him.

"Who's Jeff Mulligan?"

"I don't know."

I'm not letting you off that easy, Max.

"His name is in that precious file you keep locked up so tight."

"How do you know?" She had him again. There was definite concern on his craggy face.

"The day you saw me looking in, I peeked, just a little." There was a short silence, as Max carefully weighed what he had to say.

"Girly, I hope you're just saying that."

"Why?" *Come on, Max, spill it!*

He threw the last hunk of sandwich into his mouth and followed with a splash of apple juice. This time she'd lost him for sure. But there was one more question she had to ask.

"What's the secret, Max? What's in that file?"

"Lunch is over. I gotta get back to work. I don't have time to shoot the shit all afternoon."

Damn him!

When Dana had finished eating she headed back into the basement. Max was in the press-room, pretending to be busy. After Dana had gone downstairs he came back to the office.

Tiny beads of perspiration glistened on his forehead. *I was right about this one, Max* thought. She's too damn smart for her own good. He slammed his fist into the desk, his fragile white knuckles stinging with pain. And for the first time all day, he smiled.

It was 1:55. In five minutes Dana had to leave for home to meet Todd as he came in from school.

It had been a long day. Her eyes burned, and her fingers throbbed from thumbing through so many stacks. She was going through her last stack of the day when she found it:

BRUTAL WEEKEND TRAGEDY
HITS CRANDALL

Roger Dreiser, son of Philip and Edna Dreiser, went berserk sometime yesterday morning, going on a rampage of terror.

Roger, who is a high school all-American, removed his father's pistol from a drawer in the downstairs study and went up to his parent's bedroom, where he shot his father twice in the chest.

Philip Dreiser was rushed to Community General hospital, where he was immediately operated on for the removal of the bullets. He was in guarded condition for the first twenty-four hours following the operation, but sources tell us that now he is doing quite well.

All cards and gifts should be sent to

the Dreiser house and not to the
hospital, as Mr. Dreiser will be leaving
Community General on Friday to begin
his convalescence at home.

(cont. P.6)

Dana had found something. Not what she
was looking for, but still another part of the
intricate puzzle.

She couldn't read on. She had to meet Todd
and didn't want to be late. She stuffed the
newspaper into her handbag and proceded upstairs.

When she reached the office, Max, wrapped
in his trusty gray cardigan, was seated behind
his desk, reading.

"I'm leaving now, Max."

"All right." She headed for the door.
"Dana!"

"Yes." His abrupt call stopped her in her
tracks.

"You're a good newspaper woman. Too
good for Crandall." A fatherly expression
passed over his face momentarily, and she
thought of her own father back in Allentown.

"What do you mean?"

"Just that, girly. You *deef* or something?"

"I suppose that was a compliment?"

"It was."

"Thank you." She smiled, but wondered
what the old man was up to. He was sharp.
There was a reason for his sudden softness.

"Girly, I'd like you to have a set of keys.
This way, if you feel like doing some research

in the evening after I'm gone, you can let yourself in."

She crossed the room to his desk. "Thank you."

"Don't mention it."

"I really have to run, Max." She turned and was off again. She was halfway out the door when he called out to her.

"Just don't make a fucking mess!"

She closed the door gently and climbed into the Pinto wagon.

As she drove home, she weighed Max's gesture. He's a strange old man, she thought, smiling. She liked Max.

But what the hell is he up to?

Chapter 20

Todd was at the dining room table having an after school snack, a bologna sandwich and a glass of milk. Dana was on the phone.

When she came in from the office she immediately began trying Helen Grote, but the phone continued to ring unanswered. Maybe they moved already, she thought. But if they had moved, their phone would have been disconnected, and that didn't seem to be the case.

Dana had dialed the operator, just to be certain that the Grote phone was in proper working order.

"Miss Gray, can I help you?"

"Yes. I'm trying to reach the home of David Grote, and I was wondering if I was calling the right number."

"I believe you want directory assistance, ma'am. The number in Westchester county is

555-1212." The operator sounded professionally annoyed.

"No. I know I have the right number. I was
wondering if it was working. . ."

"That's repairs. . ."

"I don't want repairs! I simply want to
verify that it's working, because when I call
there's never any answer."

There was a brief silence.

"What's the number, ma'am?"

Dana read off the number.

"Checking," the operator said, and Dana
heard the distant hum of a ringing phone.
"What's the party's name and address,
ma'am?"

Dana gave her the information.

"Yes, the number you have is correct, and
the phone is in proper working order. Try
again later. Thank you." Before Dana could
utter a sound the connection was broken.

That was twenty minutes ago, and now
Dana was trying again to no avail. She rested
the phone back on its cradle and stepped into
the dining room to join Todd.

His sandwich was gone, and he was
draining the last of his milk. He smiled up at
her as she entered, his mischievous blue eyes
reminding her of Rick. The boy looked more
like his father each day. In a way, this surprised her. He looked so much like her just a
few months ago. It seemed she was watching
"herself" go out of him daily, as if she were
losing him.

"How's school?" she asked, just to make

conversation. Todd was a good student, as enthusiastic about learning as his father had been. School was never a problem.

"It's all right. You coming to the game Saturday?"

"Of course."

"I'm pitching again."

"I know."

"I'm gonna be real good. Maybe as good as Adonis. You'll see."

No! Not like Adonis!

"Just have fun, Todd."

"All right," he said, looking away.

"You do have fun when you play, don't you?"

"Sure." His voice dropped.

"Do you think Adonis has fun?"

Silence.

"Do you?"

"No! But he wins. I want to win, too. I like Little League, Mom, and I want to be good. The best. I want Dad to be proud of me."

Dana went to her son and hugged him. Stiffening, he pulled away.

"I'm getting kind of big for that mushy stuff, Mom." She was shocked but she tried not to show it.

"I always hug you! I love you."

"I know."

"You love me?" She tickled his sides, and he couldn't resist a laugh.

"Yes. Just don't kiss me around the team. Okay?"

"Okay."

She suddenly felt as if Dreiser were winning. He was taking her son. *So, this is how it starts.*

"Do you really want to play Little League?"

"Yes," he said softly.

"Have fun. Okay?"

"Okay."

She stood and walked to the back door. Pulling back the curtain, she stared out into the yard.

Of course she wasn't losing him to Dreiser. She was losing him to something far worse. Age. Todd was growing up, and with growing up came growing away. Just yesterday he was a baby, dependant on her for everything. Now, he didn't need her nearly as much. It was all happening so fast.

The movement in the next yard jarred her thoughts. It was Ronnie Roberts swinging a bat, practicing his home run swing.

"Ronnie is outside," Dana called. "You want to go play with him?"

"No!" There was something permanent about the "no" that made Dana turn around.

"Aren't you guys friends anymore?"

"No."

She came and sat at the table across from him.

"A fight?"

"No."

"Tell me." She touched his arm, and he stared up at her with the most godawful hurt look in his eyes. "Todd, what's the matter?"

"Ronnie's changing."

"What do you mean?"

"He doesn't play with toys anymore, and he's always reading books on numbers."

"There's nothing wrong with reading, is there?"

"No. He's just so smart. He gets smarter everyday."

Do I detect a pang of jealousy?

"I think that's good," Dana said.

"But he's mean! He talks mean, and he looks mean. And when he's not reading, he doesn't want to do anything but play baseball. Besides, I think he hates me."

Todd wasn't normally prone to exaggerations. This made his statements about Ronnie weigh all the more heavier on Dana. She thought of Jimmy Warren, Adonis Dreiser, and all the other strange little boys she'd seen playing Little League.

"He doesn't hate you, honey." She tried to laugh, but on the inside she was weighing what her son had said. *Maybe he does hate Todd?*

She got up and went back to the phone. She'd try the Grote number again until someone answered—anyone.

As she waited for an answer, she pulled the aged clipping from her purse:

BRUTAL WEEKEND TRAGEDY
HITS CRANDALL

Suddenly Dana wished they were all still living back in the city on Second Avenue. But today that seemed so far away.

It was one of those rare evenings that Rick didn't come home early. Just a few months ago anything short of a death in the family could not have gotten Rick away from the office before 8:00 P.M. Now, he was home nearly every evening, playing ball with Todd and going to meetings, and Dana didn't feel good about it.

This is what I wanted, isn't it? She questioned herself. *NO!* More involvement is what she wanted, not Little League. Why couldn't they build model airplanes, fly kites, or any other of the many father-son activities?

She remembered how happy she was when they discovered Little League. Of course that was before she suspected the boys of Crandall of being monsters or something.

She had to laugh at that one. *Monsters! That's silly!* But her laugh was only on the surface. Deep down in her subconsciousness, it wasn't silly at all.

She checked the clock. 7:36. Todd would be going to bed in about an hour. After she had tucked him in, she planned to run next door and confront Tom Roberts about Ruth's absence. The sick mother story could not hold up any longer.

Now, she picked up the phone and dialed the Grote residence again.

"Hello." David Grote's voice snapped through the line, and Dana felt a sudden chill. Her voice caught in her throat.

"Hello? Hello?"

"Hello, Mr. Grote?" she finally said.

"Who is this?"

"Dana Evans."

A brief silence.

"What can I do for you, Mrs. Evans?" His voice was tinged with ice.

Dana hadn't planned on what she was going to say, and now she had to think fast.

"I'm sorry to disturb you, Mr. Grote, but Max Richter asked me to call and ask you and Mrs. Grote if you wouldn't reconsider, and let us do the interview." She knew this would get back to Max, but it was all she could think of.

"No, Mrs. Evans, we haven't reconsidered. I'll tell you what, though—you needn't call us again. If we ever reconsider, we'll call you first."

"Mrs. Grote called me a few weeks back, and. . ."

"What?"

That's right, buddy!

Dana was fishing, and she had the distinct feeling she was getting a nibble.

"Your wife called me a few weeks ago, Mr. Grote, and from her conversation I thought you two were reconsidering."

"When did she call you?"

Squirm, Mr. Grote!

"When?" She was playing with him now.

"When did my wife call you, Mrs. Evans?"

"Oh, a few weeks ago . . . on a Saturday. We talked of Thomas' heart murmur. . ." She waited.

"You did?"

"Yes." She waited again.

"Well, what about it?"

That confirmed it. Thomas did have a heart murmur.

"I was thinking that maybe the heart murmur was the reason he ran away. You know, his parents not letting him play baseball and all."

"Mrs. Evans. . ."

"Dana."

"Mrs. Evans, you're barking up the wrong tree. Thomas' heart murmur turned out to be something quite normal in young boys. It was nothing serious, and the doctor said he would outgrow it. Now we appreciate your concern, but we're really not interested in talking to the Guardian at this time."

"Mrs. Grote said she was. Can I speak with her?"

"Mrs. Evans, I'm trying not to be rude, but you're making it quite difficult. My wife just ran down to the market. I'm sure she has nothing to say to you, but if she does, I'll have her call you as soon as she comes in. All right, Mrs. Evans?"

"Fine."

"Thank you, and goodnight." The connection was broken.

David Grote had turned out to be a wealth of information. Not only had he confirmed Dana's suspicion that Thomas had a heart murmur, but he lied about the whereabouts of his wife. Dana had been calling all afternoon, and Helen Grote hadn't been at home all day. She didn't just run down to the market. She'd been out for a long, long time. Again Dana felt a distinct chill.

"She's becoming a pest, and she was asking questions about this heart murmur thing."

"What questions?"

"She thought it was the reason that Tommy ran away."

"What did you tell her?"

"That she was barking up the wrong tree."

"Good."

"Then she asked to speak to Helen, and I told her Helen was out."

"You did well."

"I don't think she's going to quit. If she starts snooping around, she might find something out, and it won't be my fault. I've done everything you asked."

"I know you have. Now don't you worry about Dana Evans. She'll be dealt with. All right?"

"All right."

The Roberts' house was pitch black, and it was a school night. Ronnie Roberts should have been in bed, and there certainly should have been some lights on in the house. But there was no answer at the door.

Dana rang the doorbell one last time before heading back home. *Where the hell are they?* Something was terribly, terribly wrong.

* * *

He didn't like being outside of Crandall this time of year—especially this year. This was an all-important year for Crandall, for Little League baseball, and of course, for himself. He wanted to be in Crandall if he were needed, but this, too, was important.

He hadn't seen her in three years, and she was coming to the end of her college career. He couldn't be there for her moment of glory, her college graduation, so he came now, just for the day.

He stood in the bathroom of his hotel room, splashing musk after-shave over his face. He pulled a crisp white shirt and dark tie from his suitcase. This was a special occasion, and he wanted to look good.

The phone rang.

"Yes?"

He listened.

"I'll be right down."

Downstairs, in the Cork, one of the few hotel restaurants in all of Boise that you could get a good meal, Jenny Lee Harmon sat with her parents. She was going to see the old man again. When they lived in Crandall he had visited them often and had become like a grandfather to her. He wasn't important to her anymore, but she knew she had to see him.

Jenny Lee would rather have been studying. Her study group was meeting that evening to finish cramming for a Calculus III exam the next day. Maggie, her best friend on campus, and some of the others ribbed her about not being prepared.

"One failed exam can louse up that perfect index of yours," Maggie had said.

Of course Maggie was joking. They all knew Jenny would do well, whether she studied or not. Her presence in the study sessions was needed to help the others. Jenny always made out all right.

The old man entered the restaurant and looked around.

"Table for one?" a cheery voice called.

"No, I'm with them," he said, pointing to the trio.

The girl had changed. She appeared more mature, woman-like.

A fatherly pride spread through him as he walked towards them. He was overwhelmed with emotion.

They spotted him and smiled.

"How was your trip?" Jenny Lee's father asked. He rose and shook the man's hand.

"Just fine," he answered, nodding at the mother. Then he turned to Jenny Lee. "And how are you?"

"Real good, gramps." It was a flash of her former self, which at first surprised him.

"Real good? I hope that's not what they're teaching you in college." He donned a mock scowl.

"Of course not, grandfather." She rose and hugged him. It was void of emotion.

This was her only flaw—the inconsistency in the language pattern. Still she seemed perfect—just perfect. The entire program had been a success.

"So you're graduating college. That's quite an accomplishment," he said, taking his seat.

"I know. Thank you, sir."

"What do you plan to do with that precious education?"

"I'm going to attend graduate school, sir."

"Are you?" He knew the answers, but he wanted to hear them from her.

"Yeah. U.C.L.A."

He felt like a proud parent, and honestly knew what it felt like to have a child grow up and graduate college.

He turned to her father. "Is everything all right?"

"Oh, yes." He smiled again. "We couldn't be happier."

"Good . . . Jenny, you're about to become a celebrity. You know that?"

"Yeah, it'll be great."

He paused before going on. "I want you to make your parents and all the people of Crandall proud of you."

"Yes, sir."

"The Giants miss you at shortstop."

"It was an honor to play there, sir."

The talk was finished. They all settled back to enjoy a fine dinner. Throughout the meal he glanced over at her. He almost felt like crying. In a few short weeks her name would be known across the nation, and perhaps in a few years his would be tagged on to hers. After all, it was his guidance that made eleven year old Jenny Lee Harmon the youngest Phi Beta Kappa college graduate ever.

* * *

"Slow down, honey!"

Dana had jumped on Rick as soon as he walked through the door. She'd promised herself she wouldn't mention anything to him until she had documented proof that Little League was bad for Todd, but so much had happened today that she had to say something.

She started right in when he arrived a little after ten. She followed him up to the bedroom, telling him of Roger Dreiser shooting his father, Max not wanting to talk about it, and of her conversation with David Grote.

"Hey, slow down!" Rick called.

"Honey, I know you think I'm being paranoid, but I'm not. There's something wrong in this town, and it has to do with Dreiser and the boys."

"Dana, what are you talking about?"

"Even Ronnie Roberts is different. Haven't you noticed?"

"I've noticed he's been playing better lately."

"Is baseball all you can think of? He's different, Rick! I noticed it the Saturday he walked over to the field with you and Todd. He seemed so . . . mechanical."

"Dana, you're talking crazy." Rick was standing by the chair, undressing, and Dana was seated on the edge of the bed.

"Even Todd has noticed it!"

"It's that damned newspaper again, isn't it?"

"No, it isn't!"

"Then it's the Jimmy Warren thing. It's still bothering you."

"I admit that bothers me, but. . . ."

"So you want to take our son out of Little League because of one bad incident."

"Rick, why won't you listen to me?" She felt desperate now and was practically off the bed.

"Because you're babbling on like a feeble-minded old woman." The statement knifed into her.

"Rick, I love Todd, and I love you. Believe me, there's something wrong." She looked searchingly into his eyes. He saw her anxiety.

"Honey, I want to believe you. . . ."

"There's more. Ruth Roberts is not at her sick mother's."

"What? How do you know?"

"Because her mother is dead. Ruth told me herself. She died before Ruth and Tom got married."

Rick looked surprised. "Why do you think Tom would tell such a lie?"

"I don't know, but it's just part of the strange goings on in this town. Rick, I don't like it here."

"We can't just up and move."

"Why not?"

"It's not that simple. We'd lose money."

"So?"

"Honey, you're pretty upset about this thing, aren't you?"

"You bet I am!"

"All right, for starters I'll talk to the tiger about not playing baseball. I'll tell him how you feel, and if he wants to quit, no problem. If he doesn't, he'll stay on, until you can show me that Little League is really bad for him. In the meantime, I'll get in touch with Tom Roberts and root out the truth about Ruth. Hey, that sounds like the title of a hit tune—The Truth About Ruth."

"Oh, brother!"

He smiled, and she smiled back. They exchanged hugs.

"Thank you. I really do love you," she said.

"Me, too."

He cradled her in his arms, and for the first time in a long while she had the feeling that things between them could be good.

Chapter 21

It was late, and Mike Perotti senior was taking the shortcut through Crandall park. He was going this way because Tom Selby had thrown him out of the pub, telling him to go home and sleep it off.

"You better not drive, if you know what's good for you," he said, and Mike knew that if he took the car Tom would have the police on his ass. *The bastard!* And he wasn't about to walk around the park, so here he was.

Entering from the rear, he cut across the baseball field, walking past old Teasdale's dilapidated mansion.

Teasdale was gone now, the old man kicking off just before the start of the season. And when Mike Perotti had heard the news about Teasdale, he had smiled and said "good."

The old bastard had wrecked the field, leaving it like a swamp for the Throgs Neck game last year, nearly costing them a victory.

Mike Perotti immediately had started a movement to replace Doc Teasdale. The old bastard was too old and too much of a drunk to properly care for the field. Now that they had some young fellas from Rye coming in to care for the grounds, everything was in great shape. Now it was a field any man could be proud to have his kid playing on, even if the kid *was* a crybaby.

Mike Perotti cut across the lush grass of the outfield, slowing down as he reached the dusty, red clay of the infield. Damn, the dirt felt good under his feet. It reminded him of when he was a kid in Yonkers, playing ball over on McLean Avenue, scooping up grounders at third base and throwing out everyone, like Gimpy, Lefty, Guido, Sal and even Ron Bastione, who drilled fastballs too hard for anyone but Mike to handle. He could handle 'em all, just like his idol, Brooks Robinson.

Stopping at third, Mike took his position by the bag and pretended to swoop down for a hard grounder. His movements were jerky, his feet tangling together like Mrs. Olaf's spaghetti, and he spilled to the ground.

"Shit!" he mumbled, staring up at the sky.

A large gibbous moon drifted slowly across a nearly cloudless sky. It was well past 11:00 PM, and Mike Perotti senior was drunk.

"Shit, fuck," he said, remembering. I was good, like Brooks Robinson—not like the money hungry jerks they got playing today.

"Nettles!" he screamed, his voice cracking the silence. Hell, the Yanks have Nettles, and the guy can't string two good seasons together to save his life. "Clete Boyer," he said, mumbling again. Now there was a guy who knew how to represent the Yankee pinstripes—a real third baseman, not that money hungry fag they have out there now.

His mind drifted to the news he'd heard recently about Kenny Boyer, Clete's brother and a great infielder himself. Kenny discovered he had lung cancer last November, and the guy was toughing it out like a real trooper. If it had happened to one of those punks playing today, he'd probably cry himself to death.

The subject of crying made Mike think of his son. The kid was a baby, a fucking crybaby, and that's all there was to it.

Sure he beat the living shit out of the kid—sometimes he had to. The kid was making an ass out of him, embarrassing him in front of everyone, and he couldn't stand for that.

The boy should have been one of the special ones. They'd lived in Crandall since the boy was nine, and now he was twelve. *Christ!* Three fucking years, and the kid still wasn't ready. And no wonder. How many evenings had he come in to find the kid practicing that damned clarinet, instead of developing his eye or his throwing arm. Just today he'd come in from the union hall, and the kid was studying for a spelling test. A SPELLING TEST! CHRIST! Didn't the boy understand that his future was at stake here—all of their futures?

And the old lady wasn't helping none—no, siree! She was encouraging the kid. Well, not anymore. Mike had taken a sawed-off broomstick (just like the ones he used to play stickball with) to the kid this afternoon, not stopping until he'd drawn blood. The kid would practice baseball from now on. He was sure of that!

Mike Perotti stood up, brushed himself off, and was about to swoop in for another imaginary grounder, when he saw someone approaching home plate. Mike craned his neck in the direction of the approaching figure. Moonlight illuminated a boy dressed in a Giants uniform, wearing a batting helmet and toting a bat on his right shoulder.

"What the hell are you doin' out here?" Mike screamed. He knew Dreiser didn't like the kids staying up late, especially during the season.

The boy stopped just outside the batter's box and knocked the dirt from his cleats with the bat, just like the pros do. He took a few practice swings and stepped up to the plate.

"Answer me, boy! What are you doin' out here? You should be home in bed."

"Brooks Robinson, born May 18th, 1937, played eighteen years: from 1955 through 1973." The words fell mechanically from the boys lips.

Did he say Brooks Robinson? My idol!

Brooks Robinson or not, the boy didn't belong out here. Angrily Mike stormed towards him.

As he approached he noticed dark foreboding eyes staring out at him from under the peak-billed helmet. Someone else might have been scared, but not Mike Perotti.

Mike was ten feet from him now, and the boy checked his swing, the muscles in his young face tightening, as if he were readying himself for Nolan Ryan's fireball.

"Do I know you?" Mike was two feet from the boy when the kid began winding up for a big swing. Mike Perotti kept coming.

"What's your na..." The words caught in his throat as he watched the bat swish fiercely through the air. It caught him flush in the midsection, his hands grabbing his stomach, as he doubled over in excruciating pain.

"Brooks Robinson, lifetime batting average 271, 9354 times at bats, 2539 hits."

Hits?

Mike was practically to his knees when he saw the bat coming for his head.

Adrenaline is a wonderful chemical. When you're scared as hell, your adrenal glands squirt a mess of it into your bloodstream, and it can do amazing things. For instance, it can make a drunk man practically stone sober in a matter of seconds.

If Mike Perotti had been as drunk as he was a few minutes earlier, he wouldn't have reacted quickly enough, and his head would have cracked off the side of the bat, like one of those slashing singles hit by Pete Rose. Instead, Mike somehow pushed himself up, just a little, and the blow caught his shoulder. He rolled with the blow, hoping to ease the hurt, tumbling along the dusty infield as scorching pain ripped through his arm.

When he stopped rolling he looked up at the boy, and wanted to yell: "Hey, you crazy or something?" But he figured that was a pretty dumb question, and besides, from the look on the boy's face, that bat was answering all questions.

Quickly the boy approached, the bat poised for another homerun swing.

Fear suddenly rose in Mike. He knew if he didn't do something soon, Mike Perotti senior could kiss this life goodbye. So, struggling to his feet, he did the only sensible thing a man in his condition could do. He ran. Aimlessly at first, heading back out towards left, then center field.

What am I doing?

He knew he couldn't run like this forever. He was no spring chicken, but he had to get to safety. The alcohol was still in his system, and he knew he wouldn't be able to run for long. Already his breath was short and raspy, and the liquor that floated in his stomach now flamed into a burning brush fire.

He slowed, trying to catch his breath, and realized that he was headed in the wrong direction. He was headed towards the pub, and in his condition he'd never make it that far.

I've got to make it home.

Home was closer. He knew he had to head back towards the front of the park and the boy, but that was his only chance.

He turned and saw that the boy, practically on top of him, the bat on his shoulder, was poised for still another strike.

"What's with you, kid?" Mike called, but the dark eyes stared on, expressionless.

"Brooks Robinson: Most Valuable Player 1970 World Series; Most Valuable Player 1966 World Series; Most Valuable Player 1964 World Series. . ."

He's spouting them damn statistics like a fucking computer!

Now fear was raging in Mike. He started cutting back towards home plate and the front of the park, but the boy moved diagonally, attempting to cut off his escape route. Mike couldn't dodge back and forth for long, and if he stopped—even for a moment—the kid would make hamburger out of him.

His movements turned sluggish, as his tired legs became stiff and achy. The pain in his gut, caused by the blow of the bat and the burning liquor, intensified, and he wished he could stop at the drinking fountain and splash his belly with some cool, refreshing water. His arm, though, was the worst. His shoulder felt as if it had been knocked out of its socket, and even the slightest movement wracked his body with pain. So Mike ran with his arm clasped tightly to his side, sort of like a mummy. But he had to go on.

His only hope was to surprise the boy, head towards him. He had to get out of the park.

The kid could only hit him once as he went by. If it were in the back or the side, he'd have a chance.

I've got to make it home. HOME!

The phrase echoed through the depths of his consciousness.

Mike Perotti senior put his head down and charged towards the boy like a runaway train.

"All right, you son of a bitch!" he screamed.

The boy held his ground, taking the bat slowly back behind his head. "Brooks Robinson: 2,488 games at third base. . ."

Stop it!

Mike kept coming—FASTER! Even though agony wrenched his guts, and his legs felt as if they'd crumble beneath him at any moment, Mike charged forward in one last giant surge of energy and self-preservation.

". . . career assists 5,315. . ."

". . . career double plays 531. . ."

He was two feet, one foot from the boy, as the bat started its deadly swift assault. It cut through the night silence with a loud "wooosh!" Just as it was inches away from Mike, he jumped back, feeling the wind of the swing as it grazed his arm. Then he was off again, past the boy, heading towards the front of the park and home. The boy couldn't wind up and swing at the same time. And he couldn't swing—not hard—while he was running. If Mike Perotti wanted to stay alive, he was going to have to keep moving.

It was then that one of his weary legs betrayed him, and again he found himself on the ground, this time with a snoot full of soft, brown earth. He dragged himself to his feet. . . .

God! I wish I could just lie here for a while!

. . . .and started off again as he heard the tiny footsteps approaching.

"230 errors in 7966 chances."

The bat whizzed through the air just behind him.

He was running on automatic now, through the front of the park, past the statue of Edgemont Crandall, and out onto the street. *Just three more blocks.*

Home.

The street was deserted, many of the homes dark. The town was spooky at this hour. Still, some of Mike's fear abated. He knew that if the boy approached him he would let out a loud yell, and someone—*someone* would come to his aid.

He slowed to a trot as he reached Oakwood Avenue, his breath wheezing past parched lips. He glanced over his shoulder for the first time, and the street behind him appeared deserted. He stopped and looked back. The street was empty.

Slowly he dragged himself the rest of the way home. As he started up the walk, he saw it—the tip of the bat sticking out from the hedge in front of his house. The fear rose in him again, but he was home now, on *his* turf, and along with the fear came anger.

"So you wanna play rough, huh?"

There was a loose stone in the walk, one

he'd been planning to fix for months. Now he pulled it up and approached his home with the giant projectile in his hand. When he got close enough he was going to throw the stone into the boy's face, splattering it into a bloody pulp. *That'd show him!*

He was beside the hedge now, and still there was no movement. Quickly reaching out with his sore arm, he grabbed the bat, yanking forth with all his might, as the searing pain knifed through his body.

The bat came out easily.

Then he remembered seeing the bat sticking out of the hedge that afternoon. His son had stuck it in there a day or so ago. It was still there. The boy hadn't practiced his swing.

"Disobey me, will he!" The fear immediately filtered away, leaving only the anger, anger now directed at Mike Perotti junior.

Mike Perotti senior unlocked the door, headed into the house and up the stairs. As soon as he was through tending to his wounds—even before he called Dreiser—he was going to have a talk with his loving son. He couldn't allow the boy to constantly make a fool of him. He would talk to his son, and this time the boy would listen.

Chapter 22

It was Saturday morning. Dana and Todd were seated at the dining room table, Dana sipping coffee and Todd munching a Pop Tart. Rick hadn't yet shown his face for breakfast. *The coward!*

Todd had chosen to remain on the team, and Rick hadn't encouraged him otherwise.

"Did Daddy talk to you about Little League?"

"Yeah."

"What did he say?"

"That I didn't have to play if I didn't want to."

"And?"

"I want to play."

"Really?"

"Yeah, Mom."

And that was that.

Dana knew she had to find a concrete reason why Todd shouldn't play. If she didn't, no one was ever going to listen to her.

She'd been at the office every day since finding the Roger Dreiser story. She had to find a reason for the boy's brutal act and also more information on his death. She knew what she needed was there, but the papers were so scattered that tracking down the information was a slow and tedious process.

Rick finally came downstairs, and Dana started right in.

"You won't help me, and Max won't either!"

"Dana, hon. . ."

"He gives me the green light to pursue a story, but he doesn't offer any assistance! And you!" She glared at him.

"Dana, I'm on your side, believe me."

Oh, brother! That was hard to believe.

Max's advoidance of discussing Roger Dreiser or the file in the basement added fuel to the fire. Dana didn't want to believe that there was a town conspiracy, and that Max was a part of it, but ever since she'd spoken to the Grotes that first time, the question of Max's involvement nagged at her.

But he gave me a key! This added to her confusion about him.

After breakfast Dana pondered over the happenings of the week. Todd and Rick left early for the field to get in a good warm-up. Todd was pitching again today, and Rick wanted to give the boy every opportunity to do well.

Dana was nursing her second cup of coffee,

shuffling the pieces of the puzzle around in her mind, when the knock came on the back door.

Ruth?

She rushed to the door and peered out. Ronnie Roberts peeked up at her from the other side.

"Hi! Where have you been?" Dana asked, forcing a smile.

The boy looked up at her with solemn eyes. The corners of his lips curled into a grin that she could tell was as forced as hers.

"Did Todd and Mr. Evans leave yet, ma'am?"

"Oh, you're playing Todd's team today?"

"Yes, ma'am."

"I hear you've been playing quite well lately."

"Thank you, ma'am."

"Where have you been for the past few days?" She asked the question a second time.

Silence. He stared up at her as if she had said nothing.

"Are they gone?" he asked.

"Yes . . . but I'm going to the field. I'll drive you over." Grabbing him by the arm, she pulled him into the house. "Wait here!" She smiled into his cool, brown eyes.

"Yes, ma'am."

Since when is Ronnie Roberts so formal?

She raced upstairs to get ready. She had to talk with him, find out about him, and maybe even get some information on his mother.

Ten minutes later when she returned to the

kitchen, he was standing exactly where she'd left him.

"Ready?" she asked.

"Yes, ma'am."

Silently he accompanied her to the car. Ronnie Roberts was never this quiet, she thought. He always had something to say. It was as if this boy was not Ronnie Roberts.

Dana remembered what Todd had said:

He's mean. He talks mean, and he looks mean.

Well, Ronnie didn't seem mean, but he sure wasn't sociable.

They drove for a block in silence. *This will never do.* Dana wanted some information, and if Ronnie Roberts had it, he was going to give it to her. *After all, I'm a newspaper woman.*

"How's your mother?" she asked as the car turned off Oakwood Avenue.

"Fine."

"Have you spoken to her lately?"

"No."

"I miss her."

Silence.

Dana was surprised that he didn't say he missed her too.

"Is she coming home soon?" Dana asked.

More silence.

"Ronnie, are you all right?"

"Yes, ma'am. Why are you questioning me?"

"Huh? Oh, I didn't know I was. Sorry. I just thought we might talk." The boy had taken the offensive, throwing her off guard.

She had to turn the attack around.

"We missed you this week. Todd was looking for someone to play with." She decided to change her style of attack.

"There are lots of boys to play with."

"He likes you." It was an obvious lie, but she hoped Ronnie couldn't see through it. She had to get some answers before they reached the field. "You were out of school a few days."

Silence.

"We were worried about you and your father."

"We were fine, thank you."

She realized that any direct questions were going to go unanswered. *Think fast, girl!*

"Oh, but we do worry. We were afraid that something might have happened to you. If it did, I know your team would miss you a lot. Right?"

"I guess."

"It was pretty boring there, I imagine?"

"The surf was pretty."

Surf?

"But it was all for a good purpose." She smiled at him, as they pulled into the park. "I guess it's pretty cool there this time of year?" The car slid between the white stripes of the parking space.

"Yes."

Dana turned the engine off and saw Ronnie fidgeting, ready to get out.

"Well, at least your father enjoyed it."

"Not really."

He was opening the door.

"I hope you brought Todd a souvenir."

"From Atlantic City? No, maybe next time." *Atlantic City?* "Thank you for the ride, Mrs. Evans."

"You're welcome, and good luck today."

Ronnie was out of the car and running for the field. Dana sat wondering why Tom Roberts would take his son and spend half a week in Atlantic City.

The boy was ready. This time Rick was sure. He'd been watching him carefully, watching his young arm get stronger, while his confidence grew like ragweed in mid-July.

He'd met the challenge. This time the boy would do well, and Dana would see how wrong she was about Crandall and Little League. They could truly benefit from this thing, and he was going to show her. Women didn't generally understand these kind of things, but Dana was different.

As Rick took Todd's last few warm-up pitches, a feeling of gratification washed over him. A triumphant feeling spiraled through him. The boy was ready.

"Good," Rick mumbled, as Todd's fastball fired into his glove. "Good."

Mike Perotti junior was in deep thought as he approached the baseball field. He was reviewing the finer points of the game according to his father. His dad would be watching again today, and he had to be good.

Despite the pain in his arms and legs, he had to be great.

It was strange what his dad had said about being attacked in the park. It was as if his dad were getting what he deserved. Just that day he had beaten Mike with a stick, and then that night someone had beaten him.

Mike Perotti junior wanted to believe that he had a fairy godmother. Of course he knew he didn't. If he did, she would have protected him the second time.

That second time came the same night when his father had come home. Mike was asleep, and his father woke him up, taking out the anguish of his own beating on his son. The second beating wasn't as bad as the first, because his father's swinging arm hurt so bad. Still, it was more than enough, and Mike Perotti junior was certain that if he did have a fairy godmother, that day she was out to lunch.

Out to lunch!

He smiled, digging some humor out of his dismal thoughts. Of course he didn't have a fairy godmother. That same afternoon he'd told a few guys on the team how his father—a Brooks Robinson fanatic—had taken a stick to him, and he was sure that night one of the guys was sticking up for him. He'd asked them all about it, but everyone said "no," it wasn't him. Still, Mike was certain that one of the guys had bludgeoned his father, just as his father had beaten him.

Todd was pitching well. It was the third inning, and the score was 4-2 in favor of Hutchinson's. He'd struck out four batters already and was working on a fifth.

Todd sailed his fastball over the outside corner of the plate, and the umpire yelled "strike three!" A chorus of cheers went up from the parents behind the Hutchinson dugout, and from the other side Dana heard: "Kill the umpire!" It was loud-mouthed Mike Perotti. His right arm was in a sling, but his voice was in top form.

Dana looked over at Todd, who stood waiting for the next batter. She realized he'd been playing well, better than ever, but he wouldn't smile. He was becoming like the others, taking the game too seriously.

Dana then turned her attention towards the dugout. Dreiser's powerful gaze grabbed her. His expression was all business. Her flesh began to crawl. There was a secret lurking somewhere behind the man's eyes, but now wasn't the time to deal with it.

She looked past him towards her husband.

She expected to see a father's pride beaming out from Rick, but it wasn't there.

Rick also was deadly serious. There wasn't an ounce of emotion in his eyes. He looked at the boy the way a horse owner might view one of his herd, the way a pimp might regard a prostitute. It seemed to Dana that to Rick this was just another business.

The man is all work.

The thought repulsed her, but she couldn't shake it. Theirs was not a genuine father-son relationship. The only relationship that they had was baseball. If it weren't for baseball, there would be no relationship at all.

Dana wondered if Rick was trying to live out some childhood dream through his son. And the thought that many months ago had worked its way into her subconscious, once again inched forward.

Saturday evening Rick and the other Little League coaches had a meeting at Dreiser's home. The mini-season was drawing to a close, and it was time to start discussing selections for the tournament team.

It was a quarter past eight, and Todd was in his room playing with his Star Wars men. Dana had just turned off the TV and was headed upstairs. She'd been watching a special on El Salvador and was thinking of how sad it was to live in a country without any real hope, when the phone rang.

She went to the bedroom to answer it, and it took her several seconds to realize she was talking with the overseas operator.

Overseas! It must be Ted! And in a minute she heard his voice.

"How's my favorite little sister?"

Even through the crackly static he sounded good.

"Doctor Stephens, do you make house calls?"

"No, but I make phone calls."

"Dry." His sense of humor hadn't changed.

"I got your letter, and I just wanted you to know that I haven't forgotten you."

"I haven't forgotten you either." That wasn't exactly true. While Ted was always somewhere in the back of her mind, with all the excitement in Crandall she hadn't thought of him or the family much in recent days. *Maybe that's good!*

"Sis, this is costing me a fortune, so I'm not going to talk long. I started to reverse the charges."

"You better not have."

There was a blast of loud static in the line, and the next thing Ted said was obscured by sound.

"What?" Dana asked.

"I met a girl."

"Is it serious?"

"Kind of. Her name is Colette, and I'm thinking of staying over here for a month or so and trying on the continent for size."

"A French girl?"

More static.

"What?"

"No, she isn't." Ted was shouting now. "I came all the way to Sweden to meet a girl from Terre Haute. You'd really love her."

Dana laughed. "I'm glad for you, Ted. I hope it works out."

"Me, too. Anyway, that's why I called—to share my good fortune with my sister."

"Have you spoken with any of the family?"

"No, I can write the others. I just wanted to

share my good news with you."

He'd flattered her, and again she felt as if she were part of a family. "Thank you."

"In the morning Colette and I are going to Norway together."

"Sounds like fun." She was really happy for him.

"How are things there?"

"Wonderful," she lied. She wasn't going to spoil his good news with a storm cloud.

"Well, I want you to know that I probably won't be getting back home for awhile, but when I do, I still plan to stop in New York."

"Great."

"I better go now, sis." Then he thought of something. "Say, remember that Dreiser fellow? The coach?"

How could I forget him! "Yes."

Just then some loud static crackled in.

"These overseas connections are horrible. It took me the better part of an hour to get through. I don't think I'll be calling again, barring an emergency."

"All right. You were mentioning Dreiser." When Ted had said the name, Dana's heart began racing like a wild stallion.

"Oh, yeah, Dreiser. Remember I couldn't think of where I'd heard the name before? And I was telling you how that kind of stuff comes to me at the weirdest times?"

"Yes."

"Well, wouldn't you know that it would come to me just like I said. It was the day after I met Colette, and I was standing at her door kissing her goodnight. Sounds kind of Tom Sawyerish, doesn't it?" He chuckled.

Dana couldn't speak. She was waiting for him to tell her somethingbout Dreiser. *Anything!*

"You there, sis?"

"Yes. What did you remember about him?"

"Nothing important. It's just a coincidence, that's all. Your coach's name is Philip Dreiser, right?"

"Yes." Her muscles tensed in anticipation.

"Just a coincidence, sis. It can't be the same man."

"Why not? He isn't dead, is he?"

"No, I don't think so. He just dropped out of sight. . ."

This is it!

"The Philip Dreiser I'm talking about is a doctor. I read one of his books in school. He's a famous behaviorist who pioneered something on emotion controls—not a small town Little League coach."

"Oh?" Dana was flabbergasted, and it took her a few seconds to catch her breath.

"I better go now, sis, before I have to go back to work just to pay for this phone bill."

"Ted," Dana blurted. "How can anyone control emotions?"

"Drugs mostly."

She nearly dropped the phone.

"You all right, sis?"

"Yes. I was just thinking what a strange coincidence the names were."

"Well, it won't be a coincidence if I show up

at your house in the morning and tell you you have to support me." They both laughed, but Dana's was forced.

"Then I guess you do make house calls," she said.

"Yeah. Take two aspirin, and call me in the morning. And, sis—take care of yourself—and wish me luck."

"Good luck, Ted."

A few seconds later they signed off, and Dana immediately went downstairs to the kitchen—to locate the special vitamins Dreiser had sent for every boy who was playing Little League.

Waves of excitement filled the air.

As he entered the huge tent, he could feel the electricity flowing from the crowd.

A tall, heavy set black man ushered him to a seat. The ushers all wore white gloves and forgiving smiles.

"Bless you, brother," the usher said, as he deposited the man at a long row of folding chairs, most of which were occupied. "Move all the way in, brother."

Another trip, the man thought, as he took the seat beside a coppery woman in her mid-twenties. Her eyes were shut, her hands clasped as if in prayer.

The man hated the trips. Having to come to Gary so soon after Boise annoyed him, but he knew it was necessary.

"I touched him in Indianapolis," the woman beside him said.

He nodded.

He glanced around at the faces in the tent and saw expectation, even desperation, on many of them. These people had come to see miracles.

"He's Jesus' own. I touched him in Indianapolis and felt the power of God shoot right through me. Zoom, just like that." She slammed her fist into her open palm.

The man said nothing.

The huge tent was nearly filled now, bursting at the seams.

Hurry, ladies and gentlemen, to the greatest show on earth.

A racially mixed choir, in flowing white robes, began marching in from the wings, women from the left and men from the right. The organ picked out a slow marching beat, and the tent swayed to the rhythm. Hands clapped, as the choir started a soft "I Love to Praise Him."

"I love to praise his holy name," the woman sang swaying and waving her right hand to heaven.

The voices swelled.

The energy in the tent became phenomenal. They were building for something special, and the old man caught himself swaying with the crowd.

Jim Ewing made his way to the stage, as the tent continued to fill. Jim was going to warm the crowd up for his son.

"That's his earthly father," the woman said,

excitement in her voice. "He's the one takes care of him."

"I know," the man said.

He knew all too well.

Jim Ewing had been a Presbyterian minister in a small Ninth Avenue church in Mount Vernon, New York. But Jim didn't live in the ghetto of Mount Vernon near his church. Jim's congregation paid for his home in Crandall.

Things were going along fine for Jim, but as luck would have it—Jim's good luck, the old man thought—Jim got sexually involved with a young black girl in his congregation. Soon after, her father showed up in Crandall, saying that his daughter was pregnant and that he would destroy Jim—physically!—unless he married the girl. Jim did.

The family would have wasted their lives away in Crandall, but Jim was ambitious, and the man knew it. When he went to Jim with his proposal, Jim naturally accepted. Now, the Ewings were nearly millionaires.

"There he is. The disciple of Jesus."

The woman jumped to her feet, as everyone rose to catch a glimpse of the nine year old evangelist, with mysterious eyes and kinky brown hair.

By the time Jody Ewing was seven he had memorized the complete books of the Bible, old and new testaments. Discipline, the old man thought. At eight the boy began writing his own sermons, and now he was a legend.

The boy had been their youngest student and an apt pupil. No Little League baseball for him. His father wanted him to bring the gospel to the world and, at the same time, make his family rich.

The boy, in a white linen suit, mounted the pulpit. "Brothers and sisters, I'm soooo happy to be here with you tonight." His tiny voice boomed over the amplified PA system. "And yes, *He* is here with us, too."

"Amen," the woman said, clutching the old man's arm. "I'd pay my last dollar to hear the word of God."

There were tears in her eyes, and tears in the old man's eyes, also. It was truly a miracle.

Chapter 23

Mary Ellen Piatek had the nicest tits in town. They weren't the biggest (close!), those belonged to Mrs. Daily, the librarian. But Mary Ellen's were much, much nicer.

Jim Perkins knew tits. He was a tit man from way back, and he'd been watching Mary Ellen since she was in the ninth grade. She was fourteen then, and he was twenty-three, so of course he couldn't make a play for her.

"Jailbait!" That's what the guys laughingly called all the young foxes like Mary Ellen. So Jim kept his distance, but Mary Ellen's succulent tits were in his dreams many a night. He knew that in time she'd be available to him.

That time came last month, when he ran into her at the Adam's Apple down on Second Avenue in the city. It was like a dream come true. She was twenty-four now, a respectable age, and those tits had continued to blossom.

She didn't know him, and he pretended not to know her.

"You look awfully familiar," he said to her. He knew it was a weak opening, but when she discovered that she really was familiar to him, it would all seem so natural.

That night, over Bloody Marys, Jim and Mary Ellen discovered that they lived in the same town. *What a coincidence!* And that's when they made this date for the drive-in.

Now, as Jim adjusted the speaker on the window of his white Trans Am, he imagined himself releasing those gorgeous tits from the restraining bra and fondling them throughout the movie. The car was good for attracting lots of young head, like Mary Ellen, and maybe she would even come across tonight, on the first date.

Lots of the younger girls Jim went out with came across on the first date, and if Mary Ellen felt the urge to express herself sexually, it sure was all right with him.

They'd smoked a joint on the way to the drive-in, one Mary Ellen had rolled herself. "Good shit," she told him—and it was. If Mary Ellen were feeling anywhere near as high as Jim, tonight he'd hit the jackpot.

As the movie started Jim slipped an arm around her back and deftly undid the bra clasp through her sweater.

Practice, man, practice!

She giggled slightly and snuggled closer. She was ready. Tonight we're going to make it good, Jim thought. And then he was sorry he'd even taken her to the movie. He could have saved the five bucks by just taking her back to his place.

Dana was excited. She finally had something that would make folks listen. Dreiser was drugging the boys.

She knew she was being a little premature. She didn't have proof that this Philip Dreiser was the same man Ted had mentioned. Ted had called it a coincidence, but Dana didn't think so. Dreiser's giving the boys drugs seemed to fit right in.

After talking with Ted, Dana had gone to the kitchen, found the "vitamins" and flushed them down the toilet. *God, the man was shrewd,* she thought. No one would ever suspect him of experimenting on the boys.

Suppose I'm wrong? She couldn't avoid the question and go around accusing Dreiser of being such a monster if she weren't positive. *They'll put me in a straight jacket for sure!* She wouldn't say anything, not yet. She'd mention it to Rick tonight and tell him she was going to follow it up. *How?* She didn't know yet. But she was going to find out the truth about Philip Dreiser.

Dana was seated in the living room, waiting for Rick to come home. The TV droned on before her, but the happenings on the screen were far from her thoughts. Her mind was on the boys.

She thought of the strange look in Jimmy Warren's eyes. Now that same look was also in Ronnie Roberts' eyes. The drug must work slowly, she thought. She'd noticed minor changes in Todd, but nothing serious yet. Todd could still be saved from the drug's horrible effects. Now that she had gotten rid of the drugs, Todd had a chance to return to normal.

Her mind raced quickly now, going over the number of strange occurences in Crandall. They all could be related to this drug thing. Thomas Grote didn't run away, and that's why his parents didn't expect him back—he didn't want help. Thomas Grote was probably stashed away somewhere, recovering from the ill effects of some damn drug. This is what must have happened to all the runaways.

Of course the heart murmur thing didn't fit in yet, but she knew after she gave it some thought, everything would make sense.

She remembered her dream of Dreiser taking Todd. "Well, you're not going to get him," she said out loud.

If Rick wouldn't listen to her, even after she had the proof, she'd take Todd and move back to New York. The city was where they belonged in the first place. Small town life just wasn't for her.

Images of her childhood danced in her head, a childhood spent in a small town. She thought of Ted, Ronald and little Liz. Mother had been her friend then, someone she could run to with a problem. But not today.

She pulled her thoughts back to the present. Now, she was sure she knew how

Roger Dreiser had died and understood why Max wouldn't want to talk about it. But what about the locked file in Max's basement? She was now more curious than ever to find out what was in the file, but she'd have to be careful with Max. If he was in on a conspiracy, he wouldn't give up any information that would hang the conspirators. Still she trusted Max, but she'd watch him carefully, playing it by ear, and if she discovered that he were in cahoots with Dreiser on this thing, she would take them all to the proper authorities.

Dana got up and checked the large starburst clock on the dining room wall. 8:15. Rick would be in soon, and when he arrived she'd sure have an earful for him.

She returned to her seat in front of the TV. Excitement bubbled up inside of her, and she felt that she'd burst if she didn't tell someone soon.

At least Todd's safe, she thought again. Of course he'd be even safer when he was no longer a part of the team.

But suppose I'm wrong?

For the second time the thought inflicted itself on her. But she forced it out of her mind. She wasn't wrong—couldn't be wrong.

Dana silently stared at miniature images sliding across her TV screen, and suddenly she stiffened. Familiar footsteps were coming up the walk, stopping in front of the door, and now she heard the key being inserted into the lock. It was time to spill forth all of the things that had been bottled up inside of her since she'd spoken with Ted earlier that evening.

She stared up from her spot on the sofa. Slowly the door swung open, and Rick walked in.

Mary Ellen Piatek was a tease, a good-for-nothing tease, and that's all there was to it.

After the movie was over she politely refastened her brassiere and asked Jim to take her dancing. *Dancing!* There he was practically creaming all over himself, and *she* wanted to go dancing! There was only one thing Jim Perkins wanted to do with Mary Ellen, and he sure as hell couldn't do it on a dance floor.

Jim pulled the 1980 Trans Am into his space behind the apartment building on Halldale Road and gunned the engine before shutting it off. The evening had been a waste. Sure Mary Ellen had let him squeeze her tits during the movie, but afterwards he had to take her to several clubs to try and get her in the right mood to come across.

They wound up at a little bar call the Church Key, on North Avenue in New Rochelle, a few miles outside of Crandall. There Mary Ellen downed six Bloody Marys. You'd think she'd have been drunk, but she wasn't. She wasn't ready either. By 12:30 Jim had just plain given up.

"Come on, Jim. Take me dancing!" *Dancing!* The bitch had already cost him thirty-five bucks, and that was where he drew the line.

"I'm taking you home."

"Home! It's early yet!"

"Wanna come back to my place?"

"No! I wanna go dancing!"

"I gotta umpire tomorrow. I'm taking you home."

At her door she kissed him, hot and passionately, then politely asked when she would see him again.

"I don't know."

The kiss was enough to start his juices flowing again, but this time Jim knew better. Mary Ellen Piatek was a tease, a good-for-nothing tease.

Hell, he didn't plan on ever seeing her again. He had spent the better part of the forty bucks he'd get for umpiring that weekend, just showing her a good time. *And for what?*

The money was supposed to help ease his heavy car loan. Of course this weekend's money was just about spent, and he still had one more game to do tomorrow morning.

Jim Perkins climbed out of the Trans Am, locked it up tight and set the burglar alarm. You couldn't be too careful with a car like that. Unlocking the back door of the two story apartment building, he headed upstairs. He wasn't even tired yet, but what the hell, he'd get to bed early so he could be bright and alert for the game tomorrow—as if it mattered to him.

Jim had been umpiring for the past three years. He didn't do it because he loved it or because he liked being with little kiddies.

Hell, he hated the brats! Jim umpired because it paid forty bucks a weekend, and the work was easy.

"Shit!" he grunted, as his key found the lock. He'd spent his weekend earnings on Mary Ellen Piatek. She should be here with him now, filling his mouth with her gorgeous tits. Instead, he was alone. And he'd be working tomorrow gratis. "Shit!"

He entered the darkened apartment and fished around for the light switch. He didn't see the youth waiting in the darkness behind the door, so, without warning, the first blow of the Louisville Slugger crashed into the back of his head.

He let out a low, surprised yelp and would have commenced to scream louder, but the next smash careened into his face, jarring loose six or seven teeth, and Jim Perkins was too busy choking as he stumbled to the floor.

The boy with the bat worked quickly, and in seconds Jim Perkins was unconscious—in minutes he was dead. He didn't even hear the only phrase the boy uttered as the bat came slicing through the air again and again and again.

"Kill the umpire!" the boy proclaimed. And of course, that's just what he did.

Chapter 24

Dana talked incessantly for nearly twenty minutes, telling Rick what she had recently learned from Ted and giving her own theories on what Dreiser had done to the boys. When she finished there was a long silence during which Rick stared at her wide-eyed, his mouth agape, as if he'd just seen a ghost.

"Rick, I don't want Todd playing with those other boys," Dana went on. "I got rid of those vitamins, or should I say drugs, that Coach Dreiser sent over. That man is not going to get our son!" She'd said all there was to say, and now that she was finished a calmness washed over her, like the quiet moments of early morning before the breaking of dawn.

"And Ted told you that Dreiser was a doctor, experimenting with drugs?" Rick had finally spoken, and when he did, his voice was colored with disbelief. Dana noticed it immediately.

"No. Ted said there was a doctor named Philip Dreiser, and he was famous for his pioneering in emotion control. When I asked how he could control emotions, Ted told me drugs."

"And with that little bit of information you threw away forty-two dollars worth of vitamins?"

"Rick, it's the same man! I know it!"

"Dana, why do you have it in for Coach Dreiser? His son died, and he adopted a boy who I admit is a little strange, but that isn't any reason to condemn the man! The man's wonderful. He's added something to the boys' lives that all kids need. Discipline!"

"You're talking like a Nazi."

"Dana, the boys are better off. They all get better grades in school. And have you noticed there's no juvenile crime in this town? That's because the boys listen to their parents! Dana, what you're saying just doesn't make sense."

"I know it sounds crazy, Rick, but. . . ."

"You're damned right it sounds crazy! It sounds to me like Dana Evans just joined the ranks of the cuckoo birds!"

"Rick, I'll prove it!"

"How?"

"I don't know yet. A picture maybe. If he's written a book, his picture will probably be in it."

"Dana, before you get off on this thing, I have to tell you that it looks like Todd will be picked for the tournament team. I don't see any reason why he shouldn't play."

Rick, who had been seated on the sofa across from Dana, now rose and walked over to the mantel. There was a finality in his voice, and Dana noted the defiance burning in his eyes.

"Rick, I'm not crazy. I'm not making this up. You're so involved in Little League that you can't see it. But there's something very wrong here!" There was a pleading in her voice that she couldn't control. She was so sure of herself; this time she was certain.

"I told you before, I'd listen if you could prove something, but now these wild accusations are getting way out of hand. Dana, I was at a meeting this morning with a group of men who are interested in just two things—helping the boys of this town to grow into fine young men, and winning a Little League championship. And if that's a crime, then I'm also guilty!" He stopped speaking momentarily and stared at her. His ice-blue eyes were penetrating, and she was forced to look away.

She suddenly felt foolish for voicing her accusations. Now that she'd spoken, she saw how ridiculous it sounded.

But it's true! I know it!

"I know I'm always jumping the gun," she finally said, "but will you at least look for signs that something here is wrong? Will you be open about it?"

Rick smiled. "Honey, I have been open about it. At first you told me that Dreiser was trying to mold all of the boys into his dead son. Now you tell me he's feeding our kids drugs—right under our noses! Dreiser's been in this town a lot longer than we have. Don't you think that if he were drugging the boys someone else would have noticed it by now?"

"I suppose so."

"Honey, I'm being open, but maybe you're not."

Was it true? Had Dana been allowing personal feelings to jade her viewpoint of the town and Little League? She didn't want to believe it. She wasn't that type of person. But maybe Rick was right.

Then he spoke again. "Honey, maybe you should talk to someone."

"What do you mean?"

"Maybe there's a problem you need to discuss. Something from your childhood."

What is he saying?

Rick came back to the sofa and sat down next to her. He took her hand in his and stared quietly into her face. His ice-blue eyes had softened, mellowing into cool, flaccid pools. In them she saw compassion, even pity.

"Rick, you don't think I'm insane?" She could feel the tears building behind her eyes and fought to hold them back.

"No, honey, not insane. But it couldn't hurt to talk to someone."

There it was, out in the open. Her own husband thought she was a lunatic, a raving maniac. Her eyes burned as she willed the tears not to fall.

"I'm not crazy," she mumbled. And then

she could hold the tears no longer.

"I know hon." Rick threw his arms around her, clutching her to his chest, as he slowly rocked her back and forth. "I know you're not, honey."

The tears came in droves, spilling continually from her eyes, the salty brine dripping from her cheeks. Her husband had indicated that she needed a psychiatrist. *A psychiatrist!* He thought she was crazy; he said he didn't, but she could tell. And what made it so bad, what made the pain so terribly unbearable, was that a ray of doubt had been instilled within her. And she, too, began wondering. *Maybe I am?*

Sunday's game was between Harvey's Cleaners and Walgreen's Drugs.

Dana awoke to rays of warm sunlight washing over her face. She'd fallen off to sleep after one in the morning only to awaken several times. Her sleep was restless, her mind wrestling with the question of her own sanity.

She had awakened around four, bathed in sweat, her hair matted against the pillow. She had been dreaming of her mother. In this dream her mother again was taking Todd, but this time Dana let him go. She was too weak to fight.

Now, as Dana lay in bed, the warmth of a new day gently stroking her face, she again thought of her mother.

Throughout her childhood her mother had

been overbearing, forcing her pristine views of the world on her family. *Am I like her?* Dana had remembered hearing that people often turn out to be reincarnates of their parents, even when they were trying to become their opposites. She wondered if this was happening with her. Were her own views so important that she would bend the truth to suit her own needs? Again she wondered what it would have been like to have had a forceful father.

She looked across her sleeping husband at the clock on the night table. 7:34. Todd didn't have a game today, so Rick would probably want to sleep late. Suddenly Dana wanted to be out of the house and away from her family. She did not want to be there when Rick woke up.

She eased herself out of bed and padded over to the window, catching the onset of a glorious day. Many of the flowers in her front garden were coming into an early bloom. There had been enough sunlight and rain this spring to make Dana's garden a palette of blooming color.

She glanced across the street at the white stucco. It was quiet, peaceful. Could the man who lived there be as evil as Dana thought? It puzzled her, but she didn't want to think of that this morning. This morning she wanted to enjoy the beauty of the day.

Quietly she went to the door and let herself out of the room. Rick never stirred.

In the hall she heard sounds coming from

Todd's room and knew that he was once again playing with his Star Wars men. She went to his room, knocked softly, then pushed open the door. The boy sat on the floor, surrounded by Micronauts and figures from Star Wars.

"You're supposed to wait until I say 'come in,' " Todd said, staring up at his mother. "I don't just walk into your room!"

She'd always walked in on Todd, but now it bothered him. He wanted his privacy and wanted her to respect it. She knew that this was all a part of his growing up, and that he wasn't trying to hide anything, but still it bothered her.

It wasn't many years ago that Todd had walked in on her and Rick making love and thought that they were wrestling. She had overheard him telling some of his little friends: "Mommy and Daddy were wrestling on the bed!" Then one day he walked in, and the embarrassed look on his face told them that he knew what they were doing. Since then Rick had asked him to knock, and now Todd was putting the same restriction on his mother.

"I'm sorry. I'll wait from now on. Okay?"

"Okay!" And then he smiled and went back to playing.

Dana noticed the way Todd meticulously lined up the men. He was so much like his father, looking more like him everyday.

"Mommy's going out. Can you get your own breakfast this morning?"

"Sure. Can I have a bologna sandwich?"

"No. There's Cheerios in the cupboard."

"All right," he said, returning to his game.

Not long ago he would have asked where she was going and could he come along. Now he was content to let her go alone. He was quickly growing up and away.

Dana left her son at play and went to the bathroom, where she took a brisk hot shower. A half hour later she was dressed and heading out the front door. Rick was still asleep. She left word with Todd that she'd return before noon. Then she got in the Pinto wagon and drove.

She headed towards the Hutchinson River Parkway. The parkway appeared totally different from the last time she'd traveled it. Now the trees were filled with fresh, green leaves, and the grass along the road lay in lush carpets. Dana wound up at the Colonial diner, in Mount Vernon, where she breakfasted on toast and coffee. At a quarter of nine she headed for Crandall park.

There must have been an angel sitting on Philip Dreiser's shoulder. Either that, or fate was willing him in the right direction—towards fame. And fame shortly would be his. If things continued the way they were going, the whole world would soon know the name Philip Dreiser.

This morning they'd received another stroke of luck when Ned Perkins came to take his son to breakfast. There was no answer at Jim's door, so Ned persuaded Eva Gardner, the building manager, that something might be wrong on the other side of that door and that maybe she should let him in.

"You wake me at 7:30 in the morning for that! Ned Perkins, you know that boy of yours as well as I do. He's out carousing somewhere, and you know it!"

Still Ned insisted on being let in, so Eva handed him a ring with a dozen or more keys.

"It's one of them. Just drop them in the mailbox when you're finished."

That was a stroke of luck. Eva Gardner never came upstairs, never opened the door, so of course she didn't see the bloody pulp that was once Jim Perkins lying on the living room floor.

Then there was more luck. Instead of calling the county Sheriff's department, Ned called local Sheriff Guy Francis, who in turn called Dreiser.

Within a few minutes of meeting, Dreiser convinced the other two that something like this could be bad for the town. So Jim Perkin's body would not be found within the township of Crandall—and Dreiser breathed a sigh of relief.

It was obvious who had committed this horrid act, but it was going to be tough explaining it to his mother. It was too bad, but there was no way around it. He had to tell her. The boy would have to be eliminated.

Dana arrived a few minutes after nine and discovered that the game was being delayed because the scheduled umpire didn't show, and they had to wait for his replacement.

The day was as warm and beautiful as Dana had expected, so instead of sitting in the bleachers and waiting for the game to start, she strolled around the park, absorbing the beauty and fragrance of the early blooming flowers.

Her mind wandered to the previous evening. Now that she had time to reflect, her feelings on the matter began to solidify. She didn't believe she was going insane, or that she was being insensitive. Though she didn't have proof of Dreiser's guilt, she certainly wasn't convinced of his innocence.

She was going to watch him. And first thing Monday morning she was going to the library to see if she could find any books written by Philip Dreiser.

"Hello, Mrs. Evans." The voice from behind jarred Dana's thoughts. She turned on the smiling face of Eunice Graham. *Oh, no!*

"Hi," Dana said, expecting the worst. She'd never mentioned the article on the Graham boy to Max, and now she was going to have to lie to avoid an ugly confrontation.

"Have you seem my Petie play lately?" Eunice Graham was walking towards her and smiling.

"No, I haven't." *That was true.*

"Well, watch him today, and then tell Max Richter what a great player he is." Eunice Graham smiled confidently as she spoke, and Dana had the feeling that the woman was building herself up for a big letdown.

"All right, I'll do that," Dana replied, realizing that the pressure was off. "How is he feeling?" Dana asked.

"Just fine."

"And the heart murmur?"

"Nothing serious. In fact, now that he's back, he's better than ever."

When Dana got back, the Walgreen's team was already on the field warming up.

Dana found a spot behind the Walgreen's dugout and carefully watched the boy at second base. He was a pathetically thin, brown-eyed boy, with a baseball cap that was too large and an intent stare.

Dana noted that the youth looked competent enough; he didn't drop or fumble the ball, and his throws to first were accurate. But then she thought of Jimmy Warren—a dark-eyed fireball, whose rocket throws and fine catching made him a standout on an already good team. She didn't see how Petie could possibly play second base on the tournament team. Then the game started.

Petie Graham batted third in the bottom half of the first inning. Stepping up to the plate, he belted the first pitch deep into center field. The ball rolled past the center fielder, who bobbled the pickup, and by the time the ball was returned to the infield, Petie Graham had himself a home run.

Dana glanced over at Eunice Graham in the bleachers. The woman had been staring at her, and now smiled an "I told you so!" smile. *Luck!* Dana thought.

In the second inning, a boy on the Harvey's team connected with a single. On the very next play the ball was blasted over second base. The play should have gone for a double, but Petie swooped in with an amazing backhand snare, stepped on the bag, and threw the boy out at first. *Double play!* Jimmy Warren couldn't have done it any better.

Throughout the game Petie was sensational. He batted a triple his second time at bat, and later on he hit a single. As the game went on he seemed to improve. Dana was quite surprised, and each time she looked over at Eunice Graham, the woman beamed knowingly at her.

I guess I should speak to Max about the boy.

For the final out of the game, Petie swooped in for a hard grounder, handling the ball routinely and throwing the runner out at first. A chorus immediately went up from the stands, but Petie didn't smile. Instead he removed his cap, wiping his sweaty forehead on his sleeve as he trotted for the dugout.

Dana's eyes widened in amazement, and she let out a low, involuntary whistle. *I'm not going insane!*

Stunned, she watched the boy walk towards the dugout as teammates slapped him on the back. She had noticed earlier that his cap was too large, and now she knew why. Petie Graham recently had gotten a haircut.

Chapter 25

There was a baseball special on TV that Sunday afternoon about guess who? Brooks Robinson. *What a break!*

Mike Perotti senior called his son into the living room and plopped the boy down in front of the TV.

"Now watch this guy!" he said.

The boy, who'd been acting like a scared rabbit lately, said nothing. He sat quietly in front of the TV screen, as George Plimpton and an aging, pot-bellied Brooks Robinson relived the great third baseman's career for the Baltimore Orioles.

"Did you hear that? Sixteen golden gloves in an eighteen season career. This guy was the fucking best!" Mike Perotti senior took a gulp of his fourth Rheingold of the day. He was glad his son had a chance to see the legend in action. That's what the guy was—a fucking legend!

"You watchin', Mike? You hear that?" He was even happier to have a chance to see again some of Robinson's past spectacular plays—like the great catching and hitting exhibition Brooks put on in the 1970 world series against the "Big Red Machine."

Mike had been in his early twenties then, and he'd been watching Brooks since he could remember. The guy was aging, but he was still fucking spectacular! *I hope Nettles and Brett are watching, too!*

Mike knew that his son could be just like Brooks—even better. He was sure the boy had inherited at least some of his talent, and with a lot of practice and a little help from Dreiser, the boy had a chance of dancing into the record books, just as Brooks Robinson had done.

All the extra practice the boy had been getting showed on the field Saturday. No, the kid wasn't great, but he was definitely improving, and if he kept practicing—and Mike was sure he would, heh, heh—the kid would improve enough for Coach Dreiser to notice him. Once that happened all of their futures would be secure.

"You're as good as that guy, Mike— better!" Mike senior said, encouragingly. You had to encourage kids, he knew that. He'd read a book—or at least started it—on psychology once, and he knew how to get the best out of kids. And the best was what he demanded from his son.

Now that the boy was on the right track, he

could begin to pressure Coach Dreiser into helping the kid. Hell, he didn't move his family to Crandall just because it was such a nice place. He moved there because he wanted glory for his boy, the glory that had eluded him.

He could have been out there right now, playing the way Brooks Robinson did in the early seventies. But getting mixed up with beautiful Angela Cianci had put an end to his baseball. She had put him in a hypnotic trance, and he'd forgotten what he'd worked so hard for since he was a little kid.

All he wanted to do was impress her. So he bought a car—a 1967 Chevelle, black, 327-375 horse power—and he took a job. It was probably the worst mistake of his life. Now Angie's beauty was gone, and Mike was strapped with a kid and a house that demanded every penny he earned, and then some.

"It won't happen to my kid!" he mumbled, as he watched Brooks Robinson make catch after spectacular catch. *The fucking greatest!* He was going to make damned sure his son didn't fall into the same trap as he had. The boy was on his way to becoming a great ball player. The kid would reap fame and fortune for the whole family. All he needed was Dreiser. A little help from Dreiser, and the kid couldn't fail.

"You're just as good as him, Brooksy!"

When the boy was born he wanted to name him Brooks, but Angie refused. And she had been right. Now the world wouldn't think of Robinson when they saw his son playing. The name Mike Perotti would be chiseled in time.

Mike Perotti junior—the greatest fielding third-baseman in the history of baseball.

Monday morning after breakfast, Dana drove over to the office of the Guardian to drop off her editorial copy from the weekend. While there, she told Max about Eunice Graham wanting them to do a story on her son.

"He's really good!"

"Just what we fucking need!"

"Well, he is!"

Then she filled him in on her drug theory, telling him of her talk with Ted and watching his eyes for any flicker of cognizance. There was none.

"You've got some fucking imagination, girly!" Of course, he didn't take her seriously.

Leaving the office, Dana headed for The Food Warehouse in White Plains. She had to do some serious shopping. Her weekend had been filled with Little League, and if she didn't market soon, her family would be dining on bread and water.

Shortly after noon she stopped by the library on Main Street and searched the card catalog for the name Philip Dreiser.

DREISER, PHILIP R. Modern Modes In Operant Conditioning.

She was in luck. The library stocked his only book. Now if only there were a picture in it, she'd have proof.

Dana went to the designated shelf to search for the book, but it wasn't there. Quickly she went to the librarian's desk.

Matronly Mrs. Daily sat behind her desk, poring over the morning New York Times. She prided herself on looking like a typical librarian, and this morning wasn't any different. Her graying hair was coifed in a neat, crisp bun, and the glasses that sat on her nose were attached to a chain, so that when they weren't in use they dangled from her neck like some overgrown pendant.

"Hello, Miss." Dana said. The librarian slowly raised her head.

"Yes, may I help you?"

"Yes. I want to borrow a book called 'Modern Modes In Operant Conditioning,' but it isn't on the shelf."

"Oh, yes." The librarian smiled. "I wasn't even aware of the existence of the book until this morning. Is it required for some adult education class at the high school or something?"

"Not that I'm aware of."

"Well, I can tell you that our only copy is out. It was checked out this morning."

"Oh?" *That's strange!* "Well, maybe you can reserve it for me."

"I sure can." She handed Dana a card and a pen. "This card will cost a quarter. Whenever the book is returned we'll notify you to come in and pick it up."

"All right." Dana filled out the card.

"It may take as long as a month. If you're in a hurry you might try the Yonkers library on Central Avenue. They have quite a large selection. You won't be able to borrow it, not being a Yonkers resident, but at least you can use it there."

"Thank you," Dana said. It was an excellent idea. She didn't need to borrow the book anyway. "You say it was checked out this morning?"

"Yes. The first time it's been out in years. I didn't even know we had the book."

Coincidence? Dana hardly thought so. "Do you remember who borrowed it?"

The librarian eyed her suspiciously. "A man," she answered, defensively.

"Oh." How could they have known she was looking for the book? She had only mentioned it to Rick and Max. Could she have been right about the old newspaper man?

Mrs. Daily's head went back down to her paper, and Dana knew that the question and answer period was over, so she set the card on the desk in front of the librarian and walked out.

Later that evening, as Mrs. Glenna Daily filed away the order cards for the day, she thought of the young woman who'd requested a book earlier.

Dana Evans! She couldn't forget her. Often she'd been able to tell the kind of book a person wanted by the way the person looked or dressed. Today she was wrong. She never thought the well-dressed young woman would be interested in such a book. *Something about operating conditions.* She had Dana pegged for the latest Janet Dailey romance.

Glenna Daily (no relation) thought it even stranger that Max Richter would want the book. Wasn't he only interested in Little League?

She debated on whether or not to call Max Richter and tell him of the woman who was also interested in the book. *Maybe he'd bring it back sooner!*

"Oh, well!" she sighed, dismissing the thought. "It can't be *that* important. She can wait!" she commented, clicking shut the file, and it wasn't until much later that the coincidence of the name Philip Dreiser crossed her mind.

Around the same time, Max Richter was finishing up for the day when his phone rang. It was Philip Dreiser. Max had dreaded the inevitability of this call, and now it had come.

"What can I do for you, Coach Dreiser?"

"Max..." There was a pleasant, almost disarming ring in the coach's voice, but Max knew the coach only could be calling for one thing. "How have things been going for you?"

"Fine."

"We don't see you at the games anymore. We miss you."

"I'll be out there, along with everyone else, once the playoffs start. Besides Mrs. Evans has been doing a great job lately, hasn't she?"

He knew the answer.

"Max, we both know that she hasn't. I can't let you stall me any longer. Mrs. Evans is a threat to the town—and to Little League. Something must be done about her."

Max Richter silently listened, as Philip Dreiser outlined what must be done.

That same evening, after dinner, Dana drove over to the office of the Guardian, let herself in, and went down to the basement, where she again pored over stacks of newspaper.

That night Dana's diligence finally paid off. She had been there for all of five minutes when she found the tiny column:

HIGH SCHOOL SENSATION
DRUG OVERDOSE VICTIM.

Dana's eyes practically leapt from their sockets, as her heart raced wildly. This is what she had suspected. Roger Dreiser had died from a dose of his own father's drugs. She read:

> Roger Dreiser, son of coach Philip Dreiser, was found this morning lying unconscious on the floor of an upstairs bathroom. Roger was rushed to County General Hospital, where he was pronounced dead on arrival. Autopsy attributes the cause of death to heroin overdose.

Heroin? I don't believe it!

Dana read the tiny article several times, then checked the entire paper for more on the boy. There was nothing.

His death may have been drug related, but it couldn't have been caused by heroin, Dana thought. Somehow Dreiser had gotten to someone at the coroner's office. He couldn't cover up that it was a drug related death, so he compromised, to keep the lid on his experiments.

Dana wasn't satisfied with her findings, but it was enough to show Rick and Max—at least for now.

For the next two hours she searched the papers, hoping to find more. After a while her eyes started to burn, as the print jumbled together into indecipherable blurs. She couldn't read anymore, so she carefully folded the relevant newspaper under her arm and started up the stairs.

A few minutes later the lights were out, the door was locked, and Dana was heading for her car.

She climbed in and turned the ignition key. The engine wheezed, sputtered, then died.

"Shit!" she mumbled. She tried again but it wouldn't catch.

Eventually the decelerating whine of the engine told her that she was killing the battery. She didn't know anything about cars, so looking under the hood would prove futile.

Maybe I should call Rick, but he knows as much about cars as I do, and he'd have to leave Todd alone to get here.

That's when she decided to walk home. It was a calm warm evening, and a brisk walk was just the kind of exercise she needed.

She grabbed her purse and the newspaper and started down Eastchester Road. A few bicyclists passed as she turned up Harney Road, their headlights silent beacons slicing through the night.

There were no homes on either side of Harney Road for a quarter of a mile. This stretch of Crandall, for some reason, had been left undeveloped. The road here was lined with wild growing foliage, that brought to Dana's mind her youth on some of the country roads of Pennsylvania.

There were few street lights along the road, and their illumination was dull at best. Dana walked on, not really thinking of the darkness or danger. Had she been in New York City she would have been terrified, but this was the suburbs, and even a dark deserted stretch of road, such as this, felt safe. Besides, the car cruising behind her illuminated the way well enough, and she only had to travel another block and a half before she'd be on a well-lighted street.

The lights that loomed ahead were inviting signs of life, but she was in no hurry. This lonely stretch of road gave her the chance to think things over.

As she walked, Dana thought oft the information she'd found in the paper. Rick could put her off no longer. *Not if he wants to keep us around!* She had proof, and she wanted her son removed from Little League.

She was a block away from the bright lights of Harney Road now. Not much further, she thought, as images of her and Rick arguing flashed through her mind.

She knew Rick would protest, but she'd conceded enough. There was a lifetime of giving in to her husband, but this time Todd's safety was at stake, and she was going to keep him from playing at any cost.

Abruptly the highbeam from the car behind flared up, and Dana realized that the car had never passed her. Dana, bathed in scorching light, turned to discover the reason for the highbeams. *Maybe I know the driver!*

She squinted into the blinding haze and realized that she couldn't even distinguish the make of the car, no less who was in it.

The car stopped as Dana turned toward it, the two silently facing each other like gunfighters in a showdown. Suddenly the most horrible thoughts raced through Dana's mind. *A mugger! Worse, a rapist!*

Quickly she crossed the road to let the car pass, but as soon as she started moving the car rolled on in slow pursuit.

A blast of fear ripped through her, and Dana gazed ahead, gauging the distance of the flickering lights. *A block. Too far to run from a car!*

She darted back across the road, and the car followed. She started to slowly trot, as tiny droplets of perspiration dripped from her armpits. The hum of the engine grew, as the car increased speed. *This can't be happening!*

She dashed across the road again, now running full speed along the shoulder. Sharp brambles of jagged growth stabbed out at her from beside the road, but she continued running, hugging the shoulder. That's when she heard the screech of rubber, and the roar of the car's engine.

She spun around, frozen in sudden fear, and saw the car lurch forward, barreling towards her.

"No!" she screamed, her eyes wide with terror.

The car, inches from her, swerved, the left fender grazing her and hurling her from the road into the overgrowth.

"Help!" she screamed, as she crashed into the brush.

Her side now ached from where she had been hit, and her arms and face were a mass of scratches from the brush. She lay there for an eternity of seconds, praying that someone would drive along the empty stretch of road. Then, the opening and closing of the car door cracked the silence, and slow footsteps approached.

A killer! The thought tore into her head. *But why would someone want to kill me?* One answer knifed through her subconscious. *This isn't a random happening. This is planned!*

Dana quickly got to her feet, the pain in her side increasing. The footsteps drew nearer.

She had to retreat deeper into the woods. She had to escape.

She painfully made her way deeper into the brush. And as she limped into a clearing ten or fifteen yards from the road, she heard the crackling of twigs and dead leaves behind her. She eyed the heavy growth around her, not knowing which way to flee—but flee she must. Slow, heavy footsteps were approaching, and with them, she was sure, came death.

Chapter 26

Mike Perotti had been up late, figuring. The old financial situation was pretty bad. He'd been laid off for over a month now, and the few odd jobs he found around town weren't nearly enough to push him over the top. That's why Mike was figuring. Hell, he needed to do something to pass the time, something other than worry himself into an ulcer over the bills. So Mike Perotti senior figured out his son's future.

The boy could make a fortune; what with salary, bonuses, endorsements and commercials, he could clear a cool million after his second or third season.

The money, of course, had to be managed wisely, and that's where Mike senior came in. The family would live comfortably—Mike was even thinking of buying himself one of those fancy Italian sports cars—and there'd be plenty left over for the kid to sow some wild oats.

The kid wouldn't have a girlfriend—at least no one steady—'cause he couldn't afford to be serious about anything but baseball. That had been Mike's mistake, and he'd make damned sure that the kid didn't do the same thing.

Mike Perotti slurped the remains of his Rheingold and smiled. The alcohol that spiraled through his system made him feel good, and this figuring made him feel even better.

There was just one more thing he had to do this evening—and every evening, if necessary—to make the day complete. He had to talk to Dreiser, had to remind him of how far the kid had come and where he was going.

He wasn't about to let Dreiser off the hook. It had cost him plenty to move to Crandall, and now that he was here he intended to reap the benefits.

Dreiser could turn the kid into a veritable superstar. Hadn't he done it with his own kid? Dreiser had the secret, the formula, and Mike senior was going to hound the hell out of him until the old man saw that he meant business and wouldn't take "no" for an answer.

I've paid my dues! Mike Perotti senior thought as he picked up the phone to call Dreiser. Ten years from now the whole family could be on easy street. *And we will be, too!*

He dialed the number and waited for the phone to ring.

* * *

Philip Dreiser, dressed untraditionally in a white shirt and gray slacks, sat in the Warren family living room, sipping water from a large glass tumbler. He'd been there most of the evening explaining his position to Pat Warren, but she sat across from him, a puzzled look still stamped on her face.

"But what went wrong?"

"It can't be explained. In a hundred cases this thing's successful, then in the hundred and first something goes wrong, not for any particular reason. I assure you that this is no one's fault." He crossed his legs trying to look relaxed, but he could tell that Patricia Warren was going to be a tough one.

"You said when he came out of the hospital that he was fine."

"We thought he was."

"Well, just send him back to the hospital again and give him some more of whatever it was you gave him."

"I'm afraid it isn't that easy."

"Why not?" she blurted. She was visibly upset.

"It just isn't. It didn't work, Mrs. Warren. It didn't take on your son. You knew there were risks when we started."

She jumped up. "No, I didn't! You told me that it was successful ninety percent of the time," she said, shaking an accusing finger at him.

"And it is. Even better than ninety percent."

"You can't have him!" Her eyes blazed out

from their sockets, and what was a totally composed lady a few moments before now stared down at him like a wild woman.

"You knew the risks," he said, shaking his head.

This was the toughest part, telling the parents it didn't work on their child. They never promised success. They made sure that they explained all the risks to the parents, but of course the parents only centered on the benefits, sweeping the risks under the rug—until times such as now.

"Can't you try again?" There was a pleading in her tone, which annoyed Dreiser. He hated begging.

"You knew the risks," he said sternly. He stood and, now towering over her, glared down at her.

"Jimmy's all I have." There were tears in her eyes. "When his father died eight years ago, I swore that I'd devote my life to Jimmy. I wanted to make him everything that his father would have been proud of. Please don't take him! He's all I have."

"Mrs. Warren, there are others to think of. Your son's presence is a threat now. We must think of the town."

"But he's all I've got. He hasn't killed anyone, has he?"

"No."

"Then why take him? Give him another chance. Give me a chance. Please!" She stepped towards him, her outstretched arms reaching out, but he backed away.

"You knew the risks," he said. It was an old tune, but it was all he had to fall back on. "Now we must do all we can to protect Crandall and all its inhabitants. It's the town I'm thinking of."

"Well, think of me! You talk as if my boy is a monster!" Slow tears trickled from her eyes.

"I'm sorry, but there's really nothing I can do at this point. You knew the risks," he repeated, a grimness gripping his words. "You knew the risks."

Rick and Todd were watching M*A*S*H when a delirious disheveled Dana came stumbling through the front door.

She'd thrashed around in the brush for nearly an hour and had somehow gotten away.

Rick sent Todd up to his room, as Dana launched into her incredible tale—incredible, but true. She knew too much, she told him. She knew too much, and someone had set her up to be murdered. There was no doubt in her mind who that someone was. It had to be Max Richter.

Chapter 27

Dana lay in bed. She finally was calming down thanks to a sedative administered by Doctor Fritz Warner, a kindly old, white-haired gentleman, who loved to make house calls.

Dana had come in hysterical. Wild-eyed, she'd ranted for nearly twenty minutes before Rick could make any sense of what she was saying.

He was scared.

He didn't know what had happened to his wife, but he knew from her condition that she wasn't exaggerating. Someone had tried to kill her.

He called the local police department and spoke with Deputy Haig, who gave him Sheriff Guy Francis' home phone number. He called Sheriff Francis, then Doctor Warner, and waited for the men to arrive.

As Rick nervously listened to Dana tell her

story to the sheriff, he finally realized what she had gone through.

"Did you get a look at the car?" Sheriff Francis asked.

"I couldn't see it because of the headlights. They were blinding."

Doctor Warner routinely attended to Dana's wounds, as she and the sheriff spoke.

"You're going to be fine," the doctor said, using his best bedside manner. "I don't think that bruise on your hip is serious, but I'd like you to come over to Community General in the morning for some x-rays. Just a precaution," he added, nodding to Rick.

"Okay," Dana said.

"Mrs. Evans, is there anything you remember about the person?" Sheriff Francis continued.

"No! I told you I didn't see him! Aren't you listening?" She again was becoming agitated.

"Then how do you know it was a *he*?" Warner asked.

"I don't!" She hadn't mentioned Max and wasn't going to.

"All right. Enough questions for the night," Warner said. "There'll be plenty of time tomorrow, Guy." The sheriff nodded and closed his notebook.

That's when the doctor gave her the sedative.

Now that she was in bed, she could feel the tension slowly draining from her muscles.

Rick, who had been closing downstairs, walked in.

"You okay?" He looked concerned.

She smiled. "I am now."

"Good." He went to the bed and hugged her. "I don't know what I'd do if anything ever happened to you." He cradled her in his arms for a long moment.

"Rick, I don't want Todd playing Little League," Dana whispered.

"All right, honey. We'll talk about it in the morning."

"I'm serious, Rick. I didn't say it earlier, but it's Max Richter who's behind this."

"What? Why didn't you tell sheriff Francis?"

"It's Max Richter, and he's in on this thing with Coach Dreiser."

"Dana, no," Rick said, shaking his head.

"It's true!" She was ready to blurt it all out, to tell him she'd suspected Max for a long time. She wanted to tell him about Max's file, and his giving her the key, and also that Dreiser's son died of a drug overdose. She wanted to tell him everything, but she was suddenly feeling so very tired.

"Dana, let's talk about it in the morning."

"NO!" she said, her voice rising as she spewed out the last of her energy. "I don't want Todd to play!"

She saw the annoyance and anger on Rick's face. "Dana, he's going to play!"

"I'll take him and leave!" she gasped, as wisps of sleep began to shut down her consciousness.

"You can leave, but Todd stays here with

me!"

"No!" she wanted to scream, but when she opened her mouth, nothing came out.

They couldn't have her son. *They couldn't!* And with her mind clinging to this thought, Dana allowed the drug to take her.

On Tuesday morning Rick didn't go to work.

Dana didn't wake up when the alarm went off, and Rick decided to let her sleep. He got Todd out of bed, washed up, then went downstairs to fix breakfast. He scrambled eggs in butter, threw in some parmesan cheese and a diced bell pepper.

"How come Mommy didn't fix breakfast?" Todd asked as he dawdled over his eggs.

"Your mother isn't feeling well."

"Did someone really try to kill her?" The question leapt from the boy's throat.

"I don't know. I think so," he said somberly. The boy had to know. He couldn't keep him in the dark about this thing.

"Will the police put him jail? Will he fry?"

"Todd, where did you learn to talk like that?"

"TV." The boy smiled.

He explained to his son, as best he could, what had happened. Then he sent the boy to school.

At 8:40 he fixed another batch of eggs and brought breakfast up to his wife. After Dana had finished one cup of coffee, fiddled over her eggs and nibbled at a corner of toast, they continued the previous night's argument.

"Rick, this is serious," she told him.

"I know, but it has nothing to do with Little League."

"It does!"

"You don't know that, Dana. You yourself admitted you never saw who it was. It could have been someone from out of town."

"No," Dana said. "Rick, I'm on to something, and they want me out of the way."

"Honey, I think you should talk to someone."

"I'M NOT CRAZY!" she screamed. "I'm taking Todd out of Little League."

"No." There was anger in his eyes, but she didn't care.

"Don't fight me on this, Rick. I won't give in this time."

"Todd is going to play!" There was finality in his voice.

"No, Rick." Dana fought to hold her ground.

"You can't stop him!"

Later that day Rick drove Dana to Community General Hospital. When the service station returned Dana's car, they said they could find nothing wrong. Rick told Dana it must have been the starter.

They drove in near silence.

When Dana arrived at the hospital, Doctor Warner treated her as if she were his prize patient. She'd checked in at the desk in the clinic and was seated in the crowded waiting area for only five minutes when her name was announced over the loudspeaker. As she started towards the offices in the rear, she could feel the angry looks burning into the back of her head.

"How are you, Mrs. Evans?" Doctor Warner smiled, as Dana came through the door.

"Not bad, but I think I've just made a room full of enemies."

The silver-domed Warner noticed Dana's limp and commandeered a wheelchair for her use. He was a kind man, with soft reassuring eyes that Dana liked. He wasn't pompous or gruff, like many doctors.

The x-rays proved negative. *Thank God!* But Doctor Warner told Dana to stay off her feet for the rest of the week.

"I'll try," she said smiling.

"You will!" he said with a chuckle. "Or I'm sure we can find a bed around here for you, where I can watch you myself."

He gave her a prescription. "Sleeping pills, but only if you need them." And she went home, where she spent the rest of the day relaxing.

Dana and Rick had little to say to each other.

"What do ya mean he's not home!"

Mike Perotti had been trying to reach Coach Dreiser for three days, and each time he called, Mrs. Dreiser told him that the coach wasn't home. He'd called early and late, but he just couldn't seem to reach the coach.

This time it was five AM, and she told him the coach still wasn't home. He didn't believe it.

"Well, where the hell is he?" he bellowed into the phone.

"I'm not certain. But when he returns I'll give him your message."

"He hasn't returned any of my calls."

"I'll give him your message."

"Did you give him any of the others?"

"Yes, I did."

"Christ! It's important!"

"I'll tell him, sir."

"Mike Perotti senior, you got that? Tell him Mike Perotti senior called and is waiting for him to return the call!"

He hung up.

The receptionist type blandness that was in the woman's voice annoyed him, and he was highly pissed at Coach Dreiser for not returning any of his calls.

I'm not important enough for him to talk to, huh! Well, we'll see about that!

Mike Perotti considered himself a man to be reckoned with.

"Where the hell you been, girly?"

It was Max.

"Max?" Dana couldn't believe that he had the nerve to phone her at home.

"Yeah. What did you do, forget about me?"

"No. I was in an accident."

"I heard about your little run in."

I'm sure you did! "From who?"

"Guy Francis was around asking questions. That's a Johnny-come-lately for you. Whoever the fuck did it is a million miles away by now, and that ass is out asking questions!"

Max's pretense at innocence was annoying to Dana.

"I won't be working for the newspaper anymore, Max."

"Don't let some unknown sonofabitch scare you, girly. You got the stuff."

"What stuff?"

"Girly, I've gone out on a limb to keep you around here. You're not going to back down on me now, are you?"

What the hell is he up to?

"No, I'm not," Dana said, deciding to play the game through.

"That's the spirit. So when will I see you?"

"I have to stay off of my feet for the rest of the week. How about Monday?"

"Will you cover the games over the weekend?"

"Sure."

"That's the spirit. Monday, girly, and have that copy neatly typed."

Max signed off. Dana was flabbergasted by his nerve. She didn't know what he was up to, but if it was a fight he wanted, it was a fight he was going to get. She'd have to be careful of him; he did try to kill her. *But he wouldn't dare try it in broad daylight.* She'd make sure she was in the office only during daylight hours. She was going to play along, just for a while.

I'll give the old bastard enough rope, then I'll hang him!

It was Wednesday. The pain in Dana's side was nearly gone, only a sore stiffness remaining when she walked. Rick had stayed home earlier in the week, but they'd said very little to each other.

The atmosphere was thick with tension, filling their lungs with a pressure that threatened to strangle them. It was uncomfortable just being there, but Dana had to stay at home, and Rick wouldn't leave. Then this morning Rick suddenly got up and went to work as if everything were back to normal.

Dana was glad to have the house to herself, needing some time alone to think over her problem. She wasn't crazy. She'd told Rick everything, but he wouldn't listen. She'd heard him talking to Todd about practicing today and the coming game on Saturday. She wasn't going to let her son be a part of the team. She didn't want to leave her husband, but if Rick wouldn't listen, she'd take her son and move back to the city.

She needed to talk to someone. She needed a friend, but she had no friends in Crandall—except for Ruth. She'd often thought of calling Carly, her best friend since college, but had never gotten around to it.

Over the past few years she and Carly had

drifted apart, their lives going in opposite directions. Now she wanted to renew the bond they'd once shared.

She picked up the phone, easily recalling the once familiar number, and dialed.

"I'm sorry, but the number you have reached is out of service or temporarily disconnected."

She tried again, with the same result. She found her phone book, and looked up the number. *I couldn't have forgotten it!* She hadn't.

She dialed the information operator and asked for a new listing. There wasn't any. She'd completely lost touch with her friend and hoped Carly hadn't fallen on bad times. Now that she needed her friend, she wanted to know that everything was all right with her.

Seated by the phone, thinking of Carly, she suddenly found herself wanting to call Allentown.

She dialed the number and waited.

"Hello." It was her mother's voice. Hearing it brought back memories, not all of them good.

She hesitated a few seconds before answering.

"Hello, Mother."

"Who is this?"

"Dana."

A brief silence.

"Hello, Dana. Is there something wrong?"

"No." There was a tenseness in her mother's voice, and although Dana desperately wanted to talk, she couldn't bring herself to tell her mother of her problems.

"We haven't heard from you in years. Why are you calling now?"

"Is everyone there all right?"

"Yes. Are you still married?"

"Yes, Mother."

"How's the boy?"

She didn't even remember his name. "Todd is fine."

"Any more children?"

"No."

Silence. They'd run out of things to say.

"Why did you call?" her mother asked again.

"I just. . ."

"But why? You aren't a part of this family anymore. You left and refused to keep in touch with us. Why would you be concerned now?"

Dana had always been concerned, but for some reason she just couldn't call, couldn't take her mother's humiliating questions and accusations.

"I'm older now, Mother. Maybe we should try and forget the past."

"I can't!" she blurted. "As far as I'm concerned you're not a part of this family anymore. I'm not going to disturb your father by telling him you called."

There were tears in Dana's eyes. She wished she'd never made the call. "All right, Mother. Is Dad all right?" She kept the sorrow out of her voice. Her mother had always been able to make her cry, and she wasn't going to give her the satisfaction of knowing that she still could.

"Yes. Have you been going to church?"

"No."

"I thought not."

A few minutes later, Dana hung up, feeling more desolate than she'd ever felt in her entire life.

Thursday morning the roses started to come.

It was around ten o'clock, and Dana was vacuuming when the first dozen arrived. By noon two more messengers had come, each bringing a dozen roses. Red, pink and yellow —her favorites. There were notes with the flowers, all from Rick: "I'm sorry. Let's be friends."

At 1:30, Rick called.

"Hi, honey, did you get the flowers?"

"Yes, three dozen." Her tone was flat.

"I'm sorry, hon. After all you've been through, I've been such a bastard."

Silence.

"Honey?" he said. "Forgive me?"

"I don't want Todd playing anymore," said Dana.

"I've thought about it, hon. And if it's that important to you I don't want him to play either."

"You mean that?" Dana was pleasantly shocked.

"Yeah, hon. And I was also thinking that

Crandall isn't really such a great place to live after all. What happened to you Monday really made me sit up and take notice."

"Can we move?"

"We can if you want to."

"If I want to! When?" There was sudden cheer and excitement in Dana's voice.

"Whenever we find a place. We'll have to start looking."

"Oh, Rick, thank you. You don't know what this means to me, to all of us. Thank you."

"How about a date?" Rick asked.

"A date?"

"Yeah. You know, boyfriend-girlfriend? I want to start over. Let me take you to dinner and the theater. 'The Pirates of Penzance' is playing. We've never seen it."

"Tickets will be hard to get for this evening, and what about a babysitter?"

"I can get the tickets. You get the sitter. 'Money is no object,'" he said in a mock German accent. "Do you want to go?"

"Of course." She was smiling now. "Thank you again, Rick."

"I'll be home about six. Have Todd fed and ready for bed, okay?"

"Okay."

"We'll leave about a quarter of seven. That'll give us enough time to get to the theater. We'll dine afterwards. Got to run now. Love you, hon."

"I love you, too."

"Oh yeah, there's another dozen roses on the way—white."

She smiled.

Dana was in luck. On the classified page of the Guardian she found an ad for a babysitter and called the number.

The ad was placed by sixteen year old Marcie Douglas. When Dana called she spoke to Marcie's mother, who told her that Marcie would love to sit with Todd.

She lived just a few blocks away, and Dana promised that Rick would drop her off when they returned, so she wouldn't have to walk home in the dark.

Marcie arrived early, around six. She wanted to get to know Dana and Todd, and Dana liked her industriousness. She was a soft-spoken, brown-eyed beauty, who also seemed quite intelligent.

"So you plan to attend Vassar in the fall?" The two sat at the dining room table sipping tea, while a pajama-clad Todd finished up his dinner.

"That's my plan so far. I haven't heard anything yet, but I've got my fingers crossed."

Marcie wasn't the typical teenage babysitter, who only spoke of boys and music. She was quite mature in her approach to life, and this too pleased Dana.

"You've been skipped a grade?" Dana asked.

"Yes, in the seventh."

"We have a genius here in Crandall," Dana teased.

Marcie blushed. "I'm smart, but not a

genius. I'm nothing like Jimmy Warren."

"Jimmy Warren?" The name seemed to haunt Dana.

"Didn't you know?" the girl asked in mock amazement. She had had license to indulge in some juicy gossip. "Last spring his teacher noticed he was doing his math work in class at an amazing speed. At first she thought he was cheating, but when she tested him, she found that he could answer any problem in a matter of seconds. A math genius."

"Amazing," Dana said. "Has he changed anymore over the year?"

"Not that I know of."

"Can he still do it now?"

"I guess so. He's not in any special school or anything, and after the initial excitement, things did sort of die down. But it still amazes me. The kid was an average schmo, and then whammo!"

Dana told Rick about the Warren boy in the car, as they headed for the city.

"That's my girl. Always the reporter, uncovering the town's deep, dark secrets," he said, with a laugh.

They parked on 53rd Street and walked over to the Longacre Theater, where they saw 'The Pirates of Penzance.' Dana loved it. And during the performance Rick actually held her hand.

She called Marcie during intermission and was told that Todd, having given up trying to persuade her that he always had a glass of sherry before retiring, had gone to bed. Everything was fine.

At dinner they talked of looking for a new house and where they would look. Dana was feeling the best she'd felt in a long time.

"Honey," she said, as she sipped her coffee, "I know it's getting late, but I'd like to stop on 95th Street."

"What for?"

"I want to see Carly."

"Tonight?"

"I called her the other day, and her phone had been disconnected. I just want to make sure that everything's okay."

"Anything for my honey," Rick said, squeezing her hand.

When the Pinto wagon pulled up in front of the high rise apartment building on the corner of 95th Street and Columbus Avenue, Rick realized he wasn't going to be able to find a parking space.

"You stay in the car. I'll go up," Dana volunteered. She dashed from the car.

Manhattan, even at 11:40 at night, was alive with sound. The city was bursting with life, as nighttime strollers cruised past Dana up and down the sidewalk. She felt safe here, surrounded by people, even at this hour. She missed the city but hadn't realized how much until now. She wondered what Rick would think of moving back.

She ran up the walk and into the vestibule of the white brick building. A shiny intercom, with a row of black buttons, was on the wall to her left. A locked glass door separated her from a lobby filled with plastic flowers. A suspicious looking black man was sitting by the door.

Dana moved cautiously to the intercom and began going over the row of names, pretending to look for Carly's. She didn't want to be buzzed into the building and have him follow her to the elevator. She'd had enough excitement for one week, so she stood by the intercom and stalled.

"Don't panic, pretty mama," the man said. "I'm just waiting for my man, that's all." He flashed a white-toothed grin. Dana smiled back nervously, but didn't move. In a few minutes another young man emerged from the building, and the two left.

Dana pressed 33C.

"Yeah?" an unfamiliar male voice answered.

"It's Dana. Is Carly there?"

"Wrong apartment!" The connection was abruptly broken. Dana went over the names in the register. Carly's was gone. Carly had moved, and she had no way of getting in touch with her.

A feeling of great loss swept over Dana. *I hope she gets in touch with me.* But it soon passed. Things in Dana's life were looking up, and nothing but nothing was going to spoil the evening.

Later that night, at home, Dana and Rick made glorious, passionate love. It was the best day Dana had had in ages.

* * *

Friday afternoon Todd moped around the house, as if he'd just lost his best friend. When Dana approached him about what was wrong, he simply glared at her.

At dinner there was more of the same. Dana tried to get him to talk, but it was obvious that he was avoiding any conversation with her.

"How was your day, honey?" she asked in an attempt to draw him out.

Silence.

"Todd?"

"Oh! Were you talking to me?"

"Yes."

"Fine . . . Say, Dad, whatcha got planned for tomorrow?"

"Nothing, tiger."

"Maybe we could do something together, huh?"

"Sounds great."

"Maybe a picnic," Dana offered.

Silence.

"The three of us on a picnic could be a lot of fun. We haven't done anything like that before. Would you like that, Todd?" She wasn't giving up.

"I guess." Annoyance was in his voice. "How about you and me going to the stadium to catch the Yanks, Dad? Just the *two* of us."

Why is he punishing me?

Dana continued to try and draw the boy out, but it was hopeless.

Todd ate quickly, excused himself, and went up to his room to sulk in private.

"Rick, what's the matter with him?"

"Don't you know?"

"No, I don't! Don't play games with me. What is it?"

"I'm glad you asked, because I want to talk to you about it. I told him he couldn't play baseball anymore."

"Oh." Then Dana colored. "You told him that *I* didn't want him to play?"

"I told him the truth, that it was basically your decision."

"Rick, that's not fair!"

"I told the truth," he said defensively.

"So should I give you a medal now? Rick, parents are supposed to share the responsibility on these things."

"Honey, I didn't see how I could. Just two days ago we were talking about tomorrow's game. Telling him that *I* didn't want him to play would seem inconsistent, and kids need consistency, right?"

He had all the answers.

"So you made *me* the heavy."

He smiled sheepishly. "Sorry. But, hon, I've been thinking. Why shouldn't he play?"

"Rick, you know how I . . ."

"Sure, sure. But we're going to move soon, right? How much could it hurt if he played for a few more weeks? And it would mean so much to him. You saw him down here—he was miserable! The season's almost over, and if he doesn't make the tournament team it will be over for him next Sunday."

"But you said he *would* make the team."

"There's a chance he will, if they need

another pitcher. But you see how unhappy he is. He'll hold it against you for a long time, hon. And for what? A few weeks of baseball. He's not taking the vitamins anymore, and we're alert. What could happen?"

Rick spread his arms out across the table like a lawyer making an impassioned plea to the jury. Dana listened to all he had to say, and he was right. Dreiser couldn't take Todd from them in two weeks time, and in a month or two they'd be gone. Todd wouldn't be playing Little League in Crandall next year, that was for sure.

"What do you say, hon?" Rick asked, his face tense with anticipation.

"I say, Rick Evans, you should either be a lawyer or a salesman. You're very persuasive."

His face lit up. "Does that mean he can play?"

"Yes."

"That's great, honey!" He jumped up, smiling like a little boy who'd just heard from the tooth fairy. His excitement was contagious, and Dana had to laugh. "I'm going up and tell him right now. He's going to love you for this, hon."

Rick ran from the room, and Dana could hear him happily bounding up the stairs. A few minutes later a shriek of glee reached her ears. It was Todd.

Her two men were upstairs laughing, and the house seemed filled with happiness. So why did Dana have the feeling that she'd just been manipulated?

Chapter 28

The Perottis arrived at the field just after seven, to begin their long warm-up process for the game at nine.

Mike Perotti senior had finally tracked down Coach Dreiser the previous evening, banging on his door just before midnight.

The coach answered.

"Good evening, Mr. Perotti. This must be pretty important for you to come by at such a late hour." The coach's voice was filled with reproach, and Perotti started to back down. But then he remembered all the times he couldn't reach Dreiser, and sudden anger boiled up inside of him.

"You're damned right it's important!"

The coach smiled, and Mike had the feeling that underneath that smile Dreiser was laughing at him. "Come in," the coach said.

Mike entered, and as he brushed by, Dreiser caught the distinct odor of liquor.

"What can I do to help you, Mr. Perotti?" The two were seated in the living room across from one another.

"You can watch my son tomorrow!"

"I always watch all of the boys. You know that."

"Yeah, well keep a special eye on Mike. The kid's got it. He should make the team this year. It's his last year."

"Was that your important reason for coming here this evening?" Beneath Dreiser's quiet composure there was seething anger.

"Yes."

"Mr. Perotti, this could have waited until morning. And now if you'll excuse me, I need my rest." The coach was rising.

"The boy's good! You need a good third baseman!"

The coach started for the door.

"Damnit!" Mike said, jumping up. "We didn't move to Crandall for nothing!"

The coach stopped. "Why did you move here, Mr. Perotti?"

"You know damned well why I moved here!"

"Wasn't it because Crandall is such a lovely town?"

"This is Mike's last chance!" Mike blurted.

"I'll see you in the morning, Mr. Perotti." Dreiser headed for the door again, and Mike followed.

"You can help him, coach!" It was a plea.

"I'll see you in the morning!" the coach repeated slowly.

Mike left.

Now he and his son stood on the thick, green grass of the infield. It was a warm, humid morning, and the sweet smell of freshly cut grass was everywhere.

The coach will see Mike junior today, the father thought. He'll see him, and he'll be impressed. The boy began his stretching exercises.

Mike watched his son carefully, commenting on every little mistake. They had worked too hard to miss this chance. And Mike was going to make sure they got all they deserved.

By nine it was apparent that the day was going to be a hot one. The sun had quickly steamed the morning mist off the grass, leaving a dense layer of humid air over the field.

Already Mike Perotti's T-shirt was blotched with sweat, and he pulled his first frosty Rheingold of the day from his cooler, hoping for some thirst-quenching relief.

Dreiser stood on the third base line, watching the grounds men as they chalked the base lines. He too was thinking of removing his heavy sweatshirt, as beads of perspiration skidded across his body.

Dana, dressed in jeans and a light summer top, arrived with her family. She looked at the boys warming up around the field, and instead of children, she saw monsters.

There was an intensity that hung over Crandall Park, like the humidity of the day. It hovered just above the trees and threatened to come down and squeeze the life out of everyone.

The laughter and happiness normally associated with a beautiful day in the park wasn't here. The boys' warm-up was serious, and the few that laughed or tried to make light of it were looked on with distaste by their peers.

The intensity was in the parents, also. They watched their children's performances as if their lives depended on it. Dana was repelled by what she saw, but she comforted herself with the knowledge that it all would be over soon. They were leaving Crandall. *Thank God!*

Pulling a pen and note pad from her purse, she started to walk away from her family, who were standing by the dugout.

"Hey, where ya going?" Rick asked.

"Just snooping around. I might be able to get a good story from one of the parents."

"For the paper!" he said in amazement.

"Yes." Rick looked disturbed.

"After what Max did to you, you still want to write for him?"

"I'm a little nervous about being alone with him, but no harm can come to me out here."

"I don't like it!" Rick said, throwing his clipboard to the ground. His reaction surprised Dana. "I don't want you near that guy!"

"I'll be careful, hon. You really care, don't you?" She smiled.

"You better believe it!" He went to her and put his arms around her waist. "I don't want anything to spoil it for us. We've come too far together." He pecked her cheek, and she blushed.

"Rick Evans, I love you, and I promise I'll stay as far away from Max Richter as I can." She hugged him and dashed off.

She glanced back over her shoulder and saw Todd beginning to take his warm-up pitches. He was pitching again today. The boy was serious—too serious about baseball.

The people of Crandall had done this to him. There was too much emphasis placed on performance and winning, with absolutely no room left to just have fun. If the boys of Crandall were enjoying themselves, you couldn't have proved it by Dana. To her they seemed like robots, marching around in a mechanical daze. She knew it was the effect of the drugs and was thankful Todd no longer took them.

She pictured herself in the future, a future without Crandall.

By 9:15 the game was under way.

Todd was pitching against Adonis Dreiser. If he needed to win this game in order to make the tournament team, Dana knew his chances were slim.

The Hutchinson's team, in their green, white and yellow, took the field first, and Todd strolled out to the mound like a real professional.

The first pitch brought a line drive, hit by Mike Perotti, up the third base line. Toby Fowler quickly scooped it up, bobbled it slightly, then made a perfect toss to first for the out.

"Come on, Brooksy! Run, boy, run!" Mike's father screamed.

Todd struck out the next batter, gave up a base hit, and then an infield pop fly, which he caught himself for the third out.

The Hutchinson's team ran off the field, switching places with the blue and white of Harvey's.

Adonis, of course, was masterful, serving up strikes like a mechanical pitching machine.

Todd's team was playing well; they'd gotten two good hits, and Todd had struck out five batters. But still, at the bottom of the fifth, the score was 5-0 in favor of Harvey's, as Adonis continued to thwart the boys with his deft pitching. Also, Mike Perotti junior hit a two-run homer.

Then Todd got on with a walk, Adonis' first of the day.

You blind, or somethin', ump!

And Toby Fowler cracked one towards third. Mike Perotti junior moved in quickly, scooped up the ball and proceeded to throw it to first. But wait! His glove was empty. He'd missed the ball and didn't even know it. The ball now rested on the soft grass of left field, and slow-footed Herbi Jensen stumbled over to get it. By the time the ball was returned to the infield, Hutchinson's had two runs, and

Harvey's definitely found itself in a game.

Mike Perotti senior shot a furtive glance over at Dreiser, who was standing by the Harvey's dugout, and the coach glared back at him.

Harvey's went on to win the game 5-3. It seemed like a routine win for Adonis Dreiser, but two very important things happened that day:

1) Coach Dreiser decided that the future of Crandall baseball rested on the arm of Todd Evans; and,

2) He also decided that Mike Perotti junior would not make the team.

BOOK THREE

Chapter 29

There had always been a fire burning in Max Richter's eyes, a dying flame that time somehow had not been able to douse. Dana originally had noticed the flicker and was amused, even pleased, that this old codger could still be so cantankerous.

Monday, when Dana arrived at the office of the Guardian, she noticed something different about Max. The fire had been refueled. He seemed more vivid, more alive, more full of piss and vinegar than ever before.

He greeted her with a warm smile, and a hearty "How the hell are ya, girly?"

"Fine," Dana answered.

"Come on downstairs. It's about time you and me had a little talk."

And that's when the alarm went off in her.

"What about?" Dana asked cautiously.

"About us, of course. We have to stop

meeting like this," he said, almost falling off his stool with laughter.

Dana remembered promising Rick that she wouldn't be alone with Max, and from the way he now was acting, she knew she didn't want to be.

Max stood, rolling up the sleeves on his gray cardigan. "We got work to do." He started for the rear. When he realized that Dana wasn't following, he stopped abruptly and turned.

"I'm not going," she said, looking defiantly into his eyes.

"What the fuck has gotten into you, girly?"

"I'm not going to be down there alone with you, Max."

"Don't stop trusting me now, girly. We need each other."

"Sure," she replied, her voice laced with sarcasm.

"They've gotten to you. Haven't they?" There was genuine concern in his voice.

"Who?"

"All of them! Girly, the pressure's picked up. You're onto something. I don't know what it is, but whatever it is, it's scaring the hell out of them."

"Max, my family and I are moving away from Crandall. Whatever it is that I've uncovered, I don't care about it anymore."

There was a brief, awkward silence. Never had Max been at a loss for words around Dana.

314

"You're a newspaper woman, girly, and a damned good one!"

"And I want to stay one! Max, you're not going to flatter me into going downstairs."

"Wait right here. I have to show you something." Quickly Max shuffled from the room, and Dana heard him going down the creaky stairs.

He was an old man. She was sure he couldn't overpower her. Still, she felt safer upstairs. If he tried anything the sound would spill out into the street. Someone would hear.

Minutes later Max returned with a book clasped in his right hand.

"Girly, you're the one who put me onto it. I should have shared this with you sooner, but to tell you the truth, I was going to cover it up."

"Max, you must be getting senile. All morning you've been talking in riddles."

"We've got 'em, girly!" He half-smiled. "You and me, we've got power in this town now. The power of the press!"

"I suppose you're going to stop filling the paper with Little League."

"You're damned right I am!"

"None of this is going to get me downstairs with you, Max. You might as well give up."

"I've got a surprise for you, girly. Haven't you been looking for this?" He showed her the book.

She stepped closer, and read the title: "Modern Modes In Operant Conditioning" by

Philip Dreiser. Dana's eyes widened.

"So it was *you* who borrowed it!"

"I couldn't have beaten you there by more than an hour, but I had to get it. I was doing it to save the paper. At least that's what I told myself." Dana took the book. "Then when I got it, and all the pressure started, I knew we were onto something big—really big!"

Dana quickly thumbed through the book, then turned it over to look at the rear dust jacket. She was in luck.

When she saw the picture, excitement pumped extra blood through her veins, her eyes widening to the size of silver dollars.

There on the rear cover of the book, wearing a dark conservative suit, white shirt and dark tie, was a very distinguished looking picture of Doctor Fritz Warner.

Dana and Max were seated at the card table in the basement. Max was talking.

"Then one day last week they sent a little committee here, to recommend that you be banned from the paper. Dana, your husband was on that committee."

"What?"

"It surprised me too, but there he was, with Dreiser, Eunice Graham and some of the other parents."

"But why?"

"There's got to be something to this drug thing, and you're probably about to uncover it. Girly, in case you haven't discovered it yet, Roger Dreiser died of a heroin overdose."

"I know."

"I figured you would by now." There was a look of mutual respect on both of their faces. "Girly, I don't blame you for not trusting me, but try to see my side. The Guardian is all I have. With no newspaper to take up my time, why I'd just shrivel up and die. Girly, I knew there was something wrong in this town five years ago. That's when we had our first two runaways." He paused.

Dana now understood the renewed fire she'd seen in Max. He had a story, and he was going to cover it, no matter what.

Max continued. "The parents were so eager to cover everything up that I knew the boys couldn't have just run away. I thought they were sent away—or maybe even killed.

"Over the years I kept track of the boys. There's been nine, all eleven or twelve years old, and none of them has ever returned."

"Why didn't you do anything, tell anybody?"

"The town supported the paper. Dreiser explained to me that if the paper weren't run satisfactorily, they'd stop supporting me and put me out of business. I got scared. Where could I go to start a new paper at my age? So I started running Little League stories, and everyone was happy—until you came along."

"Are you sorry I came, Max?"

"Hell, no! I was shriveling up anyway. Having a paper that can't print the news is like having no paper at all. I want to print the truth!"

"Is your file a runaway file?"

"Yes."

"Can I see it?"

Max got up and unlocked the file cabinet. "You can see it anytime you want. I want to go after them, girly, and I want to nail them. You and me, together." Max paused, choosing his next words carefully. "Girly, something's been eating at me, and I have to tell you. We both know that what happened to you last Monday night was planned. I want you to know that many of the parents in this town are in on this thing. And whether you believe it or not, your husband is with them."

There's too much happening too fast, Dana thought, as she sat at the chrome and glass dining room table.

Roger Dreiser dying of a drug overdose, Warner's picture on the book, and Max declaring that Rick was in on the conspiracy—this was too much for Dana to digest all at once. All the pieces of the puzzle began to jumble together inside Dana's mind. She'd thought the puzzle was nearly solved, but now that there were so many new pieces, she doubted if the thing could ever be solved—at least not by her.

An eerie feeling began to come over her. It started slowly at first, but the more she thought of the puzzle, the more it increased. The whole thing brought to mind a movie she'd seen on TV not too long ago. It starred Donald Sutherland, one of her favorites, and had a really weird plot. "Invasion Of The Body Snatchers," it was called. That's what seemed to be happening in Crandall. The boys were being changed. *Who would be next?*

Dana dismissed her fear by reminding herself that they would be moving soon.

Rick had to mean what he said!

She didn't know why Rick went to the newspaper office, but it didn't matter. He now realized that they could be happier elsewhere, and that was all that was important.

He had a change of heart after he saw Max, obviously.

Then she thought of her son. They were not going to get Todd. They could have Adonis Dreiser, Jimmy Warren, Petie Graham, and she was very sorry that Ronnie Roberts was one of them now, but they couldn't have Todd.

Suddenly she needed to be close to her only child. He had been in his room playing since he'd come in from school.

Dana rose and went upstairs. She needed the reassurance of Todd's boyish grin. She needed to know that he still belonged to her.

She knocked at the door.

"Who?"

"Mommy."

"Come in."

Dana pushed the door open, and the first thing she noticed was that the boy's room was immaculate. For some unknown reason a cold shiver snaked up her spine.

Todd was seated atop his toy chest, staring

out of the window.

"What are you doing?" Dana asked.

"Thinking," the boy answered. Dana noticed a bit of reluctance in his voice.

"About what?"

"Baseball—the playoffs. They start next Saturday."

"Don't be too disappointed if you don't make the team, Todd."

He looked at her as if she were crazy. "Didn't Daddy tell you? I'm on the team!"

She tried to cover her sudden surprise. "Oh, yes. I forgot. Congratulations, son." She forced a smile.

"Thank you," Todd answered, returning her smile with a quiet stare.

This was twice in one day that Dana had discovered Rick working against her. She couldn't believe he was in on this thing with Dreiser. He just didn't see what they were doing. He was too caught up in his own Little League dream.

"Why aren't you playing with your Star Wars men?" Dana asked, in an attempt to change the subject.

Again, the incredulous stare. "That's kid stuff, Mom. I don't play with them anymore."

Dana realized she wasn't going to find the reassurance she needed. There was no doubt about it—Todd was changing. And Dana's flesh suddenly was laced with goose bumps.

Max Richter turned off the press. Slamming his fist into the table, he smiled, tap-dancing across the floor as best he could.

"Fred Astaire, eat your heart out!"

Max was happy, happier than he'd been in years. He liked Dana Evans. Hell, he even loved her. She made him feel young again, like a college student stepping into the world of journalism for the first time, wanting to set it on its proverbial ear.

He remembered Woodward and Bernstein's fantastic investigative reporting, uncovering the Watergate scandal back in the seventies. But the news of the eighties was filled with Reaganomics, and that didn't make for a very interesting story.

Now, Max knew that he too was on the verge of uncovering something really big. No, it wasn't on the level of a Watergate conspiracy, but if what Max and Dana thought were true, it was big—national headlines big!

Richter and Evans, what a team! We might even write a book about it.

Max Richter hung his apron on a hook by the door and turned off the lights in the press-room. He'd spent enough of his day in the office. He was going home to get some rest, and while he was there, he was going to map out plans for uncovering this conspiracy.

Next weeks headlines would get things rolling: WILL THE REAL DOCTOR PHILIP DREISER PLEASE STAND UP! He chuckled to himself just thinking of the furor the article was going to create. The

presence of Dana Evans had put some fun
back in his life. He was really glad he'd hired
her.

That's when he heard the knock.

Dana was starting to get a very bad feeling
from this whole thing—a feeling as if, maybe,
she had been used.

Rick came in around six, unusually bright
and cheery. He'd picked up two new accounts
that day, one of which was a major acquisition
in the home furnishings industry. It was a
good sign. Rick was becoming respected in
the business.

"That's wonderful, honey," Dana said,
throwing her arms around him and giving him
a big kiss. "I'm sure that will take some of the
financial burden off of our moving twice in
one year."

"Yeah, I guess you're right."

There was something wrong with the coolness of his answer.

At dinner, she asked him outright, "When
are we going to move?"

"I don't know, hon. Soon," he said,
brushing her aside.

Dana didn't get upset. That had been her
mistake in the past, and she wasn't going to
make it again. She waited until Todd was in
bed. She sat in the living room, pretending to
watch TV, as Rick came down from tucking
him in.

Her plan was to attack with cool reasoning.

"What are you watching?" Rick asked,

flopping down in the high-backed leather easy chair.

"I don't know. I wasn't really paying attention."

"When was the last time Todd got a haircut?"

"I'm not sure. A few months, at least."

"Well, I think it's about time the tiger visited the barber again. He's really starting to look shaggy."

They had small-talked enough.

"Rick!" Dana blurted. "When are we going to start looking for a new home?"

"Soon, hon."

"When?" Her voice was starting to rise. She noticed it and checked it. *Under control, girl.*

"A couple of weeks. Okay?"

"Why not Saturday? Todd's team doesn't play until Sunday."

He stared at her blankly.

"Rick, I hope you didn't tell me we'd move just to get me off your back."

"No, hon, I didn't."

" 'Cause if you did, it's not going to work. I want to move, and I want to start looking for a place on Saturday!"

"Why so soon?"

"Soon!" Her control was slipping. "I want to get the hell away from this town. Rick, the town is evil! I can feel it!" She stopped. This was not the type of reasoning that would win Rick over. "Did you mean what you said about moving?"

"Yes. Of course."

"You said we'd be gone in a few months. I want to start looking Saturday."

"All right."

It's working!

"And why did you ask them to ban me from the Guardian?"

This time she saw a bit of anger creeping into his eyes.

"Look, Dana, I'm not going to have my wife talking to me this way!"

"I'm not going to have my husband sneaking behind my back!"

"Sneaking!"

"You knew Todd was picked for the tournament team, but you deliberately kept it from me."

"Dana, I've taken enough of your accusations." Rick's smooth complexion reddened. "The truth is, I'm not sure we should move. Dana, something's happened to you since we've come to this town. You've been acting strange. I think you need help."

He's calling me crazy again! Before, this would have been enough to make her cry. But this time he wasn't going to throw her off the track by upsetting her.

"There's nothing wrong with me, Rick. There's something wrong with *you*, and a lot of other people in this town. You've all gone Little League mad! I'll ask you one more time. Are we going to move?"

"We'll move after you get help. I see no reason to take Todd and. . ."

"Then I'm moving without you." There was an ocean of tears behind Dana's eyes, but she had it under control.

She rose from the sofa and started up the stairs.

"Dana, it's for all of us that I'm doing this. I didn't want you on the paper because I thought it was harming you. I'm looking out for you, Dana—for all of us. Can't you see that?"

She stopped on the stairs.

"You won't be sleeping with me anymore. You can sleep down here. If you change your mind about moving, we can discuss your sharing quarters with me again. For now, you'll sleep down here." She started up the stairs again.

"Dana, you can't mean that! I'm thinking of all of us!"

Dana proceeded up the stairs to the bedroom, where she slammed and locked the door.

Chapter 30

Normally, Max would have thought it strange for Doctor Warner to be accompanying Coach Dreiser to his office. But since he'd seen the picture on the back of the book, he knew, somehow, the two were linked together.

"What can I do to help you gentlemen?" he asked, as the two filed solemnly through the door.

Dreiser spoke. "Max, we have to discuss an issue of grave importance with you. It concerns the future of our beloved Crandall."

The future of Crandall, indeed!

The two men sat half atop Max's cluttered desk, while Max stood off to the side, studying them. They looked troubled, and Max noted how stiffly Doctor Warner sat, his hands stuffed into his jacket pockets.

"First, Max, I want to level with you about something," Dreiser began. "This Little League championship is very important to me. I've done a lot to insure that this season would run smoothly. Now that it's over, and the playoffs are about to start, I don't want anything or anybody trying to undermine my work. I'll do anything to stop them, Max. Anything!'' Dreiser spoke from his guts, and Max knew that he meant every word he said.

"Are you refering to Dana Evans?" Max asked.

"I am."

"I'm tired of people telling me what the fuck to do about Dana Evans. She works for me!"

"I realize that, but. . ."

"I won't fire her!" Max was fuming. He'd taken enough guff from Dreiser. He was his own man, now.

"Max," Warner broke in, with his smooth, melodious voice, "Dana Evans is a threat to the future of Crandall. We know things about her that you don't."

"What things?"

He ignored the question. "Max, we know how much you like it here at the Guardian. With people like Mrs. Evans around, there won't be a Guardian for long—or a Crandall either, for that matter."

It was an impassioned plea, to which Max answered, "Bunk! That's a bunch of horseshit! You talk as if Dana Evans is a communist or something." He chuckled. "She's on to something about this town, and we're going to find out what it is!"

"Don't get in our way, Max," Dreiser said.

His voice was powerful, threatening, but Max took little heed of it. Today, Max was feeling the best he'd felt in ages, and he wasn't going to let anyone spoil it.

"For a long time I've been letting you tell me what the fuck to print in my paper, but that's all over now." Max went into the press-room and returned with the headline. "We're gonna stir up something in this town the likes of which you've never seen!"

He showed the men the headline.

"What does this mean, Max?" Dreiser asked. He appeared relaxed, but there was definite agitation in his voice.

"You tell me," Max said smiling. "You're on trial here, not me!" Columns of laughter sprang from his throat.

Dreiser looked at Doctor Warner and shook his head.

"I'm sorry. I know how you feel about this sort of thing."

"Won't you reconsider, Max?" Warner asked. "You can print anything you like, but don't let the Evans girl influence you."

"I've been acting like a Casper Milquetoast —a coward. Dana opened my eyes to what was going on around here. She ain't afraid of you, and I ain't either!"

"Let her go, Max."

"Hell, no!"

"Max, you're forcing our hand. Coach Dreiser and I like you. Don't make us do something . . . drastic."

"Are you threatening me?"

The two men stared on silently.

"Get out!" Max boomed, pointing to the door. "Get the hell out of here!"

Doctor Warner rose sharply, removing his hands from his pocket. In his right hand was a hypodermic syringe.

"What the fuck is that for?"

"Don't fight us," Dreiser said. "It will be painless."

"You're an old man, Max. You couldn't live forever."

"OUT!" The word was flung from Max's throat. He began to shuffle towards the door, but Dreiser was quickly behind him, his powerful arms restraining Max easily.

"Stop it! Get the fuck off!" Max fought, but he was no match for the two.

Warner rolled up Max's sleeve and easily slipped the needle into his soft, saggy flesh. He looked into Dreiser's eyes. "Five minutes."

Suddenly there was a horrible rumbling in Max's chest, as if someone had climbed down his throat and was walking around inside of his heart.

"What did you give me?" he gasped. The drug was taking effect, as the pain threatened to wrench Max's heart from his body.

They released him, and he slipped slowly to the floor.

"Help me!" he begged, as thunderous spasms rocketed through his chest. "Please!" The plea came from the depths of his soul.

Neither man moved to his aid.

Max's body twitched and jerked across the floor, like a freshly-killed chicken at the live poultry market. His mouth opened and closed, releasing low, inaudible sounds, while his eyes lost focus on the world. A few moments later, he lay dead.

Dreiser bent to check his pulse.

"It had to be this way," he said, looking into the eyes of his accomplice.

"I know."

"We have much work to do," he said, rising.

"Yes."

Quickly the two men went into the press-room, where they began resetting type in preparation for the next issue of the Guardian.

The first game of the playoffs was against the team from Rye. The teams played on a neutral field in Purchase, and it seemed the whole town of Crandall was present.

Max's absence was conspicious—at least it was to Dana. She missed the old bastard.

She'd gone to the office the day after she'd last seen him, Tuesday, only to find it locked up tight.

This isn't like Max, she thought. The old bastard's lying down on the job.

She pulled the office key from her purse and stuck it into the lock. It wouldn't turn. She checked the keys on her ring. *This has to be the one!* That's when she became suspicious.

She hadn't used the key in a week. Max could have changed the lock since then, but she didn't think so. *Someone has changed the lock.* And then she thought the worst. *Someone in this town has harmed Max and then changed the lock!*

She went to nearest phone and called the sheriff's office.

"Sheriff's department. May I help you?"

"Yes. My name is Dana Evans..."

"Sheriff Francis here. What can I do for you, Mrs. Evans?"

"Something's wrong with Max Richter, and..."

"Mrs. Evans, I'm sorry to tell you this, but Max Richter died of a heart attack some time last night."

"Heart attack! Where?"

"He had it in his office, ma'am. I'm sorry." There was professional remorse in his voice.

"Who found him?"

"Doctor Warner, ma'am. He just happened to be passing by, saw the light burning, and thought he'd drop in. A few moments earlier and he might have saved him."

Warner?

"The lock on the office door has been changed. Do you know anything about that?" Dana's mind reeled from the impact of what she had just been told.

Poor Max, she thought. She wanted to forget the whole thing and break down into tears of sorrow for her friend. But if Max had been killed, which she firmly believed, her life was also at stake. She had to push on.

"I don't know anything about that," Sheriff Francis replied. "You can take it up with the president of the town council."

"Who's that?"

"Dreiser."

It was all too neat. "We're not licked yet, Max," she mumbled as she hung up the phone. Tears trickled from her eyes.

Next, she phoned Dreiser and demanded that he give her the key to the office.

"I'm sorry, Mrs. Evans. The town council has taken over operation of the Guardian. You've been relieved of your duties, but I want to thank you personally for all that you've done."

She phoned the coroner's office and demanded that an autopsy be done on Max's body.

"Miss, autopsies are done on all mysterious deaths. Mr. Richter's will be performed some time today. You can call back later for the results."

She did. The official cause of Max Richter's death? Heart attack!

Now as Dana sat watching the boys in their Dodger blue uniforms, the events of the past few weeks ricocheted through her mind. The whole thing had become a nightmare.

She and Rick were definitely on the outs. He had been sleeping on the sofa for over a week now, yet he still stood firm in his position.

When he and Todd had come home last Thursday, Todd had one of those hideous haircuts. "Rick, how could you!" Dana's position in the marriage became clear to her. She knew what she must do—file for divorce.

Divorce. It was an ugly word, for it meant failure. Her marriage was failing, and she didn't see any way she could save it.

Rick was stubborn and self-centered. She hadn't noticed it before, or hadn't really wanted to. Today, however, she saw Rick in a different light. He wanted to live out his childhood fantasies through Todd. He didn't care that the town would destroy them all—had started destroying them already. He only cared about himself.

Dana watched the game with little interest. She only hoped that Crandall would lose. *Maybe then, Rick would come to his senses*. Of course, both thoughts were wishful thinking.

Crandall went on to win 10-2, the boys playing with robot-like precision.

Todd didn't play. He sat silently on the bench along with Dreiser and the other second-stringers, neither cheering nor rooting for his teammates, just staring. Todd was becoming more like the others everyday.

Dana had felt that her only hope of saving him was to wait for the team to lose. Now she realized she'd waited around long enough. She needed to take action, needed to grab her son and get out. *But where would they go?*

As Dana sat watching Adonis Dreiser toss strike after strike to the last few batters, her eyes absent-mindedly wandered over to Coach Dreiser (if that's what his name really was). He was standing in front of the dugout.

For a moment their eyes locked. She noticed

that his face was expressionless. *But the eyes!*
The deadly eyes seemed to be laughing,
laughing at her. As Dana sat, her eyes
trapped by the coach's powerful gaze, she
suddenly had the mad desire to run.

On the morning of the game against Rye,
Mike Perotti showed up at the emergency
desk of Community General Hospital with his
son. The boy had assorted bruises and a
broken right arm.

Mike cautiously walked up to the admitting
station, as Mike junior sat in the waiting area.

The receiving nurse was a frumpy-looking
black woman, with a West Indian accent and
a look that could kill.

"Yes?" she said, feeling Mike's presence,
not really looking up from the applications
she pored over.

"My kid, uhh . . . I think he broke his arm."
Mike looked around nervously, hoping no one
he knew had straggled in.

"Name?"

"Mine or his?"

"Both."

"Mike Perotti."

"Yours or his?"

"Both."

They carried on their little vaudeville
routine, as further basic information was
elicited, until finally she asked how it
happened.

"I don't know," Mike said, looking around
again.

For the first time the receptionist looked up.

"Were you there, man?"

"Yes . . . well, no. I was in the house, but I was asleep."

"Man, did you ask him?" The voice was tinged with disbelief.

"Uhh . . . Yes." The sweat was starting to drip from Mike's armpits. "He fell." Mike grinned sheepishly.

"Fell, man?"

"Yeah! The kid fell. Hell, he falls all the time. He's a clumsy kid!"

"Where did he fall from?" Her eyes were looking through him now.

"Hey, quit the third degree!" Mike screamed. "You guys gonna help my kid or not?"

"Have a seat," she said. She rose quickly and dashed into the back.

A few minutes later Mike's name was called.

"Okay, Mike," he said to the boy. "Remember, *you fell!*"

The boy nodded and followed his father towards the large swinging doors that separated the waiting area from the examination rooms in the back. When they reached the door a handsome young doctor, with finely chiseled features and smiling brown eyes, stepped out.

"Mr. Perotti?"

"Yeah."

"The boy will come with me. You can wait over there."

He started to lead the boy through the door.

"Hey, I'm goin', too," Mike called, starting to follow.

The young doctor stopped. "Mr. Perotti, you're not allowed."

"The hell I ain't! You can't work on my kid without me bein' there!"

"Hospital rules, Mr. Perotti." He continued to smile. "Sorry."

"Bullshit! If them's the rules, we're goin' somewhere else!" He reached for his son, but the doctor pushed him away.

"I'm sorry, Mr. Perotti. . ."

"Hey, you sonofabitch. Gimme back my kid!"

Mike stepped forward to show the doctor that he meant business and suddenly felt himself being shoved through the doors from behind. As he went sprawling to the floor, he felt powerful arms pinning him down.

"Hey, what the fuck are you doin'!"

He fought the powerful arms, many of them. He tried to get to his feet. "I'll kick the piss outa you bastards!"

Suddenly his left arm was jerked nearly out of its socket. Next he felt his sleeve going up and a sharp needle prick in his arm.

And then he began to relax.

"Gimme back my kid!" The powerful arms weren't holding him any longer. He looked up into the smiling face of the young doctor and wanted to kick the shit out of him.

He tried to get up. He told his body "up!" But his muscles wouldn't respond. They seemed to be asleep.

Sleep! That was it! Mike Perotti senior wanted to do nothing more than take a quick nap, right there on the floor.

He rolled onto his side, put his hands beneath his head, and closed his eyes.

It was going to be a catnap, that's all. Just a quick snooze, and when he was finished, he was going to kick the piss outta all of them bastards!

Chapter 31

Dinner time was the hardest part of the day. Dana and Rick would sit at the table, phony smiles splayed across their faces, trying to hide their differences from Todd. Yet they both knew that it was obvious from their actions that something was wrong.

Often Dana thought of leaving, but she hesitated in getting a divorce, in taking Todd away from his father. It was easy to think of leaving, but much, much harder to reach a final decision, for Dana loved her husband. In spite of Rick's stubborn, self-centered ways, Dana loved him.

Since Max's death, Dana had totally given up hope of uncovering whatever conspiracy existed in Crandall. Now, all she wanted to do was get as far away from Crandall as possible. She told herself daily that she was going to file for divorce, that she was going to take Todd and leave. Yet her mind created reasons for staying, clever excuses allowing her to hang onto the threads of her marriage.

I don't have any money! Where will I go? Those were her favorites, along with: *Todd needs his father.*

Dana was seated at the dining room table, picking over her dinner and finalizing her excuse for not leaving tomorrow, when the phone rang.

"It's probably for me," Rick said, stepping into the living room to talk in private.

A moment later he was back in the dining room, a puzzled look on his face.

"It's for you. A woman."

"Me?" Dana was surprised. She couldn't remember her last caller.

She went into the living room.

"Hello." There were distant street sounds, but no answer. She spoke again, louder. "Hello!"

"Dana?"

The voice was a near whisper, yet Dana recognized it immediately.

"Ruth, where are you?"

"Nearby. Listen!"

"Where have you been?" Excitement rose in her voice.

"Listen, please! You have to take Todd and get away from here. They're going to change him. Dana, they do something to the boys at the hospital. Kill them maybe. I don't know. They make . . . robots of them, I think. . ."

Ruth had launched into an endless flurry of words, but Dana cut in.

"Robots! Ruth, where are you?"

It couldn't be true. Dana didn't want to believe it—but it made sense. The boys seemed so much like machines.

"I've been kept a prisoner at Community General since I've found out. They drugged me. Dana, Ronnie never had a heart murmur. That was just an excuse to get him. . ."

"RUTH!" Dana screamed. Ruth was off again, but her babbling was making no sense.

"Dana, I'm in danger." Her voice quaked with fear.

"I'm coming for you."

"Don't tell Tom—he's with them. Don't tell anyone! Bring Todd. We have to get away."

"All right. Where are you?"

Rick's head popped into the room.

"Everything okay?"

"No, it isn't," Dana screamed. Now, finally she had the proof she'd always wanted. "Ruth, where are you?" she asked again.

"I'm at the shopping center, but I'm leaving. As soon as they discover I'm gone, they'll be coming for me."

"All right. Start walking north down Eastchester Road, towards the newspaper office. I'll cruise down the road looking for you. If you get to the paper before I do, wait there. I shouldn't be more than ten minutes."

Ruth began to cry. "Thank God I reached you. Hurry. Please!" She hung up.

Stepping in, Rick asked, "What the hell is going on?"

The frustration that had been bottled up in

Dana for so long now spilled over.

"I told you, but you wouldn't believe me! I told you there was something wrong, but you just wouldn't listen!" she screamed. "They do smething to the boys at the hospital. Change them somehow!"

Rick appeared shocked. "Are you sure?"

"Am I sure, he asks! YES! That was Ruth Roberts on the phone. She's been their prisoner. Tom is in on it, too."

"Where is she?"

"Walking towards the paper, down East-chester Road."

"You'd better get to her soon, hon."

"Now, do you believe me?"

"Honey, if what you say is true, Ruth's in great danger. Hurry!" There was a grim look in Rick's eyes. Finally she had gotten through to him.

"It'll be all right," she assured him. They moved across the room, falling into each others arms, embracing. "You just keep Todd safe. I'll be right back."

She moved away, but Rick pulled her back, giving her a long, lingering kiss. "Take care of yourself—and hurry."

"I will."

Dana reluctantly parted from her husband's arms and rushed out the door.

Rick stood by the window, watching the car pull out from the driveway and move on down the street. As the car sped from sight, Rick quickly left the window and went to the phone.

It was 8:29. Ruth Roberts, clad in the green orderly's uniform she'd received from the hospital, walked cautiously down Eastchester Road.

An early summer's sun had just dropped below the horizon, and darkness was stretching over the town. With it came a soft singing breeze from the north—and fear.

Ruth shivered slightly as she walked. She was scared, and the emptiness of the streets highlighted her fears.

She felt totally vulnerable walking down Eastchester Road, knowing she could be easily spotted in the green uniform.

She slowed her pace as she heard a car coming up on her.

Please, let it be Dana!

She turned to see a large car—*not a Pinto wagon*—cruising down the street.

She quickened her pace, moving away from the curb. It wasn't Dana. *It's them!*

The car grew nearer, and Ruth almost broke into a run.

Hurry, Dana. Please!

The car was on top of her now, traveling almost next to her. She wanted to scream: "Someone save me!"

Then it passed, quickly picking up speed until it was a specter in the distance.

Ruth practically laughed out loud. *Thank*

God!

She reached the newspaper office and tried to peer into the darkened windows. Drawn Venetian blinds prevented her from looking in. Nervously, she paced back and forth.

Hurry, Dana!

She didn't know how long she could stay still. This was her first time out of doors in what had to be months. She'd been kept a prisoner, often drugged, and now that she was free, all she wanted to do was run.

Run, run, as fast as you can, you can't catch me, I'm the gingerbread man.

Hysterical laughter died in her throat. Her sanity was fading quickly. But not yet, she told herself. *I'm not gone yet!*

She looked up and down the desolate street, hoping to get a glimpse of the Pinto wagon.

Dana, please . . . HURRY!

That's when she saw the boy.

The tall, thin, blonde-haired youth stepped from the shadows behind the building. On his face was a smile, but his eyes were lifeless.

"Who's there?" said Ruth, taking a giant step backwards. Again she gazed up and down the street.

The youth stepped closer, and Ruth could see the word "Giants" emblazoned across his chest.

"You're one of them!" she barked, her voice slipping totally out of control. She backed away another step.

The youth came closer. Now that he was bathed in the haunting glow of the street lights, Ruth recognized him. Adonis Dreiser.

"Stay away!" She turned to flee.

"Hurry!" the youth said. "Mrs. Evans awaits."

She stopped cold and turned back.

"Dana?"

"Yes. You are to come with me. Safety awaits."

"Dana sent you?"

"Yes," the youth replied, stepping still closer.

Ruth didn't believe him and continued backing away. "But why would she send you?"

"Please hurry!" There was urgency in the boy's voice. He looked down the street towards the headlights of an approaching car. "They're coming for you. I am to take you to safety. Hurry!" Again, the urgency.

Ruth turned towards the headlights, and a bolt of fear flashed through her.

"Hurry, please!" The youth stepped forward and took her hand.

"You're with Dana?"

"Yes."

Ruth peered into the depths of the boy's blue eyes, hoping for some telltale show of emotion, but there was nothing. Looking into his eyes was like staring off into space.

The car neared.

"You'll take me to Dana?"

"Yes."

Like a Judas goat leading a lamb to slaughter, the boy gently pulled Ruth into the shadows. She followed willingly.

Dana Evans checked her watch. She'd been standing in front of the newspaper office for nearly fifteen minutes. The walk from the center wasn't that long. She looked around again. Nothing.

She was sure she hadn't passed Ruth along the way. When she was driving up Eastchester Road, she thought she saw Ruth waiting in front of the office, but when she arrived she wasn't there. It was only a shadow.

Dana waited another five minutes, turning over the robot theory in her mind. It just didn't seem possible, but it had to be true. Now the heart murmur thing made sense. It wasn't drugs at all.

Her thoughts drifted to Ronnie Roberts. *No wonder Tom was so secretive.* He'd known about it all along.

Then something inside of Dana clicked, and she knew Ruth wasn't coming.

"Oh, my God! What have I done?"

Crandall was a small town, but it wasn't small enough for them to find Ruth in ten minutes. No. They had to know where she was.

And she told me not to tell anyone. Stupid!

It was all very clear now. She had ignored all the signs but could do so no longer. Max's words to her rang out in her mind.

. . . I want you to know that many of the parents in this town are in on this thing. And whether you believe it or not, your husband is with them . . . with them . . . with them . . . with them . . .

Dana suddenly had the insane urge to scream.

When Dana got in, Rick was camped out on the sofa watching an old movie.

She saw him lying there, as if nothing had happened, and tore into him.

"What did they do to her?"

She was on top of him, shaking him, and he pushed her away.

"Hey, what goes?"

"What did they do to her?"

He was sitting up now.

"What are you talking about? Where's Ruth?"

"You tell me!" She was standing over him, glaring down at him.

"I don't know what you're talking about. You didn't find her?"

"For months I've been listening to your lies, wanting to believe that you only needed to satisfy some innocent childhood fantasy. But you were with them all along."

He jumped up.

"Honey, what are you saying?"

"WHAT DID THEY DO WITH RUTH?" Her words rang out cold and hard.

"You can't really believe that robot story. It's got to be some kind of joke."

"So where's Ruth?"

"Probably waiting for you to run all over town telling everyone her wild story. After you make a fool of yourself, she's going to turn up laughing."

Dana backed away, eyeing him suspiciously. "You believe that?"

"What else can I believe? That the boys are robots? It sounds to me like the plot of the 'Stepford Wives.' Honey, things like that only happen in movies." He forced a smile, but Dana could tell that he was troubled.

"And Ruth's going to turn up laughing?"

"Sure, hon." He reached for her, and she backed away another step.

"Stay back!"

Rick opened his mouth to speak.

"Don't! This whole mystery is finally clearing up for me, Rick. One of the child's parents has to know about the change—probably has to ask for it—isn't that right? That's why Eunice Graham was so sure about Petie, why David Grote was so secretive, and why so many of the parents watch the kids so carefully. It's an investment, isn't it, Rick?"

"Of course not." He reached for her again.

"Don't touch me!" She turned and headed for the stairs.

"Dana. . ."

"I'm taking Todd and leaving." She stopped on the staircase and looked down. "We're going to New York, Rick. I want a divorce."

"Dana, you need help!"

"Rick, that's not going to work this time. I don't know why you're doing this, but they can't have Todd." Again she started upstairs.

"DANA!" Rick screamed. "I'm tired of playing Mr. Niceguy. If you want to leave, fine. Leave! But Todd stays with me!"

"I'm taking Todd!" Dana called from the top of the stairs.

"Over my dead body! Todd is not leaving this house. Do you hear me?"

"Yes."

She ran to the bedroom, and he followed.

"Don't come in here!"

He stepped in.

"Dana, you can never have Todd. Go to the authorities, go to the courts with that wild story, and see what they say. They'll laugh at you." He paused. "Dana, I love you."

He stepped towards her.

Standing by the dresser, she picked up a hairbrush and brandished it. "Stay back!"

"Dana, you're sick. You need help. If you want to stay here with us, I'll see that you get it. If you want to run, go right ahead, but you'll do your running alone. I can't help you if you don't want to be helped."

He turned and walked from the room. Dana slammed the door and locked it.

Dana slipped down the hall and stopped before Todd's room. She couldn't knock. Rick was downstairs watching TV. He would hear.

Todd's asleep anyway, she told herself. Slowly she opened the door.

She needed to be near her son, needed to know that he was still hers and that he was still all right.

She stepped into the darkened room, the light from the hall illuminating her way. The

Mickey Mouse night light smiled up at her.

She crossed to the bed and looked down at her son. The steady rise and fall of his chest reassured her.

He's bigger than I thought he was, she noted. *He's growing fast.*

She bent to kiss his cheek, and the thought that had skirted her consciousness for so long came streaming in.

Rick doesn't love Todd. He never did.

Rick was a figures man. One and one equals two. The whims and dreams of a child were beyond him. All he understood was results. He was giving his child to them because they promised results, and results were what he understood.

Her lips grazed Todd's cheek, and his eyes sprang open.

"I didn't mean to wake you."

"I'm kind of big to be tucked in, Mom."

"I know. I'm sorry."

She stood, turning to leave.

"Why do you and Dad yell?"

"Huh?" She turned back.

"Is it because of me?"

"No!"

"I don't like you and Dad yelling."

"We won't anymore."

"Promise?"

"I promise."

He smiled.

"Just promise me you'll try to have fun in whatever you do, even playing baseball. It's important to have fun."

A quizzical look crossed his face. "Okay, Mom. I'll try."

She had the feeling that he really didn't understand, that perhaps he thought part of growing up was to not have fun anymore.

She had to save him. While he was still her child and could still laugh and love and enjoy himself, she had to save him. She didn't know how, but she had to get him away from Crandall.

"She knows."

Rick Evans was seated in the coach's living room. The coach sat across from him, his vision fixed on the TV screen. A video tape of a tennis match was being played back.

"You see that girl? She's the world's youngest professional tennis player."

"She knows," Rick said again, louder.

Dreiser didn't look up. "In a few years, she'll be earning millions for her family. Tennis is a very mechanical game. Quite easy when there's no emotion involved." He looked at Rick. "It's our emotions that get in the way of a good performance. Control the emotions, and we all perform wiser and better."

"Have you heard what I said? Dana's figured out what we've been doing, and. . ."

Dreiser's powerful gaze silenced him.

"Mr. Evans. We've gone out of our way to keep your wife from finding out. Maybe she should know."

"No! You don't know my wife. She's the last of the great idealists. She'll fight this thing."

"And she'll lose."

Silence.

"Mr. Evans, are you sure she knows? She's suspected something for some time now."

"She doesn't have the facts, but the moment Todd goes into the hospital, I'm sure she'll blow the whistle."

"We're too close to stop now, Mr. Evans. And we can't afford for your wife to . . . blow the whistle. Do you love her?"

Rick paused a moment. "I love my family. I'm doing this for all of us."

"Love, Mr. Evans, is an unneeded emotion. Try and get rid of it."

Again, the silence.

"Mr. Evans, we can't afford to let your wife get in the way."

"I need a little more time. She'll come around."

"We can't wait."

"Why?"

"We're on a schedule. Mrs. Evans is your wife, and it's up to you to handle her. If you can't, I'm sure we can. Do I make myself clear?"

"Yes."

Slowly Dreiser's gaze returned to the TV. "That girl is one of ours. She came to us when she was four. Imagine, Mr. Evans! Your son could be one of the finest athletes in the world. Imagine!"

But Rick couldn't imagine. His thoughts were on his wife.

Chapter 32

The playoffs droned on, and Crandall continued to win—easily.

In early June the team from Piscataway came to town, and everyone came out to cheer for the Giants.

The town council decided to add extra seating to accomodate the crowds, and two rows of portable bleachers were set up behind the dugouts.

It was hot and muggy. The red clay of the field was dry, and although the field had been wet down just that morning, running on the base paths created a veritable dust storm.

Dana stood by the portable bleachers, behind the home team's dugout. She knew Crandall would win. She really didn't want to be there, watching the emotionless boys in action, and only came to the games to be near Todd.

She wanted to be as close to Todd as

possible. Her plan had been to take him and run, but they were never alone anymore. Rick no longer went to work, and although he pretended innocence, she knew she was being watched.

She waited for her time. She would lull them into a false sense of security. They couldn't watch her forever.

She didn't know when the change was planned, but they were not going to get her boy.

There was a commotion in the dugout.

"Come here!" Rick called to Dana from around the dugout.

"What?"

"Come here!"

He came over to her and began pulling her towards the dugout.

"Stop! What are you doing?"

"I want to show you something."

Jimmy Warren sat on the bench. He'd taken a nasty spill, and a gash had been opened on his forehead. Blood dripped from the wound.

"He's bleeding," Rick said. "I ask you, do robots bleed?"

"Rick, please."

"Well, do they?"

"I guess not."

"Admit you're wrong, Dana!"

"No."

She pulled away and started to run from the park.

"You're wrong!"

Of course, robots don't bleed! But if they're not robots, then what?

She didn't turn back. She reached the edge of the park and kept running, running down Edgemont hill and up Oakdale Street, running for home.

Coach Dreiser was glad he had another second baseman, Petie Graham. He was every bit as good as Jimmy Warren and should have been the starter. But, succumbing to Pat Warren's plea, Dreiser had allowed Jimmy Warren to stay.

It wasn't a mistake. He'd told his colleagues that just the other day, when they were in the hospital observing one of the boys.

"I think we were a little overconcerned about Jimmy Warren."

"We've never taken a chance in the past. I don't like eliminations, but we're too close to gamble now."

"Perhaps you're right, but he's been with us for so long. You've visited others outside of Crandall, and they're all fine."

"That's true."

"If something goes wrong, it must only materialize after some time has passed. Jimmy Warren is one of our first."

Dreiser sat in the dugout, going over the conversation in his mind. He was confident that it wasn't due to the time lapse. If it were, in a year or so, mishaps might start occuring all over the country, and he didn't want to believe that.

Dreiser felt content as he watched his team trouncing the boys from Piscataway. And no one was watching when Jimmy Warren slipped away from the dugout.

Mike Perotti senior sat on the edge of the hospital bed, trying to shake the cobwebs from his head. He'd been in the room since the morning he'd arrived with his son.

They had shot him up with drugs, the drugs made him feel wonderful. He didn't worry about getting a job, the bills, or even getting out of there. He took his daily injection, and let his mind wander off into its own Shangri-la.

For the past few days, however, the drug treatments had stopped. At first Mike begged them to give him his shot. "I need my vitamins." But they refused.

This morning Mike felt as if he were recovering from the world's longest hangover. His body ached all over, but his head was beginning to feel like it belonged to him again.

Fritz Warner entered and sat in the chair across from Mike.

"How are you this morning?"

"I'm all right. Hey, what the hell did you do with my kid?"

Warner chuckled.

"Good, good, Mr. Perotti. This is the first time you've asked about your son in weeks. We were beginning to think that you'd forgotten about him."

Mike thought for a moment.

"Well, where is he?"

"He's fine." Warner chuckled. "At home with his mother."

"Why are you keeping me here?" Mike tried to stand up, but his legs felt like jello, and he fell back on the bed.

"Relax, Mr. Perotti. Don't exert yourself. You haven't used your legs in weeks."

"Why am I here?"

"A precaution. You were threatening to expose our little program if we didn't help your son. We couldn't have you do that, now, could we?"

"I was just blowin' off some steam."

"I believe you were. But Mr. Perotti, you *are* a bit verbose."

"Huh?"

"You're quite talkative, and we can't afford to have you babbling about us to the wrong people. We'll release you when the season's over."

"That could be in August!"

"That's right."

Again Mike tried to rise, only to fall back.

"My family needs me."

"They're doing quite well without you, Mr. Perotti." He laughed. "I really don't think they miss you."

"Very funny."

"Mr. Perotti, you seem fine. Now how about your vitamins?"

He seemed unsure of himself.

"Okay."

Warner drew up Mike's sleeve and injected him.

The drug worked quickly. Already Mike was feeling better, and leaving wasn't so important after all.

It's too bad, Warner thought, as Mike snuggled back under the covers. It's too bad he isn't like this all of the time. The effect of the drug was only temporary. *Too bad!*

Chapter 33

Dana was in the bedroom, packing.

She'd run all the way home, reached the house panting, and suddenly knew instinctively what had to be done. Without thinking, without taking time to truck out one of her excuses, Dana went upstairs and began to pack.

She grabbed a large canvas suitcase from the hall closet and went straight to Todd's room.

She remembered when she and Rick had first seen the room. She had pictured how special it would be to Todd and how happy they would all be in their new home together.

Pipe dreams.

She began packing, taking only summer clothes and a few jackets. She couldn't take the time to pull out all of his things; he and Rick would be home soon, and it was important that Rick not know her plans.

I ask you, do robots bleed? Rick's words played in her ears. Well, maybe they aren't robots, but they're . . . *things*, and she wasn't going to let her son become one of them.

She left Todd's room and moved towards her own, stopping at the bathroom, by the landing, to grab toothbrushes.

No! Rick might miss them.

She put them back, moving on to her room where she flung clothes into the suitcase.

A series of crashes downstairs startled her.

"What?" *They can't be home already. Just my rotten luck!*

She hid the suitcase in her closet and stepped out of the bedroom, swinging the door shut behind her.

"Rick?"

No answer.

Slowly she descended the stairs, glancing toward the living room as she did. Empty.

It sounded like broken glass. Could someone have broken in the back door?

A slow chill came over her, sending shivers throughout her body.

Dana cautiously moved towards the swinging doors of the dining room.

"Todd?"

She pushed open the door.

There, on the dining room table, smashed to bits, was her beautiful starburst clock. A large jagged crack now ran through the table top.

Dana's voice caught in her throat as she looked around the room. Drawers and cabinets were pulled open.

Suddenly her eyes were agape, as waves of fear went rocketing through her. There was a baseball bat lying on the floor. A Louisville slugger.

Todd?

As she rushed back through the swinging door, her mind reeling, she saw him. Jimmy Warren stood by the front door, a kitchen knife in his hand.

"What do you want?" Dana screamed. *Now, that's a dumb question!*

She recalled what he had done to Scruffy and knew exactly what he wanted.

It's your turn now!

The boy didn't answer. He stood staring, his dark eyes foreboding. His head was bandaged, and through the gauze Dana could make out the faint darkening of a blood stain.

Dana slowly inched towards him.

Jimmy Warren didn't move, didn't flinch a muscle. It was as if he were a statue. Then slowly the deadly grin snaked across his lips.

He's just a child, Dana told herself, as she moved towards him. I should be able to reason with him, overpower him. But she knew the thing in front of her wasn't a child at all. It was a monster, created by Dreiser.

When she reached the staircase she realized she couldn't confront the thing called Jimmy Warren. Not alone. She had to get to a phone and call for help.

She began to back her way up the stairs, her eyes never leaving him.

"You're a troublemaker," the thing hissed. It moved towards her.

Dana turned and started quickly up the stairs. The boy's footsteps followed. She was midway up the stairs when she heard him starting up behind her. She lost her footing, stumbling near the top and turning her ankle, but she was quickly up.

Suddenly from behind, mad childish laughter filled the stairwell. A nameless chill danced up her back, as Dana again started her race for the top.

She reached for the landing, turned left, and started down the hall. She was in front of her room in seconds.

She fumbled with the door knob. *It's not locked!* But it slipped and jiggled around in her hand. Frantically she fumbled, but the door wouldn't open.

Come on, Dana, relax. It's just a door knob. The slow, steady footsteps were coming. *Hurry!*

Willing control into her fingers she gently turned the knob. The door swung open, and she rushed in, locking it behind her.

She leaned against the door, breathing heavily. It was then that she noticed the pain stabbing at her right ankle. Her foot was beginning to swell, and she knew she wouldn't be able to run far in her current condition.

Jimmy Warren's footsteps, slow and deliberate, beat in her ears. He was in no hurry. Dana was trapped, and he knew it.

He wants to kill me. For the first time the

thought fully penetrated her consciousness. But the door was locked, and Jimmy Warren was a child. The door could hold him until help arrived.

She hobbled to the nightstand and picked up the phone. The friendly hum of the dial tone greeted her.

Good.

She dialed the Sheriff's office.

"Hello, Sergeant Culver."

"Yes, this is Dana Evans, and there's someone after me in my home."

"Ma'am?"

"Please! I'm in danger."

The footsteps shuffled slowly down the hall and into the bathroom.

"Who's after you, ma'am?"

"A boy. No, not a boy—a monster!"

Silence.

"Please, send someone over here. Please!"

"All right, ma'am. Address. . ."

She now heard the thing moving towards Todd's room.

Is he looking for me?

Quickly she gave the sergeant her address. "Someone will be right over, ma'am."

But what if they're not in time? Then they'll find chopped Dana!

She stood and hobbled to the window, dragging her ankle like a lead weight. She peered out, hoping to discover an escape route, but there was no trellis or tree nearby. She wouldn't be leaving by the window unless she jumped . . . or was thrown!

Dana opened the window and screamed into the empty street. No heads popped out of any doors or windows. *Could the whole town be at the game?*

"Help!" she screamed again.

The footsteps came out of Todd's room and began rushing towards her.

She froze for a moment. *Did I lock the door?*

She was going to check when the knob started to turn.

"Get away from here!" she screamed. Then the mad laughter came dancing in.

The door didn't open. *Thank God!* The boy pushed and thudded his tiny body against it, but it wouldn't give.

Quickly the footsteps retreated. He was going down the stairs.

Is he leaving?

She waited, listening, for what seemed like an eternity. Then slowly she opened the door. The hall appeared empty. She stepped out and limped towards the staircase. She could hear him rummaging around in the kitchen.

Now's my chance. Feet, don't fail me now!

She started down the stairs.

Woosh! The sound of the swinging door. He was coming back.

Dana inched her way back up the stairs and headed for the bedroom. But the bedroom was a trap—a deathtrap, if he could get in.

When she reached the bedroom, she closed the door without entering. *Quiet, Dana, quiet.* Then she went into the bathroom and climbed into the tub.

As she pulled the shower curtain around, the footsteps again started up.

Please go straight to the bedroom.

She was peeking from behind the curtain when the boy reached the top of the landing. He was hefting the bat, a look of deranged glee stamped across his face.

He looked into her eyes, and again the evil grin appeared.

This is it, girl. Nice try!

He'd seen her. She had to rush him; it was her only chance.

She started to climb out of the tub, but then he turned and started towards the master bedroom.

He didn't see me!

He reached the door and immediately began to bludgeon it with the bat.

Images of Scruffy's body being kicked about flashed in front of her.

Football with the doggie, baseball with the mommy.

She choked down a burst of hysterical laughter.

The bedroom door started to give.

Methodically the boy hammered the wood, huge splinters flying everywhere. He hit the knob once, and the door flew open.

He went in.

"Mrs. Evans," he called in a gentle sing-song voice. "Troublemaker!" he blurted out.

Dana eased out of the tub and started down the stairs. The pain in her ankle was intense, and she couldn't move quickly, but the front door and safety were just moments away.

"Mrs. Evans." The voice was directly behind her. She turned. Jimmy Warren stood at the top of the landing.

"NO!" she screamed, as the boy started down. Tears were streaming from her eyes. "NO!" she repeated. "Please!" The deadly smile reappeared.

Go! she commanded her legs. Pain or not, she had to run.

She started down as fast as she could, ignoring the pain that tore into her.

When she reached the bottom, the bat whizzed by her head, flying over her shoulder. She didn't stop, didn't turn to see how far away the *thing* was. She ran to the door. *Don't fuck it up this time!*

She forced her muscles to relax, just enough to turn the lock. She turned the knob and swung the door open.

Suddenly Jimmy Warren's hand was on her shoulder, and she found herself being pulled back into the house.

"No, please!"

She fought against the boy's granite grip, as he slowly dragged her back.

"Troublemaker," he hissed, his face inches from hers.

This time she didn't scream. She gathered every ounce of strength in her body, and shoved him away. She slipped from his grasp, as he went stumbling backwards. Then she barreled out the door.

As she raced down the walk, screaming like

a mad woman, Rick and Todd walked up.

Dana suspiciously eyed Doctor Warner, as he tended to her ankle.

"Nothing serious. It's not a fracture or a sprain. Just ice it, and stay off your feet; tomorrow you can start soaking it." He smiled at her. "You've been having your share of accidents, young lady, haven't you?"

Dana hadn't noticed it before, but the sweetness in his voice seemed contrived and stagey. *And why does everyone in this town smile so damned much?*

"Well, don't worry," he said, rising. "She's okay." He nodded to Rick, who sat in the leather high-backed chair.

Dana wasn't fooled. She knew they were all seriously concerned about Jimmy Warren, and it wasn't only because he went berserk.

Dreiser and Rick had to capture the boy. Then Warner and several other doctors arrived. No police. They must be in on it too, Dana thought. They were all members of the same club.

It seemed that something had gone wrong inside the boy's brain—something unnatural, something that happened to monsters.

Still pretending to be in a daze, Dana listened to the snatches of conversation around her.

"Rick," Warner said, as he placed his things back into his bag, "I'd like you to bring Todd around for a checkup."

Dana stiffened.

"Checkup?" Rick asked.

"Nothing serious," Warner reassured. "Just routine, to make sure the boy's in good health."

"You don't have to pretend because of me," Dana said. "I know everything."

"Excuse me?" Doctor Warner appeared puzzled.

"Nice act, doc!"

Rick was up now. "Uhh, doc, thanks for coming by. My wife's still kind of out of it. She could have been badly hurt, you know."

"Hurt!" said Dana. "Your machine could have killed me! Rick, is that how you want Todd?"

"Please, doc. Step into the kitchen."

Rick hustled Doctor Warner off into the kitchen. It was all so neatly planned. The staging was perfect, right down to the last detail.

Perfect or not, Dana knew it was time to act. It was now or never. She had to get Todd away from Crandall tonight.

Dana Evans was a pest.

Fritz Warner didn't like eliminations, but eliminating Dana Evans would be a pleasure.

He thought back to the night on Harney Road. He'd only meant to scare her then, to frighten her enough to stop her snooping. Now he felt it would have been better if he had done more.

He didn't like Dana Evans. She was nothing but trouble.

Dana lay in bed.

Doctor Warner had recommended that she take one of the sleeping pills he'd given her some weeks ago. "It'll help you to sleep."

Now Rick was in the kitchen, getting her a glass of water. Dana wanted him to think that she needed the pill. It was part of her plan.

"How're you feeling?" Rick has asked after dinner.

She didn't answer.

"I'll bring you some water and a sleeping pill."

He wanted her asleep, out of the way, so he could talk openly with his buddies. Dana pretended to agree.

"Here you go, hon." Rick handed Dana the pill and water, watching intently as Dana placed the pill in her mouth.

Dana hid it under her tongue, then drank several gulps of water.

"Dana, everything's going to be okay. I love you. Trust me."

She wanted to laugh in his face.

Rick went over to the chair by the window, sat and waited.

Dana buried her head into the pillow and spat out the horrible tasting pill. It had already begun to dissolve, but she made sure didn't swallow any of the medication.

Fifteen minutes later, she began to breath slow and steady.

Is this how I sound when I'm asleep? She hoped so.

Rick got up. She could feel him standing over her. Then his footsteps retreated from the room. He was going downstairs. The sound of the TV reached up to her.

Dana opened her eyes. *Todd!* she thought.

She had to get to Todd. She wouldn't have time to get the suitcase or even get dressed. They'd get in the car—*I hope there's gas!*—and they would drive—anywhere!

She lay still for the next twenty minutes. She wanted to hurry, but intuition told her that Rick would be back. She was right. His footsteps padded into the room, and quickly she closed her eyes and resumed her deep breathing.

He'd sneaked upstairs to catch her if she was faking. Now satisfied, he left again.

When Dana heard him downstairs, she immediately got up, grabbed her housecoat and handbag, and slipped down the hall to Todd's room. The steady throbbing in her ankle reminded her of Jimmy Warren. As she passed through the hall, she heard Rick on the phone and knew he was talking with them.

Silently she opened the door. Todd lay awake staring at the ceiling.

"Shhhh." Her fingers went to her lips, as she walked in.

Todd stared at her wide-eyed, his ice blue eyes questioning. He looked more like Rick than ever before. It was frightening.

"You okay, Mom?"

"Todd, listen carefully. I want to play a game."

He frowned. "I'm too big for games."

"Todd, please!" She tried to keep the desperation out of her voice. "Remember when we used to hide from Daddy?"

"Yes."

"I want to play 'let's hide from Daddy.'"

"Why?"

"Because." It was the classic childhood answer.

"I don't feel like playing."

"For Mommy, Todd, please!" She dragged up a smile.

"Okay." Doggedly, he gave in.

A few moments later, Todd was in the living room.

"Daddy, I'm getting a drink of water."

Rick looked up from his phone conversation. "Okay, tiger."

The boy went into the kitchen. So far so good.

Todd would slip out the back, around to the front, and wait in the car. Now Dana had to escape.

Carefully, she crept downstairs. The pain in her ankle was excruciating with every step.

This part of her plan needed luck. If Rick got up and started upstairs, it would be all over.

At the foot of the stairs Dana stopped, huddling in a shadow. It couldn't hide her, but she felt safer, less visible there. She waited.

"She should sleep until morning," Rick said into the phone.

That's what you think, buster!

"Yes, the money is no problem. I'm just worried about my wife."

Hah!

"Of course, I realize we can be rich. I'm grateful. Really."

Rick looked up from the phone.

"Tiger?" he called. "What's happening in there, tiger? Hold on a sec." He got up and started for the kitchen.

Dana froze. *All right, girl, this is it!* She inched from the shadows. *Please, don't see me!*

Rick pushed open the dining room door. "Hey, save some for the next guy!"

Dana was up and limping for the door. Rick's voice, calling for Todd reached her from the kitchen. She opened the door and dashed out into the night.

Todd was in the car. Dana hopped in, and it started easily.

Then Rick appeared in the doorway.

"DANA!" He was moving towards them.

"Quick, Todd, lock your door."

"Why?"

"LOCK IT!" Her shout startled him into action, and he punched down the button just as his father's hand reached for the handle. Rick jiggled the door handle but was too late.

Rick ran alongside the car, as Dana eased out of the driveway. "Todd, open the door, tiger," he said.

Todd reached for the lock.

"Don't!" Dana commanded.

They pulled out onto the street and slowly

began to accelerate. Tears streaked Dana's cheeks, while a triumphant laugh escaped her.

"Dana, please!" Rick called.

The car gradually picked up speed. The handle was jerked from Rick's grip.

Dana watched as Rick became smaller and smaller in the rear view mirror, until finally his image was just a ghost in the night.

Chapter 34

They got on I-95 heading south, and they drove.

Several times Todd asked his mother where they were going.

"We're running from Daddy," she finally told him.

"Why?"

"It's part of the game."

He accepted her answer—at least for a while. He snuggled up in a corner and dozed. Near the end of the Jersey turnpike he awoke.

"Mommy, I'm scared."

"Don't be. We're safe now." Dana hoped her words were prophetic.

She got on the Pennsylvania turnpike. Dropping off at exit 33, she proceeded down US-22 until she saw the sign that said Allentown. She was heading for home.

She wasn't going to pop in on her parents. She remembered her last conversation with her mother and knew she couldn't handle any further rejection—not now. They would spend the night in a motel, then call in the morning.

At a quarter past twelve, the Pinto wagon pulled into the cinder-topped parking lot of the Cloverleaf Motel.

A mountain chill rippled through the air, and when Dana pushed open her door, she suddenly remembered that she was only wearing a housecoat.

"Why are we stopping here?" Todd asked.

"To spend the night."

"I wanna go home!"

"We will."

"When?"

"In the morning. Rest."

Dana got out and was immediately reminded of her tangle with death, as pain shot through her ankle. She limped up to the front door of the main lodge. The lights were out, but she knew a few loud knocks would bring the proprietor.

She knocked and waited. A light came on in the back. A few minutes later the office was illuminated, and slow footsteps came towards the door.

"Jennings?" A male voice, gravelly from drink, called out.

"No."

The door opened, and a grizzly old man with a full set of whiskers peered out.

"Hi. I'm Mrs. . . . Miss Stephens," Dana said.

"You didn't call ahead," the old man said,

as if that were a crime. He noticed her house-coat.

"No."

"You alone?"

"No. My husband's asleep in the car." Dana pointed, and he could see Todd's head nestled against the back of the seat.

"Miss Stephens?"

"Mrs. Stephens."

He smiled. Opening the door, he took a full view of Dana in her housecoat.

"You're lucky, Mrs. Stephens." He pretended to ignore Dana's attire. "We were expecting the Jennings family, otherwise I'd have never opened up. You can't be too careful, you know." He handed her the registration card.

Quickly Dana filled in the information, ignoring the man's attempts at conversation. A few minutes later she had her key and was heading for the room.

A feeling of relief finally began to come over her. Her ordeal was over. They would both get a good night's rest, and in the morning she would call her mother.

Dana awoke to Todd's shaking her. She'd had a fitful sleep and was hardly aware she'd been asleep at all.

"What?" She sat up with a start.

Golden strands of early morning sunlight spread through the room.

"When are we going home, Mommy?"

Dana checked her watch. 6:05 AM. "Soon."

God I'm tired!

"I'm hungry."

"All right."

She swung her legs over the side of the bed, and when her feet hit the floor, pain gripped her ankle.

She hadn't taken much money—it was the only thing she'd forgotten—but she'd charged the room on her MasterCard. She figured she had enough cash for gas and breakfast.

"I'll get us something to eat." She rose, then remembered that she had no clothes.

"Let's go home, Mommy."

"Soon."

She had to get out and back before too many people were up and around. She decided to pass up breakfast—at least for now. She had to call her mother and didn't want to do it from the room.

She went into the bathroom and splashed some cold water on her face. I look awful, she thought, noting the dark circles under her eyes.

She hoped it would all end soon. It was up to her mother.

"Todd, don't answer the door for anyone," she told her son, limping towards the door. She left, heading for the old-fashioned phone booth she'd spotted by the main building.

She dialed her parent's number and waited.

"Hello." It was her mother.

"Hello, Mother. This is Dana."

"Dana." The voice was cold.

"Listen, Mother, I'm coming home. I need your help."

Silence.

"Mother, please!" Excitement swelled in her. "I know there are bad feelings between us, but Todd and I need your help."

"Where are you?"

"I'm at a motel, outside of Allentown."

There was a brief silence, and Dana held her breath.

Finally her mother spoke. "Do you think you can run off, ignoring your family for ten years, and just come back as if nothing has happened?"

"I need help." She was starting to cry.

"And what about your precious husband?"

Dana had known it would be like this. She had hoped not, but her mother couldn't change.

"I'm coming, Mother. I'm coming whether you want me or not!"

"Will you be staying?"

The question surprised her.

"Yes, for a while."

"Well, things might not be the way you like them. For one thing, that boy of yours is going to church. If you don't want to go, that's your business, but I'm bringing God into that boy's life!"

That's a laugh!

"All right, Mother. See you soon."

"Don't come unless you're ready to change."

Dana hung up.

She sat in the booth, composing herself, before returning to the room.

When she got back, Todd was in bed.

"Todd, the cafeteria wasn't open yet."

"That's okay."

"Listen, I have a surprise for you. You're going to see your grandparents." Her voice was sugar-coated.

"When?" he asked, suspicion creeping into his face.

"Today."

"I thought we were going home?"

"We are."

"When?"

"Todd, please don't ask so many questions."

"I'm going back to sleep."

"Let's go see your grandparents, son."

"I'm tired. I'm going back to sleep!" He pulled the covers up around his neck and squeezed his eyes shut.

Exasperated, Dana sat at the foot of the bed. It was almost over, and she needed rest. But Todd had been through a lot, too. She didn't want to push him.

"All right, son."

An hour later she still sat, thumbing through Motel News, waiting for Todd to get up.

"All right, Todd, we have to go." She'd waited long enough.

"I'm not ready, yet."

"Todd, don't argue with me!"

"You don't love me!"

The accusation knifed through her.

"I want to go home—now!" he said. Sitting up, he glared at her.

"We're going to Grandma's, Todd. Now don't. . ."

A loud rapping at the door hushed her.

"Who?" Todd said.

"Proprietor, ma'am."

Todd jumped from the bed and rushed to the door.

"Don't!" Dana yelled, but already he was pulling the door open.

Rick and Dreiser stepped in.

Dana's eyes practically leapt from their sockets.

"How did you find us?"

"Todd called," Rick said, smiling. "The tiger and I played a little game of our own."

Dana stared at Todd in disbelief.

"I don't want to go to Grandma's. I'm going with Daddy."

"No!" Dana called.

Rick put his arm around his son's shoulder, smiling down at the boy. Together the two walked out.

Gently, Dreiser closed the door. They were alone.

"Don't make this difficult, Mrs. Evans."

"I won't."

Dana suddenly felt weak—very weak. And all she wanted was to rest.

Dreiser stepped towards her, pulling a syringe from his pocket.

"Relax, Mrs. Evans. This won't hurt."

"What is it?" she whispered.

"Just something to make you sleep."

"Good."

He grabbed her arm, rolled up her sleeve, and injected her.

"How long?" she asked.

He didn't answer, yet already sleep was overtaking her. It felt good—so peaceful. It was just what she wanted, needed—wonderful, glorious sleep.

BOOK FOUR

Chapter 35

"What will happen to her?"

Rick Evans was in Philip Dreiser's study, staring intently at the coach, who was seated comfortably behind his desk.

"What would you like to happen to her?"

Rick thought for a while. "I don't know. I don't want you to kill her."

The coach smiled. "My wife, Mr. Evans, due to certain 'therapy' has become like my right hand. There were times when I felt I'd be better off if she were dead. We all have those feelings, don't we? But I found a way to make my wife compatable. What I'm trying to say is that we're not killers here, Mr. Evans, we're scientists. We provide a service, and at the same time we benefit the scientific community."

Rick sat, nervously eyeing the coach. Finally Dreiser asked, "Do you love her?"

"I guess so. I'm not doing this just for myself. I'm doing it for all of us." His thoughts momentarily drifted to the day he'd first heard about Dreiser and Crandall. At that time, moving to Crandall seemed a wonderful opportunity.

"Don't let emotions get in the way of your plans, Mr. Evans. You've come too far, spent too much money for that. I warned you about unneeded emotions before. They're dangerous."

"I'll be all right."

"Just keep telling yourself that it will be worth it. There are children out there right now, Mr. Evans, who are making families rich, while at the same time living out their parents' fantasies. Imagine, your son, a professional baseball player."

"But I didn't know you killed people."

"We don't!" The coach's powerful eyes challenged him. "Mr. Evans, what happened to Jimmy Warren was very unfortunate, but rare. It wasn't a flaw in his programming. His brain simply rejected the computer. I warned you that this was a possibility."

"I know. But what about Ruth Roberts?"

"She's safe," the coach said, his powerful gaze boring into Rick. His mind quickly flashed to the evening Ruth had escaped. He hated using Adonis to get her back; he didn't want the boy involved, but Ruth would never have gone with an adult. "And your wife is safe, too. There are lots of things we can do with them, but killing isn't on our list. I assure you."

Rick wanted to believe. "All right," he nodded, smiling.

Dreiser relaxed. "That's better. Think of the future. Your boy will be a great ball player and a genius, Mr. Evans. A miniature heuristic computer."

"Heuristic?"

"It means the program in the computer is capable of learning. Everything he learns he'll remember forever. He'll make a mistake once and never again. It's taken years to perfect a computer that could be implanted in the brain. It's the next step in the evolution of man. The brain has evolved as far as it can without help. Man has his limitations, as do computers. But together, Mr. Evans, the possibilities are limitless. Your son will reap greater fortunes than you ever dreamed possible." Dreiser's eyes were hazing over in a state of dreamlike glory.

"I'm not worried about Todd or the operation. I'm worried about Dana."

Dreiser appeared insulted. "Mr. Evans, Doctor Warner and myself have pioneered a quantum leap in the evolution of the species called Man. Man of the future will truly be a superman. We're not going to let someone like your wife destroy all of our work."

"Do you mean she's expendable?"

"Yes!" he said, his voice agitated. "You're an intelligent man, surely you can see that we must make sacrifices!"

Rick stood. "I'd like to see my wife, Doctor Dreiser."

"Your wife is safe!"

"Fine. I'd like to see her."

Mike Perotti senior sat on the edge of his hospital bed, holding his head. He was trying to remember something.

For the past few weeks, the doctor had discontinued the injections, giving Mike his "vitamins" in capsule form. This way Mike could administer the drug himself.

Each morning a small cup full of tiny yellow capsules were delivered along with Mike's breakfast. There were just enough pills for him to stay bombed out of his mind all day, but not enough for him to kill himself.

Lately, though, Mike had been taking less and less pills, flushing the remainder down the toilet. The drug took his mind and memory away from him, and there was something very important that he wanted to remember.

This morning Mike didn't take his pill. He felt *godawful*, but his memory was slowly coming back.

He was beginning to remember what he was supposed to do. And he was getting pissed.

Chapter 36

Dreiser hadn't realized it before, but Rick Evans was a troublemaker, a uncomprehending nobody who couldn't see the whole picture. Philip Dreiser was not going to let Evans, or anyone, stand in his way. He was too near his final glory.

He'd eliminated his own son, when the boy discovered that drugs had made him a great athlete. The youth had threatened to expose him, and with the computers almost ready for use, there was no way that Dreiser could stand for such insubordination.

Dreiser moved into the hall, putting on his jacket and baseball cap with the orange "G" on the front. He'd been wrong about Mr. Evans—he saw that now. If there was an Evans that had to be eliminated (and there was), it wasn't Mrs. Evans.

He knew when Evans got to the hospital and saw what they were doing to his wife, he'd demand her release. Then, eventually, the two would team against him. Mrs. Evans, on the other hand, loved the boy. He was sure that after he'd explained to her that Todd wasn't a robot at all but a loving son in need of a parent to care for him, she'd want to do all she could for the boy, as she had in the past. Dreiser was certain Mrs. Evans could be reasoned with. He smiled.

Of course, a heroin overdose by a local, upstanding businessman, such as Rick Evans, would look suspicious. But even young men had heart attacks.

He pondered his predicament, but one thing he knew for certain: Rick Evans would never see his wife or child again.

Dana Evans opened her eyes and looked around the hospital room. She knew automatically that she was in the type of quarters in which they'd kept Ruth.

From the weight that sat on her brain, she knew also that she'd been drugged and wondered how long she'd been there.

The door opened, and a man in a white hospital coat entered. Dana's vision was fuzzy, and she couldn't make out his features. As he peered over her, she saw who it was. Doctor Fritz Warner.

"How are you today?" the melodious voice chimed.

Dana tried to speak, but the words only echoed in her mind. She seemed perturbed.

"Don't get upset. Your voice will return shortly. In the meantime, relax." He pulled up a chair and sat next to the bed.

"Why?" Dana finally said. The word cracked through her parched throat.

"That's a good place to start." Warner smiled. "For science. For the fame that has eluded Doctor Dreiser and myself for so long."

"The coach is Doctor Philip Dreiser?" Her voice was coming back now.

"Yes."

"But the book."

"Oh, you knew about that. For over twenty years I have assisted Doctor Dreiser. He's a brilliant man. Brilliant. Because of his experiments with human subjects, Doctor Dreiser deemed it important that his identity be protected. It's a risky business, and he couldn't afford to be recognized. When the publisher asked for a picture for the book, naturally I stepped forward."

Doctor Warner pulled a large hypodermic and a bottle from his pocket. He began to fill the needle.

"What are you going to do with me?" Dana asked.

He smiled. "A few experiments. You'll sleep right through them. Don't worry."

Dana wanted to stop him—had to—but she didn't have the strength.

The doctor stood, the needle poised over her. Dana knew she had to stall, while she summed up the energy to fight.

"Why did Tom Roberts go to Atlantic City?"

The doctor loomed over her. The needle started down.

"WHY?"

"Tom Roberts is a gambler. That was something we didn't know. He took Ronnie to Atlantic City, hoping the boy's great memory could help him win. Of course, they didn't allow the youth in the casino."

"Great memory?"

Warner sighed. "It's a long story. I don't have time for it right now."

Dana lay cringing, trying to get him to talk, as the needle again started its descent.

A commotion at the door startled them both.

Rubber-legged Mike Perotti had just stumbled into the room.

"I'm gonna . . . kick shit outta you," he managed to say.

As the doctor turned his head towards Mike, Dana grabbed his wrist, thrusting upward.

"AAIIIIIII!"

Warner let out a bloodcurdling scream as the point of the needle stabbed into his eye. The needle slipped in easily, like a hot knife gliding into a pound of butter.

Dana continued to push, as the doctor pulled away. He backed up and fell to his knees.

"Kick shit!" Perotti said, stumbling into

the room. He fell on top of Doctor Warner.

Up, girl!

As tired as Dana was, as much as she wanted to lie there and sleep, Dana knew she had to get up. Maybe it wasn't too late to save Todd.

She summed up all of her strength, willing her legs to swing over the bed.

Good.

She sat up. Her head felt as if it weighed a ton, and she almost fell back.

You can't stop now!

She was sitting. The room whirled.

Fritz Warner lay on the floor, unconscious from the drug. Mike Perotti's feeble blows glanced off of him.

Dana was up, on wobbly legs, heading for the door.

I have to find Todd!

It was her only thought. It was the driving force in her life. *Todd!*

Rick Evans was seated in a conspiciously empty waiting room when the smiling orderly came in. He'd been waiting to see his wife and was beginning to have some doubts about Doctor Dreiser.

Maybe I made a mistake.

"Hi, I'm John. You must be Mr. Evans."

"Yes."

"This way," the orderly said, waving his hand with a grand flourish. He turned, and Rick began to follow.

"Is she all right?"

The orderly turned, still smiling. "Oh, yeah. She's been clamoring all day about seeing you, the police, and *God* knows who else! But she's all right."

"That sounds like Dana," Rick said, now smiling himself. "That's my wife."

They started off down an antiseptically white corridor. They turned left onto a hall that was lined with doors.

Dreiser said she was fine. Dana's paranoia must be rubbing off. Rick smiled as he relaxed. Now he was certain he was doing the right thing.

"I'll tell you something, Mr. Evans. We'll be glad to get rid of her."

"I'll bet," Rick said with a laugh.

"That wife of yours sure can raise hell."

"Don't I know it."

They stopped in front of room 126.

"Well, this is it. She's in there. Just a short visit, Mr. Evans. Okay?"

"Sure. I just want to make sure she's fine."

"She is."

Rick pushed open the door, and right away he knew there was something wrong. The room was empty. *Empty!*

"Hey!!!!" The orderly shoved him in, and suddenly there were two of them. "What goes?"

"You, Mr. Evans."

"Huh?"

It was only then that he saw the hypodermic.

* * *

Dana started down the corridor, past doctors, nurses, and staff in green and white.

"Help me!" she said to a nurse in crisp whites. She was still reeling from the effect of the drug and fought to hold her balance, the pain in her ankle also returning.

"What's the matter?" the nurse asked.

"I'm looking for my son."

"STOP HER!"

Dana didn't recognize the voice, but she knew she was being pursued. She pushed the nurse aside and staggered further down the corridor.

She turned back and saw two orderlies in pursuit.

"NO!"

She was traveling as fast as she could, which wasn't very fast at all. She fled down the corridor, turning left, and then right, as the corridor seemed to stretch into an unending labyrinth. Instinct pushed her on.

I've got to find Todd. Save him!

The men were coming. They were only a few feet away.

Dana couldn't run anymore. She turned and prepared to do battle with them.

They grabbed her, overpowering her easily. She was no match for them, especially in her condition.

"Please!" she pleaded. "I only want my son."

Fatigue suddenly overtook her, and she knew she couldn't drag her feet another step. She slumped to the floor.

"Up!" one of the orderlies yelled, yanking on her arm.

"I can't . . . please!"

"Up!" he said again, pulling harder.

The room began to spin, as waves of dizziness drifted over her. Then the pulling hands were gone, and Dana slithered to the floor again.

"Rest, please!"

Blackness and sleep were closing in.

Then a comforting hand rested on her shoulder. There was something familiar about the touch. She looked up.

"Hello, Mother."

She gazed up at a blue-eyed youth with a fresh haircut and a dark, unblinking stare. *Todd.*

Then she saw Dreiser.

"No!" she screamed. "Noooooo!"

When she awoke she was still on the floor. Dreiser knelt beside her.

"You just gave us some scare, Mrs. Evans."

"Is it done?" she asked. "Is Todd. . . ?"

"Yes."

She lowered her head. She didn't care if they killed her now. Her fight, her life seemed over.

"Mrs. Evans, you're frightened, you're suspicious, and you believe you've suffered a great loss. You may not approve of your son playing baseball, but I'm hoping you and I can come to terms, see eye to eye."

She looked up, puzzled. "What do you mean?"

"It *is* possible to show Todd how to be the kind of devoted son a mother could be proud of.

"He can learn from you. He's still a child, *your* child, and what a wonderful child he can be! He's programmed to give twenty-five percent of his earnings to his parents. He'll never be an alcoholic or a drug addict, a revulsion of both being programed in. But Mrs. Evans, he can still go bad—if you let him."

Dana looked up and saw her son standing a few feet away. She wanted to hug him and run from him at the same time. She was too late to save him, but he was still her son. And she loved him.

"Think about it, Mrs. Evans."

Dana Evans stared at her son for a long moment. Standing there, he seemed so helpless. Then the boy smiled at her, and suddenly the dark stare didn't seem so bad.

She held out her hand to him, and he stepped towards her.

"Todd?"

"Yes, Mother?"

"Are you all right?"

"Yes, Mother."

She looked to Dreiser. "He's still my son. He's not a . . . *Thing?*"

"Of course not, Mrs. Evans." Dreiser smiled.

"But the haircut?" She looked at Todd's nearly bald head.

"There have been some changes, Mrs.

Evans. We've worked on his brain—made it better.''

She pulled her son to her and buried her head in his chest. "I love you," she whispered.

"Will you do it?" Dreiser's voice jarred Dana back to the probem at hand. "Will you be a mother to him?"

"I'd like to talk to my husband about it."

The expression on Dreiser's face was stony. He signaled to the orderly who stood several yards away.

"Take the boy."

"Wait!" Dana cried. "Where?"

Again, the smile. "It's all right, Mrs. Evans. You need medical attention. Todd will be just fine. You can see him afterwards. Trust me."

The man led Todd away.

"Mrs. Evans, you mentioned your husband."

Alarm struck at Dana's heart. "Is something wrong?"

"Not really. But to tell you the truth, Mrs. Evans, it came down to eliminating one of you, and we chose him."

"*Why?*"

"You're a mother. Nothing can replace a mother's love."

"I meant, why eliminate anyone?"

"Together you pose a threat. With your influence on him, or his on you, you might do something . . . foolish. He wasn't a good husband anyway. Too much time at the office, unattentive to your needs. I know all about it, Mrs. Evans."

Dana stared silently into Dreiser's powerful eyes. He was masterful, unlike her father. But she'd come from a family of strong women and felt her power was equal to Dreiser's.

"Mrs. Evans, you will be much better off," Dreiser said.

Suddenly Dana sparked to life. "Better off without a husband or a father for Todd? Mr. Dreiser, you can't believe I'd be better off without the man I love?"

"I do believe it."

"But it doesn't have to be this way. Rick doesn't have to be the man he is. He doesn't have to be cold and unattentive!" Agitation gripped her voice.

"What do you mean?"

"I mean, look at you, the great doctor! You can make average boys geniuses. You can program anyone to play great baseball and give twenty-five percent of their earnings to their parents. Does your treatment only work on children?"

"Of course not. What are you getting at?"

"Rick could be the kind of husband I want him to be, need him to be—with your help."

A slow smile played upon Dresier's face.

"And in return I could be the best mother Todd could possibly ever have."

"Are you trying to make a deal, Mrs. Evans?"

Dana's face was expressionless, and for a

long moment Dreiser stood studying her.

"Mrs. Evans, I think we may have just come to an agreement. Now, how about letting me take a look at that ankle?"

For the first time all day, Dana smiled.